Sprinkle
of
Snow

# Sprinkle of Snow

## of

## Snow

SPELLBOUND IN HAWTHORNE NOVEL #2

## LORIN GRACE
## MARIA HOAGLAND

CURRANT
CREEK PRESS

$S$now has its own magic,
every flake its own brilliance.

# CHAPTER 1

Modernizing an antique store was an oxymoron waiting to happen. A sense of accomplishment filled Makenna as she entered the last of her grandmother's leather-bound acquisition ledgers into the software on her laptop. Every item in the store valued over fifteen dollars was photographed and cataloged. The project that should have taken months took over a year to complete. The notification of a video chat interrupted her celebration.

She checked the time. Rotten hawthorn berries. She'd meant to fix her hair and make-up before her video date. She removed her glasses before tapping the green icon. "Good evening, Wendell."

"You're still working?" Of course he recognized the back room of Abigail's Antiques behind her.

"Just finished up. And I mean finished, not just for the night. Every item is in the computer now." Makenna rested her phone against the pencil jar on her desk. "How was your day?"

"As you can see, I'm still at the office too."

Actually, she couldn't see—not without putting on her glasses. Wendell told her last fall that he preferred her in contacts, so she tried to avoid wearing her glasses around him. One advantage of their Wednesday night virtual dates was that she could usually hide the fact she'd worn the glasses all day along with whatever vintage clothing she'd chosen. "You've been working a lot of long hours lately."

"That's what junior partners do in law firms."

"Junior partner? You got the promotion?" Makenna slipped her glasses in her pocket and pulled on her coat in preparation to go home.

"They're announcing it in the morning. So tonight I am moving from my associate's cubical to a proper office." He'd worked so hard for this promotion, often working sixty- and seventy-hour work weeks. Between his long work hours and Abigail's Antiques, their in-person dates had declined to about three a month.

"Congratulations! When do we celebrate?"

"Are you driving into Boston or am I coming out to Hawthorne?" Depending on traffic, the twenty-five-mile drive could take an hour. At some point, the commute became a burden, and their dates glorified phone calls.

She held her phone in her left hand as she set the alarm system, careful not to let him see the code. They may have been dating for a year and a half, but until she had a ring on her finger and a marriage license, Wendell didn't need to know her business affairs, including how poorly the shop was doing since Grandma's passing.

Makenna exited the back door and crossed the alley to her house. "My car still needs to go into the shop and the cargo van is such a pain in the city. What if I ride the commuter rail in and you drive me home?"

"Can you not miss the 6:30 train? You always miss the train."

"I've only missed it when there were extenuating circumstances." It wasn't fair of him to count the night that Grandma collapsed or anything the month she died or the month after.

"Friday night, 7:45 at Atlantic Fish in Back Bay. They have reservations open." Like most New Englanders, Wendell loved his seafood. She could hardly deny him his celebration based on the fact his favorite restaurant only featured two non-seafood items on the menu.

"Sounds like a date." She unlocked the front door. The last notes of her favorite grandmother clock's chime ended as one of the Black Forest cuckoo clocks started.

"Sounds like you're home."

"Only the grandfather clock to go." Makenna smiled at her phone. Wendell's appreciation for the clock collection in the house didn't include the various chimes she set to run back to back at midnight and noon.

The eight loud bongs drowned out his answer.

"Sorry, I thought I could make it to the kitchen before he chimed."

"I was saying I need to cut our date short so I can finish packing up." Originally, their Wednesday night dates included a game or some other activity. More and more busy lives reduced them to phone calls. Not that she minded.

"No problem. Kisses." Makenna blew a kiss to the phone and assumed Wendell did the same since she couldn't see him. Her screen went black, and she put her glasses back on. She'd been lucky it hadn't been raining or snowing. The twenty yards from the back door of the shop turned into an obstacle course of puddles. Without her glasses, she usually stepped in two or three.

Makenna put a frozen dinner in the microwave and checked the weather app. Clear and cold for tomorrow. That would make the estate sales easier to navigate. As she ate her dinner, she marked various items of interest at the closest sale. She needed new inventory before the holiday sales began.

An alarm went off on Quin's phone. He searched through his task list to figure out the purpose of this reminder. "Thursday, 11 a.m.: Call Hawthorne's chief of police with the projected numbers for First Night." If only those numbers were based on something better than an educated guess.

The chamber members hoped to draw families from the neighboring towns that didn't want to drive into downtown Boston for the larger and more famous New Year's celebration. It was a gamble—one that held Quinton Kayhill's reputation and future in the balance.

Last spring, his grandfather sweet-talked the chamber board into hiring Quin as the Hawthorne Chamber of Commerce director. They'd hired him despite his having lived on the west coast most of his life. Several board members considered his California upbringing to be a strike against him along with his age. Due to the lack of competition, they'd given him a year trial in his job. If he were to remain, he must exceed the expectations of the town. Difficult to do in a town with over three hundred years of history, traditions, and superstitions. If First Night failed, by January 2, Quin would be job hunting.

His phone rang. His grandpa's photo filled the screen below the name Walter Abbott. Quin slid his thumb over the red dot to reject the call. A twinge of guilt shot through him, but he needed to keep his schedule. His grandpa could wait until tonight. The call was most likely another one complaining how he missed the low-cost, last-minute vacation. Quin had explained a dozen times he couldn't take personal calls at work. He could barely keep up with everything without stopping to listen to whatever vacation Pops had missed out on this time.

Quin dialed the police station and sat on hold for ten minutes. So much for scheduling a phone call. While he waited, he emailed reminders to chamber members to decorate their stores for the holidays. With only a week before Thanksgiving, several businesses had yet to decorate for Christmas. The antique shop still had gourds, squash, and corn decorations in the windows. Granted, there were some pilgrim dolls too. If Hawthorne was going to draw more shoppers, they needed to play up their quaint hometown feel. If only all the other towns around them didn't fit the same cute New England mold.

He pulled the warehouse club-sized bottle of mint flavored antacid out of his drawer and popped two in his mouth. Of course, the police chief answered mid-chew, forcing Quin to cover the receiver while he swallowed them quickly rather than have the first sound the chief heard be a crunch.

# CHAPTER 2

S ome people's trash might be another's treasure, but sometimes it was just dust and rubbish. Makenna walked through the picked-over Federalist Era house one last time. Most of the outstanding pieces were gone before she arrived. She picked up a handbell with a turned wood handle, the kind a schoolteacher might have kept on her desk. The clapper fell against the side and a clear note rang out. Even if the bell didn't sell, it would be a pleasant addition to the checkout counter at Abigail's Antiques.

In a side room she found a desk with a stuck drawer made and signed by a local craftsman in 1935. Newer than the pieces most of her customers looked for. It might sell. If only she had her grandmother's touch for knowing what customers wanted, maybe she could balance the books at the end of the month and not wince.

Makenna added the bell to her small pile of items in the front hall. She found the estate sales agent in the kitchen.

The balding man pulled out a large calculator. "Good morning, did you find anything you liked?"

"Not as many pieces as I expected to find today from the description of this sale."

"We had a buyer come in from Boston last night."

"I wasn't aware you held an early sale." Makenna fisted her hand behind her back. Third sale this month she'd missed because some big Boston antique dealer came early. Many of the estate sale agents held early sales for antique dealers.

The man adjusted his glasses. "Sometimes it happens."

From the back of her phone wallet, Makenna withdrew a business card.

*Makenna Wilson*
*Abigail's Antiques*
*Curiosities of Spellbinding Wonder*
*3 Covington Road*
*Hawthorne, Massachusetts*

"I would appreciate the opportunity to take part in any early sales you have, particularly in the Hawthorne area. Many of my customers want something that was locally owned." At least the tourists always asked for something authentic New England.

"You must be Abigail Covington-Hill's granddaughter."

"I am."

"Abigail used to purchase all of our best pieces."

This wasn't news to Makenna. The company holding this sale had appeared many times in her grandmother's ledgers. "I believe she did a great deal of business with you."

The man pulled off his glasses and looked her up and down. "I can't promise you anything, but I'll pass this card on to my boss. Now what did you want to purchase today?"

An hour later, Makenna parked her half-empty van into the marked space between her house and the antique shop. She opened the back doors of the cargo van and pulled out the crates of smaller items she'd gleaned from the estate sale and a private sale posted on social media. She'd have to wait to unload the desk until the Monroe boys came to help after school.

She pushed through the back door and deposited the crates, ready to be sorted and inventoried. The job would only take a few hours, not the days she'd planned on. Makenna stopped to rub her temples before entering the main shop. "I'm back. How did things go?"

"You call this an antique?" From a stool behind the counter, Walter Abbott waved a ten-inch, blue, die-cast truck she'd picked up at a sale last week. When she'd left, the truck had been part of a toy display she was preparing for the holidays. "When I was five-years-old I had one just like this. I may not be the youngest man around here, but this is insulting. That makes me older than an antique."

"Sometimes the term antique is relative. I would never call you an antique." She pasted on her most sympathetic of smiles. Walter was older than many of the items in the store—a fact she kept to herself. "Thank you for watching the store."

"This truck reminds me of all the good times I had with my brother..." He set the truck on the counter and made a show of checking the clock on the back wall. "You're late. I missed my game with Judge and Gene."

Makenna glanced at the time on the tablet she used as a register. She was an hour earlier than she'd planned. Grandma told her it was better to let Walter get his grumpy out than to argue with him. "First game or second?"

Walter harrumphed and ducked into the back room, emerging with his coat and hat. "There wasn't a first game because I wasn't there. Unless they got Keira to sit in for a round."

"Then you didn't miss a thing. Can you mind the store next Thursday when I go out again?"

"Can't. My daughter, Rebecca, would skin me alive if I missed Thanksgiving dinner."

"Thanksgiving already?" The months had blurred together since she'd become the sole owner of the store. She was sure she'd had another week to prepare for holiday sales. The 1950s calendar where the days were right even if the year was wrong agreed with Walter. "You're right, there won't be any estate sales then."

"You won't be working that day, anyway."

"Abigail's will be closed." Wendell had hinted she would finally get to meet his family, but that would only take part of the day. The rest of the day she would spend prepping for the weekend sales.

Standing in the open doorway, Walter narrowed his eyes. "You should take the day off, too." The bell over the door jingled as the door swung closed behind him.

Makenna marked Walter's hours down on the computer, knowing he never would. Last month, she'd tried to explain to him that he couldn't volunteer to work in a place of business. Her words fell on closed ears. She checked her email to find confirmations of sales, item requests, and an announcement from the chamber of commerce with the subject line, "Colonial Christmas."

She scanned through the email, wondering what idiot thought Colonial Christmas would be a good theme for the town's holiday decorations. Sure enough, it was the new director, Quinton Kayhill. Living proof that being born in the commonwealth didn't make you a New Englander.

Only three items left on the day's task list. Not bad for a Thursday. Quin tapped the box next to "Confirm First Night music," and a green check mark appeared. Underneath the item, he had individually listed the ten different bands, quartets, and singing groups who would play at the two indoor venues. There were already check marks confirming the library and the senior center.

One could never check on things too many times. Earlier that month, the company contracted for the fireworks display canceled their contract. Fortunately, Brant Whitbeck, a pyrotechnician on vacation in the area, saved the day with his fireworks. The price they'd negotiated even allowed for a second show at midnight—a unique aspect to the first-ever Hawthorne New Year's celebration, since most similar events in the area only had one fireworks display.

A commotion in the front office drew his attention. He brought up the security camera feed to see if he needed to intervene. A willowy woman in a long skirt and thick green wool sweater stood in front of the reception desk waving her arms. Her hair was twisted into a bun and thick glasses hid her eyes. Quin downed two more antacids and turned up the volume.

"I'm sorry. Mr. Kayhill is busy this afternoon. He has an opening tomorrow at 10:30." Running her normal interference on Quin's behalf, Mrs. Zimmerman looked up from her computer screen. "Will a half hour be long enough?"

The woman crossed her arms and tapped her foot. "I'm not sure. It depends on how long it takes California Boy to understand that Colonial Christmas is the most asinine idea for a Christmas celebration in New England. And these illustrations are Currier and Ives. Please tell me he isn't one of those people who can't tell the Civil War from the Revolution."

California Boy? Quin had heard one of his grandfather's friends call him by that name. This woman didn't look older than Quin, although her clothes just might be older than his grandfather. Better to deal with the woman now than to give her until tomorrow morning to spread her views around town. Quin opened the door. "Is there a problem?"

Mrs. Zimmerman spun on her office chair to face him. "Miss Wilson would like to meet with you."

"I have a few moments now." Quin held his office door open for Miss Wilson. After she entered, he closed the door, hoping to contain the sounds of her tirade. "How can I help you?" He indicated for her to take a seat and walked around the desk.

"You came up with this theme?" She slapped a black-and-white copy of the flier from the email he sent to the chamber members that morning.

"Yes." Calming the furious woman wouldn't be possible without more information.

"Then I strongly suggest you develop a relationship with your internet search engines. If we celebrate a Colonial Christmas, all our shops will be open on Christmas Day. We won't have any decorations, and most of us wouldn't attend church since Christmas isn't on a Sunday. In fact, depending on what years you are targeting by the term colonial—which, with this post-Civil War artwork it's difficult to determine—there were fines for celebrating Christmas. There is no such thing as a Colonial Christmas!"

"I'm sure I read that Martha Washington—"

"Martha lived in Virginia, not in Massachusetts. In case you need a map, Virginia is in the South. Different customs. Massachusetts outlawed Christmas. It wasn't until after the Revolution that they celebrated it even in a small measure. And Christmas wasn't a national holiday until 1870. The only thing you got even remotely New England-ish is the picture you included. Nathaniel Currier was born in Boston, which makes him a New Englander." She never paused to take a breath. "However, Currier and Ives prints are not colonial. Back to my point, every Massachusetts kid learns about the years Christmas wasn't celebrated in elementary school. Or maybe you should have asked your grandfather. Walter knows all of this." Miss Wilson glared at him from the chair on the other side of the desk. "Not to mention about twenty percent of the businesses in town decorate with menorahs and their owners don't celebrate Christmas. Although I believe some of them decorate for Christmas anyway because, you know, sales."

Quin had attended through third grade at Hawthorne Elementary and would have remembered if a teacher had told him they'd outlawed Christmas once upon a time. Those were the kinds of details that stuck in a young boy's memory.

There must be a way to defuse her ire and get her out of his office so he could finish his work. "What business do you represent?"

Her eyes narrowed. "I'm Makenna Wilson. I own Abigail's Antiques."

The woman his grandfather worked for on Thursday mornings. He'd expected someone older from the way Pops talked. Her name and business also explained a few more things. Abigail Covington-Hill's funeral had been only days after he'd moved back to Hawthorne. Makenna Wilson descended from one of Hawthorne's founding families. Or judging by the monument of Lavinia Hawthorne Covington in the center of town, *the* founding family. Grandpa had warned him not to cross them. "My condolences on your grandmother's passing."

Makenna's face softened for a moment. "Thank you. Now, back to the point. Colonial Christmas has nothing to do with the history of this town or even the state. Please change the name."

Quin opened to a fresh page on his legal pad. "I wanted traditional Christmas decorations downtown. You know, less Santa, more holly."

Miss Wilson peered through her glasses at him. The effect was much the same as the librarian in his elementary school library when she told him to hush. "Without Clement Moore's *A Night Before Christmas,* we wouldn't even celebrate Christmas. Which is not the point. The point is, you can't use Colonial Christmas. Do you have any idea what that will do to my business?"

"No?" Quin reacted the same way he had to the old librarian. In the future, he'd be sure to tread carefully around this Covington descendant. He straightened and tried to redeem himself. "How could a name of a Christmas celebration hurt your business?"

"Tourists."

Precisely who he wanted to attract to Hawthorne. Quin waited for her to continue.

"More than half of my customers are tourists looking to take a bit of the commonwealth home with them. If they hear about a colonial Christmas, they will come in asking for an antique ornament or some such thing and get annoyed when I don't have anything to offer from 1776. Which is the only year the average tourist wants items from, regardless that most anything from that time period is either in a museum or the private collection of some millionaire. Unless the tourist is a basketball fan, in which case, they know 1891 as a famous Massachusetts-related year, and no, I don't have any antique basketballs. Anyway, Colonial Christmas will have tourists leaving critical reviews not only on Abigail's Antiques but on the tourist sites for Hawthorne too. All because our chamber director grew up in California and doesn't know how to use a search engine." Her voice softened as if she'd run out of fight.

Quin supposed it would get frustrating to explain constantly to people that not everything happened in 1776. He'd had to defend the dates on the Hawthorne History page to a prospective food vendor last week who didn't believe that the battles of nearby Lexington and Concord had happened on April 19, 1775 not 76. It was a common error. "I didn't intend for the tourists to see the actual flier."

"What about the social media and radio ads? Are you using 'Colonial Christmas' in them?"

Quin winced. Only that morning he'd signed off with the ad agency. No wonder the graphic designer snickered. "What would you call it then?"

"I don't know. Old Town Christmas. Or Hawthorne Hometown Holiday. That way you can make it politically correct. Not everyone celebrates Christmas."

"I like your alteration. Are you a writer?"

Her cheeks pinked, and she leaned back in her chair. "No. I research. I am a certified genealogist and have a degree in history from Bradford." Miss Wilson pushed her glasses up. The lenses magnified the golden flecks in her hazel eyes. Most glasses made eyes appear smaller.

"If I change the title to Hawthorne Hometown Holiday, can we call a truce?" Shame he hadn't met the fiery woman under different circumstances. It would be nice to know her better.

She straightened as if pulling back on her armor. "I wasn't aware we were at war, Mr. Kayhill."

He stood and walked around the desk. "I hope we aren't. My friends call me Quin. I hope you will too." He extended his hand.

She took it in a firmer handshake than he expected.

Checking his watch, he showed her to the door. Less than ten minutes to solve this problem, saving him twenty if she'd scheduled a meeting.

Mrs. Zimmerman stood on a step stool hanging a garland.

"Christmas decorations before Thanksgiving, Mr. Kayhill?" Makenna's frown put her in the class of people that didn't even use red and green in their decorations until the day after Thanksgiving.

"The chamber is just leading out in the Hawthorne Hometown Holiday." Quin moved to Mrs. Zimmerman's side, worried the grandmother of seven might fall. Makenna followed.

He put a hand on the old step stool. "I thought I told you to let me hang the garland."

Mrs. Zimmerman's head snapped around. "Oh look, you are under the mistletoe."

In unison, Quin and Makenna looked above them. The pale green of the mistletoe was set off with a red polka dotted ribbon. Kissing the fiery woman with the enormous eyes could only lead to problems since they'd just met.

Makenna stepped back before he did, her eyes wide. She looked back up at the parasitic plant and took another step back, her blush growing. "I... I need to get back to the store."

She left before he could apologize.

Quin needed to clear his throat before he spoke. "Mrs. Zimmerman, I don't believe mistletoe is appropriate for the office."

# CHAPTER 3

*M*akenna hurried around the corner and into the store. "Thanks for watching the store, Kent."

"No problem, Miss Wilson. We'll unload the van now." Kent Monroe and his twin brother Keith exited through the backroom. She would miss the high school seniors next year when she needed to find new part-time help. If the store was still open...

In the far back corner, a gray-haired woman poked through a box of photographs found tucked in a chest Makenna had acquired last month. The unsorted photos needed to be cataloged and filed with the others. Yet another project to tackle. Most photos sold for under five dollars and weren't worth cataloging in the main system. Makenna wove her way through the furniture and knickknacks to the woman.

Careful rearranging kept the store from looking half empty. If she didn't locate more inventory soon, Makenna wouldn't be able to hide the truth for much longer. "May I help you?"

The woman turned. "I'm not sure. I don't know what I am looking for."

The lace tablecloth in the photo the woman held reminded Makenna of something. It took her a moment to focus on the idea. "I have a beautiful tatting shuttle you might like."

The woman's face lit up, and she followed Makenna through the maze to the other end of the store. Tucked into a bookshelf was a small case with a glass lid that held a variety of tatting shuttles and thimbles.

"Oh, that blue and silver one is gorgeous."

Makenna opened the case and removed the exact shuttle she'd pictured only a moment before. How odd.

"My grandmother used to tat. I loved watching her make lace just by tying knots. I've always wanted to learn. This might be just the inspiration I need."

"This shuttle dates to the early 1920s. You might only want to use it for inspiration."

"That old?" The woman turned it over in her hands.

"That's my best guess."

"I'll take it. I want to learn so I can pass on the tradition to my granddaughter while she's young enough to think it's more fascinating than her mom's cell phone."

Makenna rang up the sale. Sliding a credit card through a card reader on a tablet wasn't as satisfying as hearing the cha-ching of the old cash register. With the computerized tracking system, she'd relegated the antique register to a glorified cash drawer. Few people made cash purchases anymore, so she could go more than a day without hearing its cheerful sounds.

"Do you know where I might find a book about tatting?"

"There are videos online that might help."

"I really would prefer a book."

"Try Red Leaves Books. Turn right at the door and take the sidewalk to the first cross street, and it will be on the opposite corner. Tell Claire, Makenna sent you."

"Thank you very much. This is just what I needed. I hadn't thought of tatting in years." The bell above the door rang a goodbye to the woman.

Makenna rearranged the shuttles in the case to hide the extra space left in the box. As she did, she replayed the experience in her mind. Weird. Super weird. Even for Hawthorne and all the stories of magic she grew up with, it was weird. She'd just matched a customer to an antique she'd purchased about a month ago. Grandma always knew what a customer wanted and hinted that maybe Makenna would do the same because she was a Covington, but it had never happened before—at least, not to her.

Ridiculous. She closed and locked the case. Makenna wasn't a wide-eyed teenager anymore. Stories of witch-craft were as authentic as the women who dressed up for tourists in Salem. Thinking of the tatting shuttle was only a coincidence. It had to be.

The Monroe brothers came through from the back room. "All unloaded, Miss Wilson."

"Can you two work four to close tomorrow?" She'd have time to get ready and make the train. No trying to put on makeup during stops, hoping no one was close enough to stare.

"Sure."

"Thanks, guys. I'll text you when I have another load. Do either of you want extra hours over the holidays?"

"Now that football is over, I have extra time," Kent said.

"Not me, I start wrestling season soon." Keith shrugged into his coat.

With Kent working, Makenna could almost guarantee the female teen population would frequent the shop. As long as they bought more than they broke. "Let me know your schedule. With holiday sales and First Night, I know I can give you extra hours."

"You'll be open on First Night?"

"Only until they have the early fireworks around seven." With so many activities planned on the common, staying open later would result in more shoplifters than purchasers. It had been two weeks since the gold watch worth over two thousand dollars disappeared from its locked case along with a handful of five-dollar items she had on display. The watch had been in a case which was still secured when she discovered it missing.

Makenna locked the front door after the boys left and turned the store sign to Closed. She dreaded this part of her day when she tallied the day's receipts. Rarely did they meet the daily sales goals.

The day had been slow. Only a few dozen patrons resulted in a paltry four sales. Makenna stared at the balance sheet. What would Abigail do? There was money enough to continue for a while. The money she'd budgeted to buy more stock could pay the bills and employees since there was so little new stock to be found.

Between competing with the larger Boston stores and shoplifting, Makenna wasn't sure how she'd survive another year. The gold watch that had disappeared last week would have covered a week's worth of expenses. She could cut back on her own pay. As Grandma Abigail's sole heir, she'd inherited the titles to the house and the store.

Using a feather duster, she started her round of cleaning. One summer, she made the mistake of suggesting that Grandma use a microfiber cloth and ended up with all the dusting every summer after that. Grandma was correct, dusting things the old-fashioned way was more satisfying. If only she could sell things the old-fashioned way, or even a novel way. Sadly, the website she set up didn't get much traffic or help to keep the business going. At the rate things were going, she'd be the first Covington to fail in a business since the Great Depression. There had been a close call in 1959 when Great Uncle Carl tried to sell Edsels at his car dealership in Woburn. Another dealership bought him out, so technically he didn't fail. Makenna couldn't bear it if her cousins whispered the name of Abigail's Antiques in the same sentence as the failed Covington Car dealership.

A text pinged on her phone.

*—Bosses want to take the new Jr. to dinner. Reschedule?*

Makenna answered the only way she could. *Sure, when?*

*—Saturday. Can you be here at 6? Most of the reservations are taken.*

The train schedule would get her to South Station an hour early. *6 works. I'll drive in.*

*—Thanks. You're an angel.*

There was something ironic that after paying the Monroe brothers twice to work for her, driving in, and parking, even if she ordered the most expensive thing on the menu, the dinner would still cost less than the arrangements she had to make to be there.

She needed to stop worrying about money so much.

Since Quin called so quickly, the advertising firm didn't charge extra to change from Colonial Christmas to Hawthorne Hometown Holiday. The fact that the firm also handled all the First Night publicity helped. Mrs. Zimmerman corrected the flier and sent out a changed holiday decoration email to the community businesses.

Quin checked his to-do list. Still three tasks to complete. He wanted to blame Makenna Wilson for causing him to stay late, though she'd only been in the office for a few minutes. Even all the calls to change things couldn't explain why he was two hours behind schedule.

Maps covered the table of the small conference room which doubled as First Night headquarters. Two more vendors confirmed they would attend, meaning he'd attracted more vendors than he'd originally planned for. Not necessarily a problem, he just needed another two hundred square feet of space in the vendor area. If they could close Maple Street on the south side of the square and Autumn Road along the east side to the church, it would give them more space.

Quin traced his finger over the streets on the map. Maybe they didn't need to worry about traffic, since they were already shuttling people from the commuter rail station and the high school parking lot. What if they closed the section where the monument was? He'd have to talk with the police chief again, but considering it was the chief's idea to close some streets to prevent pedestrian-vehicle accidents, it should be approved. Quin made a note on his task list for tomorrow.

The extra ice sculptors didn't need more space than he'd allotted, and their portfolios meant the judges would have some excellent competition, to view.

He spent the next two hours working through problems. This event had to be perfect. Not only was it Hawthorne's first First Night celebration, it was his first opportunity to prove that he could help increase tourism and business to the area and stay within budget, which was admittedly massive.

He moved cutouts around the map. Something was wrong with the rendering of the square. No maple trees. No big pine. No *any* trees. In reality, there were two or three near the gazebo. Quin pulled up street view on his phone map app, which wasn't helpful as it wasn't meant to record the trees. He'd need to walk through the park again.

One advantage of seeing the area in the dark was that it would be dark during most of the First Night celebration. The frosty night air formed his breath into clouds. A streetlamp near the church flickered. Quin pulled out his phone and added a note to check with the city to make sure the streetlights were in good repair.

At night, the common seemed bigger than in the light of day. He walked past the statue of Lavinia Hawthorne Covington. Too bad there weren't actual witches. What he really needed for December 31 was glorious weather. Preferably with no precipitation and a windchill above freezing. But then, witch or no witch, a fog in spring was most likely much easier to come by than a perfect night in December.

# CHAPTER 1

Someone tapped on the front door. Makenna yelled the obligatory, "We're closed!" as she crossed the room. The person tapped again. The hunched form of Grandma Tansy stood on the stoop. Makenna pulled the keys from her apron pocket. Tansy was technically her first cousin twice removed being Grandma Abigail's first cousin, but literally no one cared about proper relationships and everyone on their side of the family called her Grandma Tansy. Most of the *town* called her Grandma Tansy.

Makenna held open the door. Grandma Tansy had a knit shawl and no coat. "What are you doing out? You'll freeze."

"I hadn't seen you around this week and figured I should check on you." Grandma Tansy followed Makenna to the center of the store and sat on the stool behind the register. "You left your blinds up, so I knew you were here."

"I'm doing fine." A little white lie was better than dumping out the whole truth. Makenna lowered the blind in the closest window.

"You didn't look that way when I saw you hightailing it to the chamber this afternoon."

"Just a minor disagreement over the term Colonial Christ-

25

mas."

Tansy chuckled. "I wondered how long it would take you to clarify that situation. So many people make so many assumptions. Just because things are, doesn't mean they were, or will be the same as we expect."

"Is it too much to ask that the director of the chamber know a sprinkle of history?" The next blind was more stubborn and refused to lower, so she skipped it.

"What you define as a 'sprinkle of history' is someone else's blizzard."

"But everyone knows that there was no Christmas during the Colonial Era, and it was only marginally recognized during the New Republic period."

"Sweetie, I hate to tell you this, but other than you, me, and the librarian, not a single person in town has ever heard of New Republic." Grandma Tansy wandered through the store.

Makenna abandoned the blinds and continued to dust, following Grandma Tansy around. "Are you trying to tell me I was too quick to correct California Boy?"

Grandma Tansy cleared her throat. "He was born here, just like you were. I remember his mother coming in to get herbs for morning sickness. Your mother didn't need them, of course, being a Covington."

"He wasn't raised here."

"Neither were you." Grandma Tansy gave the handbell a ring. "Nice clear tone. I need one of these for my store."

Makenna added the bell for Grandma Tansy to her Christmas gift list. "I still lived in the commonwealth, and I lived in Hawthorne during the summers. He only visited." Makenna held her duster in the air like a wand.

"Don't you point that at me. Not every conversation is an argument you need to win. That must be from your Wilson side; we Covingtons don't need to argue everything."

Makenna bit back her response. Arguing with Grandma

Tansy was impossible. Instead, she pulled unsorted photos out of the box. Sometimes she could identify enough information to put a photo on a genealogical site for family members to discover.

Grandma Tansy circled one of the largest pieces in the store, an armoire dating back to the late 1700s, that stood over eight feet high. "You need to move this, so it isn't blocking these chairs. Be careful of the feet, they are the kind to reach out and grab a person."

The armoire had huge carved, clawed feet at the base. By Makenna's estimation, they were larger than the lion's at the Franklin Park Zoo. "I will."

"And you shouldn't lie to me."

Makenna's head popped up from the photos she sorted. "I don't lie."

Grandma Tansy raised a brow. "You said you were doing just fine. Anyone with half an eye can see the shop is suffering and you are worn to the bone. Do you ever take a day off?"

"There is so much to be done." If she could even afford one full-time employee, there wouldn't be so many after-hours tasks.

"Is that why you are barely taking care of yourself? Putting your hair up in a bun each morning because it is the fastest? It isn't even a fashionable one like those women on Insta-gramer-ma-thing. Wearing your glasses instead of putting on contacts and your make-up?"

"The dust bothers my eyes."

"It didn't when you were a teenager and batted those lashes at every boy you saw."

"I did not." Not everyone. Just one particular boy about two years older—who just happened to be the newest director of the Hawthorne Chamber of Commerce.

"What did I just tell you about arguing and lying?"

Makenna slammed the box of photos down on the counter. "Fine. You want the truth? The truth is every time I go to an estate sale, some big store from Boston or even New York has taken all the outstanding pieces. Then they raise the prices on the poor quality pieces left behind. Mostly, the only things that have sold this summer are items Grandma Abigail purchased. I am cutting corners every place I can to save money. Yes, I am tired. But I'd rather be working than sitting in that house all alone, wondering where a new draft will pop up next because that's one more repair I can't afford. At least if I am working, I am trying."

Tansy patted Makenna's hand. "Doesn't it feel good to let the truth out?"

"Not really. What good is the truth if it only hurts?"

Grandma Tansy smiled. "The truth sets you free."

The bells in the church tower chimed seven times. She closed the store an hour ago. This day needed to end.

Grandma Tansy pointed to the armoire. "It would look much nicer just over a foot or two. And make sure you apologize to the young man."

"I think you're right." Makenna gave the heavy piece of furniture a shove. It moved several inches.

"Goodnight." The bells rang over the door as Grandma Tansy left. Makenna used her back to push the armoire another few inches. She took a half step away from the piece and was stopped by her skirt, caught in the clawed foot. She knelt to extricate the cloth only to discover her imagination worked overtime as more of her skirt was claimed by the claw.

Under his long wool overcoat and scarf, Quin shivered. According to his grandfather, today wasn't even cold yet. The

28

last time he'd been in Massachusetts in the winter, he'd been fourteen and more interested in the newest video game than going outside. It hadn't even snowed that year. What was the point of Christmas in the cold if it didn't snow?

Having counted the trees and noted their location on his map, he crossed the lawn to return to the office.

Unlike the surrounding buildings, lights glowed from the antique shop's windows. Only half the blinds had been pulled down. Quin checked his watch. The store should have closed an hour and a half ago. Despite his encounter with the owner this afternoon, he wouldn't be able to forgive himself if he passed by only to discover later there had been a problem.

He looked both ways before he crossed the street at the corner. The sign in the window claimed the store was closed, but the door opened when he turned the handle. A bell rang above his head.

"We're closed!" Makenna's yell came from behind a large piece of furniture.

"Is anything wrong? Your door was open."

"*Humph*!" The huge armoire moved an inch or two in his direction. "No, nothing is wrong!"

"Do you need help?"

Makenna's face appeared around the side of the cabinet. "Mr. Kayhill?"

"Quin. Do you need help?" He repeated the question as he wove through the various goods.

"Please stop."

"Is something wrong?" He repeated his question. Oddly, she hadn't moved from behind what he now identified as a wardrobe over eight feet high.

"My skirt is caught under the armoire."

"How did— Never mind. I'll help lift it up; then you'll be free." He took another step closer.

Her eyes grew wide. "Don't take another step."

"But you need help." Quin reached the other side of the fine wood wardrobe.

"Stop!" Panic filled her face. "Please, just go away. I don't need your assistance."

Obviously, she needed help, but not *his* help. His gaze dropped to the floor. He expected to see a corner of cloth under the carved clawfoot. Instead, blue fabric, the same as the long skirt she'd worn to his office, pooled around the wardrobe leg. His eyes rose to meet hers.

Her blush touched every corner of her face. A tear creeped from under the rim of her glasses. "Just go."

Obviously, she was in distress. Regardless of what happened today, he wasn't leaving. "Are you hurt?"

Makenna shook her head.

With only one reason for her to be hiding that he could imagine, Quin unbuttoned his overcoat and slipped it off. "Here." He extended his arm as far as he could. She grabbed the offered covering and disappeared behind the wardrobe. A moment later she stepped out, his coat buttoned up. Her bared calves peaked out from underneath. He'd guessed the problem right. Not only was her skirt caught under the massive piece of furniture, she no longer wore it.

"If I lift this up, you can pull your skirt free." Quin moved to the corner with the greedy clawed foot.

"Careful, it is very heavy."

Heavy was an understatement. Lifting the antique even two inches off the ground was as difficult as his first deadlift. Makenna yanked her clothing free, and he set the furniture down.

"Thank you." She shook out the skirt.

"Is it ripped?"

"No. If you'll wait here a moment..." Makenna dashed through the door to the back room.

Quin looked around the shop. He'd come in here often during his summer visits to Hawthorne. There had been a cute girl called Sunny working behind the counter the year he'd turned fifteen. Somewhere in an unpacked moving box, he had the odds and ends he'd purchased trying to talk to her. The girl must be related to Makenna. It was impossible to tell with her hair in the bun if her hair had the same honey color as the girl he remembered. He pushed on the armoire. The sturdy piece must weigh two hundred and fifty pounds.

Skirt slightly askew, Makenna emerged from the back room, his coat over her arm.

"Thank you for the rescue." She handed the coat back to him.

"I am curious. How did you end up like that?"

She bit her lip. "Would you believe it reached out and grabbed my skirt?"

Quin glanced at the clawfoot. "This is Hawthorne and you are a Covington descendant, right? According to my grandfather, anything is possible." However furniture eating a skirt was only possible using CGI.

"Then that is the story I'll stick with. Thank you for your help. Although I assure you, I could have handled it on my own." She walked around the checkout counter separating them.

"And walked home in the cold without a skirt?"

"I have my long coat, and even if I didn't, who would see me? All the other businesses on the block are closed. No one is ever in the alley."

Many of the downtown business buildings contained upper-level apartments with outside access. Quin looked up, quite sure this was only a one-story building. "I didn't think this building had an apartment."

"It doesn't. I live in the house in the middle." She dusted an already clean counter.

Maybe she'd hit her head when her skirt got stuck. "The middle of what?"

"Of the block. Haven't you ever noticed there is a house hiding behind these buildings?"

"I just figured it would be another business like the lawyer next door. His place was once a house. You live there?"

Makenna smiled. "It is my ancestral home. A hundred and fifty years ago, we'd be standing in the well-tended yard of Olivander Hill's home. Unfortunately, my second great-grandfather was not a good businessperson. He started selling off parts of the property. They built the house with the law firm on the first portioned-off section. The owner in turn sectioned off their property. And now you have this hodgepodge of a block. An architectural history of the city in 100,000 square feet."

"Do you know the history of everything in Hawthorne?"

Her laugh was clear and sweet—not one of the fake giggles he detested.

"I wish. There is still so much I don't know. Then there is all the folklore—like people claiming my eighth-great grandmother, Lavinia, was a witch. Yes, she snuck out and warned the minutemen that the British were to march on Concord. But conjure a fog thick enough to stop them? Unlikely. There are always fogs in April around here."

"You don't like the tales?"

Makenna shrugged. "It's fun, but sometimes it gets annoying. Customers asking for magical items. Like I have a collection of cauldrons used by Lavinia. Even if she had used one, it would be in the Hawthorne Historical Museum or Covington House B&B. It would be worse if my last name were Covington. I'm sure the tourists would ask me for spells."

"So you're saying that next Halloween, I shouldn't play on the witch angle."

"Please, no." Makenna played with the keys on a lanyard around her neck.

Quin glanced at the grandfather clock. "I should get going. I worked late, and Mom worries if I don't get home at a reasonable hour."

Makenna raised a brow. "You live with your mother?"

"Technically, I live in an apartment. It just happens to be in my grandpa's house and my mother lives in the other apartment in the house."

"So you are saying you don't live in your Mom's cellar?"

"Mom lives on the second floor, and Grandpa has the main floor. No one lives in the basement. I have the attic apartment and extremely nosy neighbors who think I am not an adult."

"And they both know when you come home." Makenna walked with him to the door of her shop. "Thank you for helping me and not making it any more embarrassing than—" She waved her hand.

"Always willing to help a damsel undress," Quin turned away, hoping he wasn't blushing. "I mean in distress."

Makenna's laughter warmed the chilly November air around him.

# CHAPTER 5

Saturday afternoon, dressed for her date with Wendell, Makenna pulled the cargo van into the parking lot of the Covington House B&B. She'd been on the hands-free phone with Liberty when Wendell called to postpone again.

Liberty met her at the door to the family wing. "There's a pair of sweats in the bottom dresser drawer if you want to change."

A few minutes later, Makenna joined Liberty in the kitchen and pulled the bags of cranberries out of Liberty's reusable grocery bag. "You gave up on trying to grow your own cranberries?"

"With everything else I need to do around here, making a bog was just too much work. And the goats got into them. I bought these berries from an organic farmer near Plymouth instead." Liberty put a twenty-two-quart stock pot on the industrial stove.

"And making how many batches of cranberry sauce on a Saturday evening isn't too much work?"

"This is the last batch. I sold more this year than last and needed to make one more to have some on hand for people who forget until the last minute. Like you're one to talk about overworking. I drove by the shop the other night well after closing and the lights were still on."

"I just need to get things running well, then I'll slow down. I finally finished the cataloguing. All those photos took forever. It will be easier now. I can take pictures before I put items on the floor."

"Same tune, different month." Liberty set out a bag of lemons.

"Hey, I'm taking tonight off." Not by choice, exactly. She would not return to the shop when the Monroe boys saw her leave all dressed up.

"Does this really count?" Liberty looked up from her recipe card. "Sorry. That was mean."

"Wendell sounded really sick. He must have had something bad for dinner last night."

"Have you counted how many times he rescheduled on you in the last three months? And I'm not counting those video calls the two of you call a date."

Makenna rinsed the cranberries in a large colander. "Don't go dumping on him. He just hit a busy patch with work. And he did finally invite me to Thanksgiving dinner with his parents."

"I'm just saying that he doesn't drive out here anymore. He always expects you to go to him, and then he cancels while you're driving in or on the train." In another sink, Liberty rinsed the lemons.

"I hadn't even gone five miles when he canceled." Only because she was running late. "How many cups of berries?"

"Thirty-two. Use the eight-cup measure on the shelf over there." Liberty zested the lemons. "The invitation to Thanksgiving dinner is still open if he backs out. I have plenty of room."

"He won't back out. He's introducing me to his parents. Thanks for the offer. Eight cups of sugar?"

"Yes. Well, at least take one of the jars of sauce with you. Half of my return customers say they never have better

Thanksgiving dinners than when they have the Covington House cranberry sauce at their table. The Williams family in Shrewsbury has been buying it since Grandma first started selling it back in the 1930s. It should impress even a Beacon Hill family."

"They live in Belmont. Anyway it is a good idea, and you'll owe me a jar after making me slave away all evening."

"Making you? I know I'm your back-up plan."

"How much water?" Makenna held the glass measuring cup under the tap where she rinsed the berries.

"Eight, but use the water from the other sink."

"Why?"

"The house well is connected to that sink. It's sweeter than the municipal water. No chemical treatments."

Makenna walked across the room to the old-fashioned sink. "It makes a difference?"

Liberty checked the pot. "I don't know. It's just how it's always been done. Remember how much trouble we went through to get the old well's water all those years ago? And the entire time we could have just walked into the kitchen."

"I thought you and Eden would break your arms trying to get the crowbar to work. A bucket on a rope is way over-romanticized as a method to get water," said Makenna.

"We were so sure the water in the well was magic. And the tea we made with it? Worst. Tea. Ever."

"Sludge. Pure sludge." Makenna poured the water into the pot.

"Then, when we couldn't get the top on and my grandpa and grandma found us..."

"I thought your grandpa was going to lock us in the cellar for a year. I was glad to only get off with polishing the silverware. Although two-hundred silver spoons is excessive."

"Ha. You and Eden got off easy since you both had to leave town. Grandpa even went soft with Claire and Keira and let them go home soon after you left. Me? I got an entire week of it. Dusting the attic!" Liberty laughed and stirred the contents of the pot. "I wish things were as simple as they were back then. And our wishes. I can't believe we did that."

Makenna shuddered. "Please, don't remind me. I already had one reminder this week. I should have chosen a generic wish like you did."

"Reminder? Does that mean you finally talked to Quin? Or did you kiss him?" Liberty grinned.

"I was at the chamber protesting his Colonial Christmas flier. And Mrs. Zimmerman was hanging Christmas garland early. Anyway, there was mistletoe—"

"No way! You got your wish!" Pink splatters flew across the counter as Liberty waved her spoon. "That makes you the first one." She wiped off the counter. "Probably. No one's heard from Eden in years."

"He didn't kiss me—we both stepped back. I haven't been so embarrassed since I crashed into him that summer when I carried an ice cream cone and covered us both in raspberry swirl." Well, until later Thursday night when he found her not wearing a skirt and... The situation still made little sense. Furniture didn't come to life or grab skirts. Perhaps the sleepless nights were catching up to her.

"Please tell me you didn't stand there just stammering."

"I left. I'm quite sure he doesn't remember me, anyway." Forgetting *him* had never been possible. Even if Walter hadn't bragged about his grandsons regularly. Quin's eyes were still kind. They had long been her favorite feature. Her friends would talk about his tan or his blond hair, but for her it was always the eyes. Even after she'd yelled at him, he'd still helped her. Oops, and she hadn't apologized or thanked him.

"Why would he recognize you? You were probably in your old lady clothes—"

"Vintage." Not once had she worn something baggy or resembling a housecoat to work.

"With your hair up and your glasses on."

"Buns are fast, functional, and fashionable." Glasses were a necessity and didn't require a defense. "How many jars do you need prepped?"

"Don't change the subject. They are all prepped. You need to take care of yourself. I know you dressed up tonight, but that was for Wendell. You should dress every day like you are going to see his."

"I'm working. Working hard." Makenna drew a circle in the air around her face. "I don't have time to do this daily."

"You worked hard with Aunt Abigail, too. But you took the time to do your hair and put in your contacts. The vintage clothes are great. An iconic statement only my best friend-cousin can pull off. Yet, often, they are wrinkled, and I am not just talking about your '80s broomstick skirts. And you look tired all the time. More than tired. Even under your makeup, I can tell you have bags. This is the first time I've seen you in your contacts in a long time."

Trying to clear the lump in her throat, Makenna rinsed the used measuring cups. "I'm only wearing one."

"What?"

"I lost the other contact, and my prescription is so expensive. Don't worry, I am still legal to drive, only seeing out of one eye." Sometimes she wished she could wear soft disposable contacts like the rest of her friends.

"When did you lose it?"

"First of September. I don't want to replace it because I am due for an eye exam in January, and I always get a new prescription." Like everyone else, her insurance didn't cover more than one pair of gas permeable contacts a year.

"So in the meantime, you suffer?"

"I am not suffering. I only see Wendell on weekends

or calls, and I can take my glasses off for those. At work, I need both eyes."

Liberty set the gas stove burner to low and turned her full attention on Makenna. "Giving you a pass on the contacts because I think Wendell is shallow to care. You let yourself go even more since Aunt Abigail's passing and you need to — I'm not sure how to say this — come back to life. I miss your laughter. I miss my Sunny cousin."

"I still laugh. I just laughed on Thursday." Mom and Dad had nicknamed her Sunny. Part of the reason she wore vintage clothes was to make people smile. She smiled, didn't she?

"The fact you know the last time you laughed is scary. I don't know when I laughed last."

Makenna placed her hands on her hips. "Two minutes ago. At me. Is it really that bad? Grandma Tansy gave me the same lecture the other night, but she's been a bit off lately."

Liberty wrapped an arm around Makenna. "I want you back again."

Makenna leaned her head on Liberty's shoulder. "I just want to sleep. I lay in bed at night and all I see in my mind is the store and the profits going down. So I get up and surf for new inventory and try to figure out ways I can sell things. Grandma had such a way with people and things, and I don't have it. I've always loved the store, but I wasn't ready to do it on my own."

"Then let's finish these up and get you home."

Makenna worked slowly. There wasn't much point to going home only to have the same worries keep her awake.

Walter shook the remote. "Why isn't there anything good on TV? A billion channels full of garbage. I don't understand why anyone would want to watch the channel that shows dogs playing all day. I've got my own dog to watch. Not that he does anything but sleep twenty hours a day.

"People use that channel to entertain their dogs when they aren't home." Quin looked up from his organization app on his phone.

"What are you doing on that phone?"

"Planning my to-do list."

"That's another thing. Everyone is always playing games on their phone. What is the point of that? It's like perpetual solitaire."

The secret to getting along with his grandfather was to read between the lines. "Do you want to play a game?"

"Only if you want to spend time with an old man."

"Pops, if I didn't want to be with you, I would not have come down from my apartment." The fact that old steam radiators didn't heat as well in the attic as they did on the ground floor prompted Quin to visit his grandfather more often than he might otherwise. It was one of those two-birds-with-one-stone things: get warm and spend time with Pops so he didn't feel so guilty.

"It's Saturday night. Why aren't you out with some girl?"

"I've only lived here a few months. I've been busy with First Night and other chamber business."

"Too busy to date? We courted women right, back in my day. None of this meeting over a phone app then having to bring the right color of carnation to meet for coffee over a twenty-minute lunch."

"You know more about it than I do. I've never brought a carnation to meet over lunch."

Walter muttered something unintelligible as he searched the coat closet. "Othello or checkers? I don't have many two-person games."

"Either. You know I'll win, anyway."

"No, you won't." Walter pulled out an ancient checkers game with mismatched pieces.

"Checkers?" Quin pocketed his phone. "You're on."

"You need a social life. I've seen those chick-flicks. I know all about those men who live with their mommy. Regular romance killer."

"I live in one of the three apartments you divided this old house into. I don't live with Mom."

"She cooks your dinner."

Quin sorted the pieces. "Rebecca cooks yours too. You don't see me giving you a hard time about it."

"When are you going to start dating? I remember when you used to have a crush on Makenna. She is still mostly available. That Boston lawyer she goes out with is a chowderhead."

"I had a crush on Makenna Wilson?"

"Sure did. Every other day you were hanging around that antique shop trying to get the nerve up to talk with her."

"Wait a minute. You are telling me Makenna is Sunny?" The uptight, know-it-all was the smiling, friendly girl behind the counter? Quin rubbed his neck to rid himself of the mental whiplash.

"Who else would she be? Don't tell me you didn't recognize her."

"She's taller."

"So are you."

"I thought Makenna's hair was brown." They had to be different people.

"When she wears her hair down, you can tell. Not bleached blond like those California girls you are used to. Her hair has more colors in it."

"I haven't seen her with her hair down since I moved back." Quin hopped one of Walter's pieces. "And those glasses. She didn't use to wear glasses, did she?"

"Contacts. Haven't seen her in them lately." Walter tapped his own readers. "You aren't one of those people who doesn't like women because they wear glasses, are you?"

"You have to ask? Before LASIK, my glasses were almost as thick as hers."

"Then you shouldn't date her; your kids would be blinder than you are." Walter jumped three checkers to earn a crown.

"From her glasses, I think she is farsighted. I'm nearsighted. It could balance out."

"So you're still interested?"

Quin countered by jumping four of Walter's pieces. "Are you playing matchmaker?"

"Nonsense. That's for old ladies. I'm just pointing out you don't need an app."

"You also said she had a boyfriend."

"Not a particularly good one. He is a lawyer out of Boston, and oily as they come." Walter moved, winning the game. "He stands her up more than half the time."

"Does she know you don't like him?"

"I told her he's no good for her. She counters with this story about how he has been so good to stay with her through the past year and a half while three of her grandparents died. Like she owes him for showing up at the funeral, so she doesn't have to sit alone. Abigail didn't like him either."

"Why do women stay with men that aren't good for them?"

"Why do you keep wearing that old, faded Chargers sweatshirt when I gave you a new Patriots one the beginning of the season?"

"It's comfortable." Quin put the pieces back in the box.

"But it has a hole in the wristband and the logo is for the wrong team. Get my point?"

"Sure, Pops, men are like old sweatshirts." Quin wanted more details about the lawyer but knew that pressing his grandfather only meant he was falling for whatever game Walter was playing.

# CHAPTER 6

Makenna unplugged the curling wand. It took almost an hour to create the beach curls she wanted. Even with stopping to take care of her burned fingers—thanks to Grandma Tansy's quick healing burn cream—she was still running on time. After months of hearing descriptions of Wendell's parents' Belmont home, she'd decided on a remade vintage navy pencil skirt and white sweater combo for a more formal look for Thanksgiving dinner. Since Wendell was picking her up, she'd inserted her one contact, knowing she wouldn't need to drive at night. After finishing her makeup, she sent a selfie to Liberty—proof she could fix herself up.

She'd taken all of Sunday off, pampering herself, and cleaned the house. Even with a rest day, she still needed makeup to cover the dark circles under her eyes. Maybe Grandma Tansy and Liberty were right. She had gotten too busy to take care of herself. If only she could find the proverbial sweet dreams her grandmother always wished for her.

According to the chimes of the clocks downstairs, Wendell was fifteen minutes late. Not a huge thing. Who knew what traffic was like between his Boston apartment and here. Thirty minutes later, the clock chimed again, and her phone rang. Wendell's photo came up on her screen.

"Hey, is everything alright?"

"I'm sorry, babe. I should have called earlier. Mother invited my great aunt who is a hundred, and she's worried about germs..." His voice trailed off. The lack of background noise indicated he was not in a car.

"Are you uninviting me to Thanksgiving dinner?"

"You can still go to your cousin's, right?"

"Sure."

"I'll make it up to you. I have tickets to the opening of *The Nutcracker* tomorrow night."

"I thought we decided to go next week. Tomorrow is a huge shopping day, and I can't leave the shop early."

"These are box seats. You'll love them."

"Did you hear me? I said I can't drive in tomorrow."

"Then take the commuter rail."

"Wendell! I. Can't. Go. Tomorrow. We discussed this. And you said you had tickets for next Saturday."

"Hey, my Mom is signaling for me to come inside. I'll call you tonight, babe."

Silence.

Makenna checked the phone screen to make sure the call had really disconnected. The temptation to throw the phone across the room was balanced out by the cost of a new one. How dare he do this to her again? He should have called her earlier.

His mom? If he called from his parents' house, he knew at least an hour and a half hour ago she couldn't come. What was up? What happened to their long talks this past summer walking around the pond? Or Wendell's promise that after he finished this next year at the law firm, they'd have more time? Their kisses under the stars? The plans to visit Italy?

Not as definite as marriage, but still they were planning.

He'd been so attentive all those weeks after grandma died. Their relationship moved forward from the friendly place it had been since they met at his law firm when she went to Boston to clarify a part of Grandpa Wilson's will almost two years ago. She'd told no one, not even Liberty, but earlier this summer she'd thought she'd be engaged by Christmas, even with Wendell's insistence that they had to take things slow due to his job. Now she wasn't so sure she wanted to be married to him.

Makenna kicked off her heels and switched for a pair of ballet flats more suited to walking to Covington House. She grabbed the jar of cranberry sauce off the counter. No way would she eat it all. Liberty could always sell it for Christmas. She pulled her favorite wool coat from the closet and grabbed the matching earmuffs. She'd be early for Liberty's dinner, which would allow her to help since her only offering was the jar of sauce Liberty made.

She hoped Liberty's grandpa, Great-Uncle Dean wouldn't make them go around the table naming what they were grateful for. At this moment, she had nothing.

"Where is the cranberry sauce?" Walter slammed the refrigerator door.

"Quin, did you pick up a jar from Covington House yesterday like I asked?" Rebecca stirred the giblet gravy on the stove.

"I forgot." He never even added it to his task app on his phone. There was just so much to do for work. Rebecca could have done it. She was only taking care of Grandpa and editing novels for the firm in California where she worked remotely.

Walter opened the fridge again. "Run over to Covington House and see if they have any more."

Quin grabbed his coat and rushed out the door. It was almost as fast to walk as it would be to drive; however, driving was so much warmer, so he hopped into his car. As he turned onto Covington Road, he passed a pedestrian with long honey-blond hair.

For a moment he thought it might be Makenna. That was ridiculous. According to Pops, she was in Boston with her lawyer boyfriend. The man had not impressed his grandfather. Hardly surprising, as few things impressed Walter Abbott.

Quin parked in the half-full parking lot at the bed and breakfast and sprinted to the front door. No one sat behind the small check-in desk. Quin rang the bell.

A middle-aged woman wearing a "Run, Turkey Run" apron came from the back of the building. "May I help you?"

"Do you have any more cranberry sauce?"

"Sorry, we sold out on Tuesday."

Even if he had remembered yesterday, he would have failed. "Thank you. Maybe next year."

"Have a happy Thanksgiving."

"You too." Quin walked back to the car. Did Massachusetts have a grocery store that would be open? A Stop and Shop or one of the big box stores in Framingham might be open. He checked his phone. Canned wasn't what his grandpa wanted, but it was better than nothing.

"Excuse me."

Quin looked up just in time to avoid walking into the woman he'd passed driving over. She held a jar of the coveted sauce.

"Makenna?" The question mark at the end of the sentence was accidental.

"Happy Thanksgiving, Quin."

"I thought you were in Boston." He winced, he wasn't supposed to know that. Pops and his gossiping.

She lifted her chin. "Obviously not."

"Is that a jar of Covington House cranberry sauce?"

She lifted it up to eye level. "Yes."

"Stupid question—why are you bringing a jar of the sauce here?"

"I didn't need it."

"Can I buy it from you? Grandpa is fit to be tied because we don't have any sauce, and I was searching for an open grocery store so I could get something. Even canned at this point would be better than nothing."

"Doubt you will find a store open within fifty miles. Last year my Aunt Tami drove all over searching for strawberries, but everything was closed. Unlike other parts of the country, we close for the entire holiday." She handed him the jar. "It's yours."

"How much?"

"Consider it a gift. For Walter." She smiled a half smile that didn't reach the eyes that for once were not hidden behind those thick glasses. "Someone should benefit from my hard work."

"Yours?"

"Liberty conned me into helping her make it the other night."

"Thank you. Especially for saving me from Pops."

"Walter wouldn't have let you forget about it for a year." Her smile grew a little as if the thought of him being pestered for a year pleased her.

"Or more...I owe you." Without thinking, he bent and kissed her on the cheek. "You saved me."

Makenna slipped around him and walked up the steps to the front door. "Tell Walter to have a happy Thanksgiving."

"I will. And you have one too!"

He walked back to his car. He'd just kissed Makenna. Not a proper kiss. But she hadn't slapped him for the gesture or seemed annoyed. Boston lawyer boyfriend or not, maybe he had a chance. He knew he shouldn't have kissed her, but he had no regrets.

Makenna slipped into the north parlor and put her hand over her cheek. What had just happened? Why hadn't she told him off? The kiss meant nothing more than gratitude for saving him from a dinner with Walter grumbling. Probably the same kiss he gave his mom when she gave him a cookie. And it definitely didn't fulfill her wish at the well years ago. Curse Liberty for bringing that up. Especially after the mistletoe incident last week, she couldn't stop wondering what Quin's kiss would be like.

Not that it mattered. She had Wendell. Maybe.

She found Liberty in the kitchen. "Give me something to do and don't ask questions."

Liberty handed her a large apron. "Cut the celery."

Dinner was a blur. Grandma Tansy mentioned Quin, and Makenna may have snorted. If she was honest, he wasn't all bad. And what was that kiss? Just a peck on the cheek. Makenna tried to make it look like she was eating more than playing with her food. She passed up the cornmeal stuffing, which she never liked, and a pomegranate salad Keira made. Seriously, pomegranates and Thanksgiving? Someone was pushing the limits of tradition.

Kiera's multi-flavored scones were somewhat perplexing. Although they looked the same everyone tasted different. Makenna's tasted like hawthorn berries, reminding her of the night she wished to kiss Quin. A memory she pushed aside faster than she passed on the green bean casserole.

Great-Uncle Dean kept asking questions about the shop and what she was thankful for. Makenna answered with a nod or single word. She did not understand what he said as her mind was so preoccupied. This was the day she was supposed to meet Wendell A. Smith's family. The Smiths. One of *the* Smiths of Boston. That was almost like getting to go to the Kennedys, only not so famous.

How could he goof on such a day? Makenna looked around at all the extra food. And what kind of chef makes a Thanksgiving feast where there isn't enough food for one more? Mini turkey? How hard is it to add a mashed potato into the mix?

After dinner she volunteered for dish duty, mostly to avoid conversations. Keira had a cousins' meeting that brought up uncomfortable questions about Covington magic and her scones. Considering the tatting shuttle incident, Makenna didn't want to think about it too deeply. If magic existed, why was she forced to eat Thanksgiving dinner with extended family? Covington magic hadn't saved Grandma Abigail from her cancer or her parents from the drunk driver. If it existed, it was only good for matching middle-aged women with tatting shuttles.

Thankfully, Keira left with Brant to deliver boxed meals. That was an interesting combo of the clean-cut motorcycle rider and her cousin—third cousin, to be exact, but nobody cared about correct genealogy.

Aunt Lisa, Liberty's mother, rushed into the kitchen. "Ginger has food poisoning or something. Claire took her to the hospital. I'm going to take Grandma Tansy; she is so upset."

Makenna held up a dish towel. "I'll stay and clean."

After they finished cleaning, Liberty and Makenna watched Christmas romance movies on the Hearthfire channel and waited for news.

Minutes before the clock in the church bell tower struck midnight, Makenna unlocked her front door. It wasn't until she took out her contact that she realized Wendell never called. Makenna put on her glasses and checked her texts. None. Maybe he'd had an emergency too.

She checked her alarm. Oh no, she had to be up early to put up her Christmas decorations at the store. If only she'd given in this year and hadn't let the pilgrim dolls have their day in the window. Which meant she had to face Black Friday with only four hours of sleep. At least she could be grateful that Aunt Ginger was in stable condition.

# CHAPTER 7

Most Hawthorne businesses were decorated and open early. Quin navigated crowded sidewalks, judging the foot traffic for Black Friday. Considering the small town didn't have a single big box store with deeply discounted deals on electronics, it appeared sales were going well. No lines at any store, but there were many more people than usual out at 9:30 a.m. on a Friday. He stopped by Sweet Memories Café to grab a muffin. His grandfather and his cronies sat at their usual table.

"Good morning, Judge, Gene, Pops."

Gene scowled. "Not much good about it from my point of view. Ginger is in the hospital and rumor says it was Keira's cooking."

Judge crossed his arms. "The girl is talented. She's just a better baker than a cook. I hope you came in here to get a hawthorn berry scone."

"That was my intention." Muffin, scone, not that much of a difference in his mind.

"Better do it. I know it isn't her fault that Ginger is in the hospital. Make sure they put it in a logo bag so people can see you aren't scared to eat here," advised Gene.

"Also," Walter said, "take Makenna something for giving you that cranberry sauce yesterday."

At Grandpa's advice, Quin risked his life on a scone. The heart attack, or whatever it was, most likely had nothing to do with Keira's cooking. The smell of apples and cinnamon tickled his nose. "And caramel spiced cider, please."

Keira smiled, although it was obvious Ginger's condition was taking a toll on her. "Anything else, Quin?"

"Does Makenna have a favorite?"

"She usually comes by for a muffin but hasn't this morning. I guess Black Friday started early for her."

"I'm walking down Covington Road next. I owe her a thank you. Will you bag up a muffin and whatever she likes to drink?"

"Two caramel apple ciders then. You both have good taste." Keira rang up the order.

Quin dug a twenty out of his pocket. "Just put the change in the tip jar." Empty tip jars rarely generated more tips. Quin hoped his offering would induce others to be generous. He had no clue what the financial situation of the café was, but a good tip day would brighten all the employees' spirits with Ginger in the hospital.

Crossing at the corner, Quin dodged two mothers pushing strollers. Fortunately, someone exited the antique shop as he needed to enter with two cups and bags. A simple evergreen wreath hung on the door decorated with a red ribbon and a sprig of red berries. Next to the door, where the fall gourds and decorated pitchfork had been last week, stood an antique sled. Blue and white ribbons adorned it and a pair of ancient ice skates. Garlands bordered the front windows.

Behind the counter, Makenna turned and pushed her glasses back up her nose. The glasses magnified the exhaustion in her eyes. Instead of a bun, she wore her hair down today. "Coming to make sure I adequately decorated for Hawthorne's Hometown Holiday?"

"I am stopping by all the businesses this morning. I heard your family had a tough day and Keira said you hadn't been in, so I brought you this." Quin set her cup and bag on the checkout counter.

She lifted the lid, closed her eyes and breathed in the aroma. Looking in the bakery bags, her smile grew. "Caramel apple cider and an everything muffin. Thank you, I was about to call over and see if Walter would bring me something. My first customer showed up before I finished decorating the windows this morning."

The bell rang on the door behind him. Makenna peered over his shoulder. She moved the pastry bag under the counter. "Thanks for bringing this by."

"Is anyone working with you?"

"The Monroe twins will be in around three for a couple of hours. Thanks again." She smiled and hurried to greet her customers.

Outside, Quin sipped his cider and returned to the café.

Judge dealt the cards at the corner table. "Back so soon?"

"I realized I couldn't eat and walk, plus most of the stores have a 'No food' policy." Quin pulled up a chair and watched the game progress.

"Do you play Sergeant Major?" asked Judge.

"Pops taught me when I was a boy. I'm afraid I don't remember much."

Gene explained the basic rules.

Quin finished his scone. "Pops, how often do you help Makenna?"

"A couple hours a week here and there. Why?"

"I just dropped off her breakfast, and she ended up hiding it under the counter when a customer came in. I'm afraid she won't get a break until this afternoon when her high school employees show up."

"And you're wanting me to leave my game and go over there?"

"Maybe after the game? Just for fifteen minutes."

"How about you play my hand, and I'll go over now. Just don't lose for me. And watch Judge. He'll try to cheat." Walter pulled his coat on.

"I do not cheat."

"Do too."

"Why just last week—"

Keira appeared with a pot of coffee in hand. "Walter? Do you need a refill?"

"No, I was just leaving. Maybe when I get back."

Keira asked the other men and moved to the next table. Quin picked up his grandfather's cards and tried not to lose too badly.

Makenna emerged from the back room having eaten a still warm breakfast and taken care of other pressing needs. "Thanks again, Walter."

"Don't thank me. My grandson insisted I get over here and give you a break. He even offered to play my spot with Judge and Gene."

"I'm thanking you because you're the one who came." She didn't want to think of Quin's involvement. He wasn't supposed to notice or take care of her.

"I'll be off now, but I'll come back at lunchtime, just to check on you."

"No need to do that."

Harrumph. "That is what you think, missy." He waved a goodbye and held the door for an exiting customer.

Makenna checked the accounting software. Walter had made two sales. Not bad for a fifteen-minute break.

A young couple came in. As Makenna wove her way over to them, she pictured an old china doll on the other side of the room tucked into a cradle. This couple needed that doll. The inspiration came so strongly, she nearly tripped. "May I help you?"

The woman's hand moved to her abdomen. The couple was soon to be a family. The husband stepped forward. "My grandmother died recently, and we are naming our daughter after her. We wanted something that we could say had been an heirloom. A toy."

"Don't you have any heirlooms?" Makenna refrained from commenting on their plan to fake an heirloom.

The man frowned. "My uncle sold off most everything when he moved Grandma into a nursing home. We never even got a chance."

"Do you know when your grandmother was born?"

"1925."

"Are you planning on putting the item in your daughter's nursery?"

"Maybe on a shelf." The wife spoke up. "I've read that many antique toys aren't safe for children because of the paints and things, so I don't want her to reach it."

"Yes, many aren't suitable for safety concerns. They are also fragile. Have you considered a doll?"

The couple nodded in unison.

"I have a couple in mind that are the right era." Makenna led them over to the corner where the display contained an old child's cradle and several toys.

The husband gasped. "That's hers!" He whipped out his phone and scrolled through his photos. First, he showed the phone to his wife, then to Makenna. The porcelain doll was an exact match to the doll in the photo, down to the stain on the sleeve and skirt.

It was Makenna's turn to gasp. The impression she had when they'd walked in flashed in her mind, as if the thought were trying to prove itself worthy, there was an image of a child's quilt.

"Wait here." Makenna hurried over to the shelf where she kept the quilts and sorted through the smaller ones until she reached a pink, green, and yellow one. There was a mismatched piece of fabric where someone had patched it with tiny stitches. The patch matched the one on the quilt the doll sat on in the man's photo.

The husband and wife were examining the doll and comparing it to the one on the camera. Makenna handed them the quilt. "I purchased both items at an estate sale in August. I am sure this quilt matches the one in your photo."

"Where was the sale?"

"Lexington, I believe. I can look it up for you."

"Did you get anything else there?"

"Most of the big items were sold before I arrived. If you come over to the counter, I'll look on my computer." Makenna listed off the other items she'd purchased: tools, a sewing box, and a few books which she'd passed off to Claire to sell at Red Leaves Books. The estate sale was one of the first sales she'd attended where most of the good things were sold to a larger store before the sale started. The doll and the quilt stood out to her, so she'd purchased them.

The husband shook his head. "I don't remember any of those other things. But I remember seeing the quilt."

"It would make a nice wall hanging. I should have painted the nursery green." The wife frowned.

"I'll repaint it tomorrow. We'll take the doll and the quilt. How much?"

"Knowing they should have been yours, I can't charge you for them."

"At least let me reimburse you what you paid for them."

Makenna read off the amounts from the computer.

The man slipped his card through the reader, and then added a tip four times the amount they'd agreed to.

"You can't pay that much. It's more than I had the items listed for."

"You don't understand. I would have paid double for something that looked similar. I can't believe I found the ones that belonged to Grandma. After scouring the stores in Boston, I'd given up. It was just by chance we drove through today. There was a wreck, and we took a scenic route."

"I am so glad I could help." Coincidence. Just a coincidence. Magic required spells and things. Makenna had done nothing more that buy a doll in less than pristine condition.

The couple left, and Grandma Tansy came up to the counter.

"Grandma Tansy, how's Aunt Ginger?"

"Oh, she'll be fine, dear. I know she will."

"What do you need?"

"I need to confess. Temptation overcame me, and I borrowed this from you a few weeks ago." Grandma Tansy held out the missing gold watch.

Only the presence of other customers in the store kept Makenna from screaming. "You *borrowed* this?"

"I just needed it for a while. It is an incredibly special watch, you know."

"Yes. I know." It was one of the single most valuable pieces in the store. Each night she'd locked it up in the safe with the other small valuables.

"Well, it was time to give it back. You need it now, and I don't anymore." Grandma Tansy turned to go.

Makenna stared at the watch in her hand. What should she do? It wasn't like she could call Officer Hastings on family. "Grandma Tansy? Do you have any more things you borrowed?"

"I may have one or two items. Don't worry, they won't sell. Would you like a twenty for them?" Grandma Tansy held up a wrinkled bill.

Makenna took the money. "I turned in a police report on this. What am I to tell Officer Hastings when I tell him the watch is back?"

"You can always say it was magic." Grandma Tansy shuffled out of the store.

Another customer came to the register with an old hand crank drill. Makenna slipped the watch into her apron pocket. As soon as the transaction ended, she pulled out her keys and opened the glass case in the counter. Makenna checked the time on the watch against her phone and set it back in the place of honor it had maintained for so many years. How had Grandma Tansy gotten it out of the display case? Makenna was sure the elderly woman hadn't been in the store the day the watch disappeared and there were only two keys to the case—one around her neck and the other in the safe.

When Walter came to give her a quick lunch break, Makenna called the police station and reported the watch returned. The sergeant on duty told her he'd send Officer Hastings around as soon as he was available.

She shot a text off to her cousins, asking what to do about Grandma Tansy. What if she'd shoplifted from someone who wasn't a Covington?

Midafternoon, a family of four, including two teenagers, came in. The teens looked around, then leaned against the claw-footed armoire and pulled out their phones.

"Excuse me. Will you please refrain from leaning on the furniture?" As soon as Makenna said it, the image of a toaster came to mind. This was the oddest thing yet. "Have you guys ever seen how they used to toast bread over a stove top?"

The younger boy moved away from the furniture and cocked his head. "On the stove?"

"Usually with an open flame."

The mention of fire caught the older teen's attention. Makenna led them to the kitchenware display and pulled down one of several toasters that had collected there over the years.

"It just looks like a metal pyramid."

"Does that mean it came from Egypt?"

"No, they made this one in the USA." Makenna placed it on her palm. "You set the toaster over a stove flame or hot coals and lay your bread against the sides. After a minute, you take the tongs and flip the bread to the other side."

"Wow, you could toast bagels on it and not get them stuck."

"Your great-grandfathers probably used something like this when they were your age."

"Can I hold it?" asked the older boy.

"Sure."

Makenna caught sight of the parents waiting a few feet away, staring at her with awe-filled faces.

The boy turned to his parents. "Look at this. The lady says this is how your grandpa would have toasted bread."

"I remember my grandma having something like that in one of her cupboards when I was a little girl," said the mother. She took the toaster from her son and examined it. "I should pull out that old photo album and show you boys. I think I have a photo of her kitchen."

"Did they do other cool things over fires?" asked the older teen.

Makenna didn't hesitate. This time as she pulled out one of the newer, 1930s popcorn pans. "Guess what this is."

She handed it to the teen who opened and closed the hinged lid. He shook his head.

"A popcorn popper. You haven't had real popcorn until you've used one of these."

His mother came over. "Is this still usable?"

"This one is."

"Can we get it, Mom?"

The mother nodded and looked to her husband, who shrugged.

"Is there anything else I can help you with?"

"I think we'll just look."

Makenna helped another customer before the family came to check out. They added an old Parcheesi game to their collection. The mother took care of the transaction while her husband stood near the door with her sons. "My boys haven't talked that much in one day in so long. I had to drag them in here. This is absolutely amazing. Who knew antiques would get our kids to talk to us?"

Makenna gave the woman the same smile that she'd seen Grandma Abigail give her customers a hundred times, because on the inside she was freaking out. She had no explanation for the inspirations she kept getting.

# CHAPTER 8

How was it at the end of the day Quin found himself hours behind? No matter which planner app, no matter how many alarms he set, it seemed that by 5 PM, he was always running late. He'd purposely kept his Black Friday activities focused so he wouldn't get behind. The only time he could find that he'd wasted in his entire day was that game of Sergeant Major, which he played for a good cause. Rushing back to the office for a 6:15 p.m. west coast phone call, Quin glanced at the blazing lights of Abigail's Antiques. Makenna was the only person inside. Had she eaten dinner? He could ask her out—just two harried friends eating together after a rough Black Friday. Absolutely nothing to do with anything else since she had a boyfriend.

Quin checked the time on his watch, which in order to keep up on things, he'd chosen specifically because it showed the minute and the second. If he could be in and out of Abigail's Antiques in four minutes, he would be on time for the phone call. Four minutes should be enough to ask her if she wanted to get dinner together.

Makenna looked up from behind the register as he entered. "Oh, it's you. I suppose you heard I caught my shoplifter?"

"I didn't know you had a shoplifter." He tried to keep up on the crime in the businesses, but he hadn't had time to check the report the last couple of weeks. He wanted to rush her with the shoplifter conversation, so he could get to the point.

"I don't. Now." Makenna tapped on the display case. "I filed a police report and started insurance proceedings all because Grandma Tansy borrowed a gold pocket watch and a few other items without telling me."

Quin studied the intricate watch in the display case. "She borrowed this watch? It looks valuable."

"So valuable it will never sell. It's been in the antique shop as long as I can remember. Occasionally, someone will buy it only to return it the next day. I don't know what got into Grandma Tansy. She kept it for more than a week."

According to rumor—not that Quin ever listened—Grandma Tansy, the self-proclaimed matriarch of the Covington clan, had been acting unusual for the last few months. No one seemed willing to state the obvious: that the old woman was succumbing to the frailties of age. "What are you going to do?"

"I was waiting for Officer Hastings. I was hoping he had some ideas. Since she freely returned the watch, I can't have her charged for shoplifting. Can you imagine the scandal? It would be worse than if someone actually got fined for wearing a goatee."

"A... What?" Quin traced the design of the pocket watch through the glass case.

"Supposedly there's some old law forbidding the wearing of goatees without a permit. But don't worry, I don't think your five o'clock shadow qualifies."

Quin rubbed his jaw. "With First Night just over a month away, I would appreciate it if you can keep our little town of Hawthorne out of the scandal sheets."

"You and me both. I'm at the mercy of cousins and aunts and uncles of all sorts since Grandma Abigail died. I'd rather not be disowned from the Covington clan. It's all I have."

The second hand on the gold pocket watch moved, but the minute hand didn't seem to. The time couldn't possibly be right. According to the old pocket watch, it was only seconds after he'd come into the antique store. No wonder they always returned it. The watch was broken.

Quin snuck a peek at his wristwatch. Less than a minute had gone by since he entered the store. He could've sworn they'd been talking longer. He really should get to the whole point of why he came in so he could get to the call. "Have you been able to eat dinner?"

"Not yet—" The bell over the door rang. Makenna froze, then smoothed her hair and red and green sweater. "Wendell? What are you doing here?"

"I came to get you for the opening night of *The Nutcracker*." Everything about the man spoke money from his shiny leather shoes to his tailored wool coat. A perfectly ironed scarf hung around his neck as a fashion statement, not to ward off the cold.

"I told you that tonight was impossible." Makenna removed her glasses and slipped them into the pocket of her apron.

"Do you know how much these tickets cost? Hurry and you'll have time to get ready. Slip on that red dress I like so much. It'll be perfectly festive for the season."

"Today is Black Friday; I can't possibly leave now. I'm open for almost three more hours, and then I need to close shop. We discussed this months ago. I can't go tonight."

"Are you standing me up?"

"I can't stand you up when we didn't have a date."

Not wanting to be caught in a lovers' quarrel, Quin made a show of checking his watch and found the time to be three minutes later than the last time he checked, although he was sure less time had passed. He mumbled something about seeing Makenna later and hurried out of the shop.

Despite the time he took to talk to Makenna, he was perfectly on time for his West Coast call. He downed two antacids before answering on the second ring.

Makenna watched the retreating form of Quin through the windows. The good thing about being farsighted was that she had absolutely no problem seeing what was going on in the street. Wendell's face, which was much nearer, was only a blur. "I'm sorry you drove all the way out here. I've been quite clear about my plans since September when we first discussed getting tickets."

"There is nothing like opening night, darling. I thought you would change your mind."

"I don't have the luxury of changing my plans when one of the biggest shopping weekends of the year falls on opening night. Even if I were to close the shop, I would still have a deposit to prepare and financials to be checked." Makenna took a deep breath. As much as she wanted to yell at Wendell, she wouldn't lose it when a customer could walk in.

Wendell brushed a nonexistent crumb off his coat. "Can't you have an employee do all that?"

"Do you see any other employees?" The Monroe brothers had left an hour ago.

For the first time, Wendell seemed to look around the room. "Well, no. What happened to all your inventory?"

Makenna toyed with the glasses in her apron pocket. "As you can see, I still have a fair amount of inventory. I've just had difficulty gaining new pieces since Grandma's passing."

With the possibility of a customer coming in, she wasn't about to discuss her financial woes with Wendell.

"I guess it doesn't matter. Closing out your inventory will make it easier to sell this place."

"Sell? Why would I sell?"

The bell above the door rang as a small group of middle-aged women entered. From the sound of their laughter and the number of bags on their arms, they were on a shopping odyssey. Makenna brought a practiced smile to her face. "Excuse me. I have customers."

Wendell blocked her path. "When do you close?"

"Our holiday hours are until 9 p.m. on weekends and special sale days."

"Fine, I'll be back later with some takeout then."

Makenna waited five seconds before pulling the glasses out of her apron so she could see the women. Part of her was glad she hadn't been able to see the expression on Wendell's face. "Good evening. How can I help you?"

Ten minutes before closing and several customers later, Wendell returned. Makenna gave him a nod as she finished with the last customer's purchases. There had been no connections between items in the store and the women like she'd experienced earlier in the day. Or if there had been, her mind had been so occupied with Wendell's statement about selling that focus on any other topic was impossible.

Locking the door behind the women, Makenna turned to Wendell. "I need another half hour to close out the sales and prepare the deposit. I had more cash sales today than usual."

He held up the takeout bag. "Dinner is getting cold."

"There's a table in the back room if you want to eat."

"I want to eat out here with you."

Makenna pointed to the "no food or drink" sign. "This isn't just for customers. I don't eat up here either." The mostly empty cup from this morning's apple cider still sat under the counter next to her water bottle, so she didn't include drink in her personal rules. A drink behind the counter was different. She knew where to set her cup so it wasn't near anything that could be destroyed.

She hurried through the closing routine. As predicted, the cash deposit was larger than expected. Makenna transferred the money to a bank bag and filled out the slip. She'd rather put the money in the night depository than leave it in the safe. Another fifteen minutes of delay that would annoy Wendell.

Someone tapped on the door. Makenna peeked through the shade. Officer Hastings was easy to identify by the light of the streetlamps because of his hat and black police-issue coat.

Makenna unlocked the door. "Thanks for coming after hours."

"I figured you wouldn't want me in here with customers. Now what is this about getting the items back?"

"The only thing returned so far was the watch. Its value was the reason I turned in a police report for the insurance company. I think the same person took the other items."

"But he or she hasn't returned them?"

"She gave me twenty dollars for them. Which covers my cost."

"Do you want to press charges?"

"I don't think I can."

"Why not?"

"Grandma Tansy returned the watch."

Officer Hastings laughed. "I understand. Can you imagine a trial involving her? The judge would end up confessing to every crime he committed, starting with stealing a cookie off his mother's counter."

"I don't think she has been all there lately either." Makenna tapped her temple. "Some of her comments are even less normal than usual. I'm not sure why she took the watch or the other items. What's more worrying is that I don't know how she took it."

"Have you gotten CCTV cameras installed yet?"

"The alarm company is scheduling out to next February. I have a spot the second week."

"You can buy Wi-Fi cameras online and put them up yourself. They aren't too expensive either."

"Why didn't I think of that?"

"If you buy some, I'd be happy to help you put them up. Order tonight, and they should be here on Monday."

"You don't moonlight selling items on late night TV shopping channels, do you? That sales pitch sold me."

"No sales. Just high school debate with Liberty as a partner."

Officer Hastings helped Makenna choose a set of cameras from a website and place the order. "Anything else I can help you with?"

"Thanks, Greg. I mean, Officer Hastings. I'm just going to walk my deposit over to the bank and call it a night."

"Would you like an escort? I'm headed that direction, then over to Maple Sugar & Spice—Josie's lights are still on too."

A few questions rolled through Makenna's mind. Why would the officer need to check on her cousin's sweet shop? Was it personal or business? Since she hadn't spoken with Josie in over a month, she wasn't going to pry. "I'd love a police escort the entire half a block."

Makenna grabbed her coat from the back room. Wendell sat at the table staring at his phone.

"I'll be back in a moment."

"Where are you going?" he asked without looking up.

"To the bank."

"Ummm-kay."

Twenty minutes later, he was still on his phone. Makenna readied the alarm. "I'm ready to go. Would you like to go over to the house?"

"What did you say?"

Makenna clenched her jaw. "I'm closing up. Come on."

Wendell turned off his phone and remembered his manners, collecting the uneaten food and holding open the back door for Makenna's exit.

At the house, Makenna took the takeout into the kitchen to prepare a plate.

"Do you want to watch a movie?" called Wendell from the parlor.

"Something short. I'm going to have another big day tomorrow." In the kitchen, she opened the first take out box. Shrimp? Not that Makenna was allergic, but she detested seafood. Several times since they'd met, she'd discussed this with Wendell. It might make her an oddity in the commonwealth, but seafood was out. When they were in a restaurant, she could choose something other than fish. The other takeout box contained a single piece of orange chicken. Hallelujah for the inventor of frozen burritos, Clarence Birdseye of Gloucester who was the first person to freeze packaged food in 1925—a Massachusetts fact Wendell wouldn't appreciate.

She took her plate and sat down on the couch.

"That isn't Chinese."

With her mouth full of beef and beans, Makenna could only nod.

"But I went clear to Newton to that Chinese place."

There was a perfectly good place around the corner, but he went to the one she'd mentioned she liked one time, even if it had more to do with the decor than the food. "And I ate the piece of orange chicken you left."

"I left you an entire box of food."

"Shrimp."

"Their shrimp is the be— Oh no, I forgot again, didn't I? You don't like seafood. I'm sorry, babe." Wendell patted the couch next to him.

"What did you do with your tickets?"

"I sold them to another junior partner at the firm. He needed to get on his wife's good side."

Makenna finished her meal and set the plate on the coffee table. Wendell rested his arm along the back side of the couch and Makenna leaned into him. Her glasses bumped his chest, and he jerked away.

She sat up. "Sorry, I forgot I was wearing them."

"Why don't you have your contacts in? You know I like them better."

She shrugged. No point in giving him details about how late she got home, or that she only had one contact. "It was just one of those days."

"You won't wear glasses next week when we go to *The Nutcracker*, will you?"

"We're still going?" Maybe he was just busy and stressed. She was. Forgetting things under stress was easy enough.

"I told you I would take you."

"Thanks." Makenna leaned back into his side, careful not to have her glasses touch him.

The movie was longer than she wanted. The tradeoff was worth it to have someone hold her for 112 minutes. And for that long not to feel lonely. She wished she could be like the girl in the movie and fall asleep snuggled in her boyfriend's arms. If only sleep could come so easily.

He kissed her the obligatory goodbye at the door. The kiss wasn't as intense as the couple in the movie, but as tired as she was, a mild kiss was a good way to end the day.

# CHAPTER 9

Before closing the driver's door to the cargo van, Makenna checked twice to make sure her coat and midi-length red dress were tucked safely out of the way. If Wendell had called fifteen minutes earlier, she could have made the commuter rail. According to Bob, Makenna's old Ford needed a new transmission—not in the budget. Nothing was in the budget. If she hadn't used her inheritance from her Wilson grandparents to pay off her student loans, she'd have more cash, but then she'd have those hanging over her head too.

To save on tolls, she bypassed Mass Pike. With the van, there was no way around paying to park in a garage. Makenna hurried the block and a half to the theater. She searched the lobby for Wendell. Not seeing him, she checked her texts—nothing—though she was ten minutes earlier than she'd planned.

Taking advantage of the spare time, she checked her makeup and hair in the women's restroom. The first thing she noticed in the mirror were her glasses. She'd forgotten to bring her contact to change out. There was no point sitting through *The Nutcracker* if she couldn't see the costumes clearly. Wendell would just have to live with her wearing glasses tonight. She needed them. Quin didn't seem bothered by her glasses. It shouldn't matter to anyone anyway. Makenna reapplied her favorite blush lip gloss and returned to the lobby.

Wendell leaned against one of the columns typing on his phone.

Makenna placed her hand on his arm. "Good evening."

"You made it. I was just sending a text."

"The show doesn't start for twenty minutes. We have plenty of time."

"But we have people to meet..." Wendell looked up from his phone. "Where are your contacts?"

"One is at home tucked in its case. The other is AWOL. I'll get new ones in January."

"Why not sooner?"

"Insurance. It doesn't really matter. I can see." It shouldn't matter to him. They were her eyes.

"But I like to see your eyes."

"And I like to see. Now who did you want me to meet?"

"Never mind. Let's go find our seats." Wendell placed his hand in the middle of her back and steered her through the lobby at a pace difficult to keep in high heels.

"Are you ashamed to be seen with me in glasses?"

Wendell didn't answer.

They climbed the stairs. Instead of stopping for the box seats that Wendell had pontificated over, they continued climbing. They stopped at seats in the far stage right side of the balcony near the back.

Makenna tripped over someone's foot trying to get to her seat. The heat from embarrassment which flooded her face differed from the heat that bubbled deep inside. If Wendell had purchased these tickets the day sales opened as he'd claimed, they would have had better seats, or she would have heard him regret the purchase.

He'd lied to her.

This was neither the time nor place to confront him. Makenna studied her program, waiting for the lights to dim. Wendell tapped away on his phone.

As the lights dimmed, he pulled out a rectangular case that opened to become a pair of opera glasses.

"I wish you'd warned me. I could have brought mine."

"I thought I texted you to bring some."

Another lie.

He took her hand as the lights dimmed and the curtain went up.

Familiar musical notes filled the theater. Makenna tried to settle in to enjoy one of her holiday traditions. Every year Grandma and Grandpa Wilson would bring her to Boston for the matinee of *The Nutcracker*. Afterwards they'd go to dinner and to Copley Center to see the tree and shop before taking the commuter rail home. Last year, she'd come with her Covington cousins for a Wednesday night performance, as schedules made it difficult to take an entire Saturday near Christmas off of work.

The music changed and Clara, her brother Fritz, and their friends received their Christmas toys. Makenna squinted to see the costumes, lamenting her lack of opera glasses. How far was the stage? For once, her bad eye might be useful. Makenna slipped off her glasses, and the dancers on the stage came into better focus. Extreme farsightedness for the win.

With the mouse king vanquished, Clara and the nutcracker prince met the snow king and queen. Makenna slipped her glasses back on as the lights came up for intermission. Not wanting to discuss Wendell's lies, Makenna excused herself and walked in the direction of the ladies' room. Since the lines were long and she had no need to stand in them, she wandered through the crowds.

She spotted Wendell on the mezzanine, talking with a small group. Politeness led her to join them. When she was five feet away, a woman in a chic black dress, standing next to Wendell, turned and kissed him full on the lips. The people around him laughed. Makenna gasped. Wendell and the others turned at the sound. The intermission buzzer rang in the lobby. Makenna hurried to her seat, determined not to miss her favorite dances.

Wendell reached his seat moments after the curtain went up. He didn't attempt to hold her hand during the second act. The remainder of the ballet was not as enjoyable as it should have been. Even Mother Ginger and her little Polichinelles failed to delight Makenna as they should have.

Duplicating traditions didn't always work. Perhaps she should wait until she could share the tradition with her own daughters. Although if Wendell proposed by Christmas, she might not say yes, and the daughters wouldn't be his. There'd better be a good explanation.

Applause filled the theater, and the house lights came up. Wendell turned to her. "Were you able to find a good parking space?"

"Yes, I parked in the garage a block north of here." Makenna stood and pulled on her coat.

"I'm parked at the one to the south. Since I know how you don't like driving out to Hawthorne late, we can forgo getting dessert." Wendell led the way out of the theater. He walked her only as far as the garage entrance where he kissed her on the forehead as if she were a child. Not a single spark.

As soon as Wendell was out of range, she wiped the kiss off her forehead. If only she could wipe him away as easily.

So many thoughts swirled through Makenna's head, it was a wonder she arrived home safely. Cellphones were not the only cause of distracted driving.

# CHAPTER 10

The meteorologist on WBZ promised no snow for the remainder of the week. Despite the correct weather forecast, Hawthorne was beginning to look a lot like Christmas, Hanukkah, and winter fun thanks to the imaginative shop decorations. The sign in the craft store's window announced seventeen shopping days left until Christmas. Quin whistled as he walked down the street on dry sidewalk. If only the last week of December could be as temperate as the first one had been. He stopped at Maple Sugar & Spice to order fifty four-piece mini candy boxes for thank you gifts from the chamber.

At the corner, he crossed the street to Sweet Memories Café to order a selection of baked goods to be wrapped and used as more gifts. Pops and his friends sat at their usual table. Quin nodded at them but didn't stop to talk. He'd been avoiding his grandfather for a week now, knowing that eventually, Makenna would come up in the conversation, and Pops would push for Quin to take her out. After seeing Wendell, Quin knew he couldn't compete. It was just as well that he'd never asked her out to eat on Black Friday.

Quin didn't date women already in relationships. At least not deliberately. One mistake was enough, and definitely in the past. To be fair, that woman had asked him out first, failing to mention not only that she was not single, but that her husband was serving overseas. Granted, Makenna wasn't married, yet. The *yet* being the word that kept him trying not to think about her.

Returning to the chamber office a few minutes early, Quin took the time to check on the to-do list for First Night. While the small town couldn't compare to Boston's or even Worcester's First Night celebrations, Hawthorne would be able to hold their own.

Besides several local bands and musicians, a small cast of local thespians had agreed to put on an original short children's play about Baby New Year getting lost. After approving the script, the church leaders said they could perform it in the old white church house that bordered the north side of the common. That eliminated several problems, the largest of which, according to Mrs. Zimmerman, was cold five-year-olds.

Everyone's favorite brown van double parked in front of the chamber, and the delivery person unloaded twenty boxes, quickly filling the small reception area. The driver asked Mrs. Zimmerman to sign for them.

Quin borrowed the letter opener from the reception desk and sliced through the tape on the top box. He held up a set of fuzzy bunny ears. "What are these for?"

"Let's find a packing slip." Mrs. Zimmerman sorted through the boxes. "Did you order the Happy All Year selection of children's party toys?"

"I ordered a Happy New Year for six hundred. It was supposed to be hats and noise makers and those messy confetti poppers that will have the parks department annoyed with me until next October."

"This says you have sixty sets of Cupids and Hearts, Shamrock and Gold, Mardi Gras Fun, Easter Bunny Bounce, Cinco de Mayo, Independence Day, Ghosts and Ghouls—which includes a special witch collection—Pilgrims' Thanksgiving, and Snowy Day Fun. Oh, and here it is—sixty New Year's Surprises."

"There must have been some mistake. I need six hundred children's party New Year's packs."

"I'll check our invoice and give the company a call. What are you going to do with all these boxes?"

There might be enough space in the conference room. "I'll move them as soon as I can. I have a ribbon cutting for the new game store at noon, and I'm meeting with the manager in ten minutes."

"Can you move the boxes in front of my desk before you go?"

The boxes were not as heavy as their size would indicate. Quin stacked four of them in the corner of the conference room and put three more under a table that had been pushed against the wall. He placed the bunny ears back in the box and folded the lid closed. He hoped there was time to get the order right before New Year's Day. The children's celebration was one of the big draws to First Night. They needed gifts to give since some of the traditional fair activities for kids were out due to the cold. Even with a heated, enclosed tent, face painting might have to be canceled if it was too cold out.

The ribbon cutting went as expected. Photos were taken, hands shaken, and Miss Hawthorne's crown didn't fall off this time. Quin waited only as long as necessary before packing away the giant scissors and returning to the office.

"Do you want the good news or the bad?"

Not the greeting one ever wanted to hear from the office assistant the moment they walked in the door. "Tell me in whatever order makes the most sense." Quin hung his coat over his arm.

"You placed the order for six hundred New Year's party kits, so this was the company's mistake."

"Is that the good news?"

"Almost. They are giving us a choice of returning what we have for a full refund and twenty percent off our next purchase. Or we can keep what we got, and they'll give us a fifty percent refund with twenty percent off on next purchase. There is no price difference between what you ordered and what they sent."

"Why can't we return this and get what we ordered?"

"That's the bad news. They only have two hundred kits left in stock."

Quin groaned. He needed more antacids for this. "That would be two hundred sixty total. That's nowhere near the estimate. There are just over three hundred and fifty students at the elementary school alone, and if anyone comes from out of town...."

"They said they'd hold the two hundred kits for us until tomorrow at 10 a.m. Pacific time."

"We looked at several other companies. What if we changed?"

"I've already checked the websites of the two others we liked, and they're sold out. The one you thought was sketchy has some, but they're double the price."

He ran a hand through his hair. "Not particularly good solutions. I guess this company is off our list for next year."

"I don't know. Have you looked in the other boxes? The quality is nice for kids' party toys and some of them are so cute. The little witches' hats would make Lavinia proud."

"What is it with this town and witches?" Quin took another box into the conference room.

"Salem had their witch trials; we got the real thing." Mrs. Zimmerman followed him.

"Do you believe in them?"

Mrs. Zimmerman laughed. "No, but my grandmother did. She claimed to have watched those Covington women do something in their gardens during the Depression and no one in town was ever without food."

"That seems like an awful agreeable thing for witches to do."

"According to my grandmother, the Hawthorne magic was only ever used for good."

Quin held up a string of Mardi Gras beads. "Some days I wish I could have some magic."

"I don't think it works the way you see on TV. My grandmother claimed it was all around the Covington women, but you had to watch carefully to see it, as it wasn't anything you'd ever expect."

"You sound like you believe."

"I've used Tansy Covington-Noyes's remedies since I was a little girl, and I'm here to tell you, if they aren't magic, they should be."

Quin stacked a box of Halloween toys in the corner. "My grandfather uses Tansy's stuff too."

"Maybe you can use these things for other events during the year." Mrs. Zimmerman used a large felt-tip pen to mark the side with a giant shamrock.

"Maybe. I wasn't planning on hosting that many events. Maybe a schoolteacher could use this stuff." He checked his watch. "I need to go distribute some more of the First Night fliers and posters. Some businesses complained that they were out. I need to hurry before they close."

"What about the two hundred kits on hold? Should I wait until tomorrow?"

"Order them. As far as this other stuff, maybe we'll have some inspiration overnight. If I'm not back by the time you need to leave, just close up." Quin searched the decorated street for inspiration. What would he do with Uncle Sam hats?

Makenna cleaned her glasses and read the email from Wendell again with the attached real estate offer on behalf of a foreign investor his firm represented. He had to have her confused with one of his clients. She wasn't looking to sell the shop or the house. Even if she were, there was no way they could be worth more than eight million dollars. The house needed several thousand dollars' worth of repairs, even if they were all little things she could live with until she had the money. Since she used the upstairs back bedrooms for storage, it didn't matter that she couldn't plug anything into the outlets without setting off the breakers.

He hadn't called since their Saturday night date at *The Nutcracker*. In a way she hoped he'd never call again. Makenna hated breakups and hoped the relationship could just fade away. She focused on the email and opened the attached documents. Business—not personal—interaction she could do.

The address was right. And the property lines were what she believed they should be. When she inherited the house and shop earlier that year, she hadn't inspected the paperwork that closely. But she'd recently paid the property tax bill and knew the valuation on the property was nowhere near what Wendell claimed.

The second document appeared to be a contract. She scanned through its contents. Weirder and weirder. A company out of Leeds, England, wanted to buy property in Hawthorne. To the best of her knowledge, nothing in town had been under British ownership since her eighth great-grandma Lavinia warned the minutemen about the march on Concord.

Only debating a minute, Makenna opened her phone and dialed Wendell's number. It went straight to voicemail. "Call me as soon as you can." After the debacle at the ballet, calling him wasn't wise, but she could talk business with him. He'd probably have someone else return the call anyway.

She reread all the documents. Halfway through the second page, a customer entered the shop. Makenna shrunk the email window on her tablet. "Quin, what brings you here? Are you finally going to buy the watch? Or just stare at it again?"

Quin stood at the case and traced the watch face through the glass, as he did every time he visited the shop. "No offense, but it's a bit spendy for my budget this time of year. Or anytime."

"You and everyone else. Given the cost of gold, it's probably underpriced as it is." The insurance company had asked for a new appraisal. Makenna had it on her list of things to do after the holidays.

"It keeps the correct time, doesn't it?" He traced the face again. Makenna wished she could lower the price for him. No one else had been as enamored with the watch for years.

Makenna checked the time against her phone. "I've never seen it not work. It was working when Grandma Tansy returned it." Quin pointed at a camera over the kitchenware section. "Is that why you have the new cameras?"

"Greg—I mean, Officer Hastings—helped me put them in."

"I still call him Greg too. We played coach-pitch baseball together."

"I give you such a bad time for not living here, I forget you were a native. Perhaps it is because of your California accent."

He smiled the same thousand-watt smile that had attracted her to him as a twelve-year-old.

"You didn't grow up in Hawthorne either."

"Haverhill is only an hour away in bad traffic—two, if I took the train. New England has always been my home. I spent every summer in Hawthorne."

"I remember. I spent many summers here too. Perhaps you remember my four older brothers. They were constantly causing problems."

"And you weren't? One summer, you had Abigail sure you were scoping out the place to rob it, you came in so often."

"You remember me, then?"

Makenna felt her cheeks warm. It had been years since she'd had that crush on him.

Quin's California tan that hadn't faded completely, and the light ends of his hair were probably natural from years of surfing. The soft gray-blue of his eyes hadn't changed over the years. She stopped the direction of her thoughts. Until she was sure about things being over with Wendell, crushing on another man was wrong. "Grandma had me watch you like a hawk anytime you came in so I could report what you were trying to steal."

"For the record, I never left the shop with something I didn't purchase." Quin smiled, showing a small dimple she hadn't seen since he'd returned to Hawthorne.

The Monroe boys came through the back room. "We unloaded everything. Do you need us to watch the store?"

If they watched the store, she could ask Quin about the property values. As head of the chamber of commerce, he might know more about building sale offers. "Would you mind? I have some questions for Mr. Kayhill."

Quin raised his brow but waited, only checking his watch once while she turned the register over to Kent. Makenna beckoned him to follow her through to the back room, where she grabbed her coat and took him out the back door.

"Have you ever seen the old Hill house up close?" The 1820s house sat in the center of a patch of brown grass.

A battered white picket fence surrounded most of the lawn, and a single hawthorn tree grew in the yard.

"Not for years. I once came through the alley with my brothers to look at the house in the middle of the block. It is rather unusual."

"I have something more unusual. Today I received an unsolicited real estate offer on the shop and the house for over eight million dollars. I don't see anything worth that much."

"Do you mind if I walk around the house?"

Makenna opened the gate. "Be my guest."

"The house needs a few repairs." Quin pointed to a loose siding board.

"I know."

"How much land is with the house?"

"Not much, about 1100 square feet of grass. Then there's the carriage house, and the alleyway next to it is the southernmost border. According to the city, I own both alleyways and the parking area between the house and the shop. I let the other businesses use it because we always have, and in return, they take care of the snow all the way to my front door."

"Originally, the Hills owned this entire block, right?"

"Yes."

"Did you know that Ben Tills, the CPA, had an offer on his building? And Mr. and Mrs. Davis had an offer on theirs?"

"Three properties?"

"Five. Monte Monroe and Linda Gee both sold earlier this year."

"So someone wants the entire block?"

"That's my guess."

"Why?"

Quin shrugged. "I thought it was just an investor wanting more real estate properties—which it would then rent back to the businesses. The veterinarian over on High Street has had his building listed for months without a nibble, so a random investor seems less likely."

"I don't want to sell, but—" She bit her lip. How much did she dare trust him with? He might know how to help her professionally. That was part of the chamber's purpose. "I'm afraid if things don't turn around soon, I won't have a choice."

"What do you mean?"

"I've had difficulty finding new inventory. Today, I ended up purchasing several pieces from the post-World War II era. Nice furniture, but borderline in the antique world. I picked up some lovely trinkets which will sell, but they won't bring much in. I can't run a shop without things to sell."

"Did your grandma ever have that problem?"

"Not that I know of. Several of the estate sale dealers remember her fondly, but they are still allowing big Boston shops first dibs even when the estate is within ten miles of here. It isn't like I have the funds to purchase every piece of inventory and compete with the high stores. Estate clearance companies have always allowed the local shops first pick."

"I don't know much about your business."

"Estate sales are my principal source of furniture. Some older houses have pieces in attics and back rooms that have literally been there collecting dust for decades. Most of the out-of-town visitors want real New England antiques. Being able to send them on a drive-by of where the piece came from has always been a big sell—along with the line that John Adams may have slept there, but…"

Quin laughed. "That *is* a good line."

"And 'Paul Revere didn't make that silver but…' Anyway, neither line is helping sales now. I do trades with other shops between here and Maine. You can only sell so many old eggbeaters."

"People buy old eggbeaters?"

"Yes, they don't break as fast as the newer ones with plastic parts."

"Back to the offer. Do you know who wants to purchase the house and shop?" asked Quin.

"Some company out of England, of all places."

"Ouch. They must not know you were a Covington descendant."

Makenna tilted her head, not expecting Quin to know her genealogy. "I didn't know you knew I was a Covington."

"The way your grandma cared for that statue? Of course, I knew. The shopkeeper has always been the unofficial historian of the town—but don't let the historical society museum know that."

"Most of the people over at the historical society are distant cousins of some kind."

Quin checked his watch again but made no move to leave. Nervous habit, maybe. "I stopped to see if you needed any more First Night fliers."

"I still have a dozen."

"I need to finish handing these out before everyone closes for the night."

Makenna smiled. "Speaking of which, I probably should go in and close up. Do you want to cut through or walk around?"

"I'll walk. I need to check some businesses over on the next street, and the alley puts me closer."

"Thanks, Quin, and you won't tell anyone, will you? That amount of money is just crazy."

"Not even Pops."

"Especially not Walter! He and his buddies are the biggest gossips in Hawthorne." Makenna laughed as she waved goodbye.

# CHAPTER 11

The news from the other building owners on the block was more disturbing than Quin expected. Like Makenna, most had received an unsolicited offer in the last few months. Since he couldn't disclose Makenna's offer, Quin didn't ask for details, and few volunteered.

Despite the Closed sign in the window of Abigail's Antiques, Quin took a chance and tapped on the door.

As Makenna came closer, her smile grew. She unlocked the door. "Come on in. I'm assuming you have news?"

"Not much." Quin followed Makenna to the counter. The watch wasn't in the case. "Where is the watch?"

Makenna studied him, her brow slightly furrowed. "It's tucked in the safe for the night. You really like that watch, don't you?"

Quin swallowed. "There's no way not to make this sound weird. You know the old saying 'time flies when you are having fun?' Around you, it does the opposite. It slows down so I can have fun, or more time, or something. But it only does it when the watch is here. Like this afternoon, we talked forever in the store, but it was just two minutes. But when we went outside, time moved normally. Crazy, huh?"

"Are you saying there is some kind of time warp? I check that watch every morning and every night against my phone. It runs normally."

"I told you it would sound weird."

Makenna bit her lip. "Is that why you check your watch so often when you're in here?"

"Yes."

"Well, at least it isn't because I am taking up too much of your time."

"I didn't mean to make you feel bad."

She waved it off with her hand. "As far as that watch… I could go all Covington magic lore on you—not that I know anything specific about that watch other than it won't stay sold or even stolen—but if you believe that sort of thing, it could have some old spell put on it. Not that I've heard of such a thing." Another look passed over her face as if she were concentrating extremely hard. "I have something to show you if you have the time."

"The only appointment I have left is with my microwavable dinner."

Makenna showed him the section of antique toys. "I don't know if you have something for Walter for Christmas, but this truck seems to have caught his fancy." The blue cast-metal truck was about eight inches long and had the tiniest speck of rust behind the bumper.

Quin took it from her and turned it over, inspecting the wheels. What was that story Pops used to tell about rolling inside of a tire down a hill? And the other one about his grandfather's rusty Model-T? He really should pay more attention. "You're sure he wants it?"

Makenna shrugged. "All I know is that every time Walter works for me, this truck ends up at the counter and he talks about his family."

"I've been looking for something for him. Nothing seems quite right." Quin checked the price and noticed it was well within his budget. "I just don't know what he'll say about a toy car."

"Fill it with some of those caramels from Maple Sugar & Spice and tell him it is a candy dish."

"Do you know what my Mom would do? 'Blow a gasket,' as Pops says." Quin mimicked the conversation he heard at least once a day. "'Dad, you know the doctor said to cut down on sweets.'"

Makenna hid her laugh behind her hand. "Don't quote me, but I'm sure Walter will love the candy dish."

"What happens if I defend myself and blame you?"

"If your mother comes in here, I'll point out that you and Walter are big boys and can make your own choices."

"I'll buy it." Quin pulled out his wallet. "Do you want to hear what I learned?"

"I'm not sure I do, but tell me anyway."

"Almost every single building on this block has had an unsolicited offer. I didn't ask details, but I learned that one seller's offer is contingent on the other properties selling."

"Can they do that?"

Quin set the truck on the counter. "I'm not a lawyer. Speaking of which, your boyfriend Wendell is the contact person for at least two of the sales. They think you must be selling out because he's involved."

"But I knew nothing until today. Is Wendell saying I approved this?"

Getting in between a woman and her boyfriend was never a good idea. "I'm not sure how to answer that. I got the impression they thought you were privy to the offer, but they didn't come out and say so."

Makenna sat down on the stool behind the counter. "I wouldn't do that; I love my house in the middle. Not to mention the company is from England. Liberty would have my head."

"Liberty Covington, B&B, right?" So many businesses and so many names. Quin struggled to keep names together with people without another context.

"The one and only defender of the commonwealth. I think our fifth-grade teacher made a mistake when she assigned Liberty to do a paper on the Revolutionary War heroines of Middlesex county. She got a bit too far into the role, and every Fourth of July since, she has dressed like a minuteman—or more precisely, Deborah Samson, who disguised herself as a man to fight in the Revolutionary War. She even takes part in the reenactments in Lexington and Concord on Patriot Day."

"I need to see that."

"I'm not sure she'll be in it this year—it's the Lavinia Covington Reunion."

"The what?"

"Every thirteen years, all the female descendants of Lavinia Covington have a reunion over Patriots' Day weekend. We read stories about her, eat way too much food, and swap stories. You should have it on the Chamber calendar. So many out of town visitors spend a lot of money at local businesses."

"Have you ever been to a reunion before?"

Her face lightened and the constant strain around her eyes disappeared. "Grandma took me to the last one. It was a lot of fun. Maybe too much fun. Liberty, Claire, Keira, Josie, Eden, and I all ended up in so much trouble."

"Who's Eden?"

"Grandma Tansy's real granddaughter. I haven't seen her for a few years."

"The big question is—what did you do?"

"You know the old well out at Covington House?"

Quin nodded. The rock well was one of the few authentic wells in the county—a point in the travel brochures in the rack they kept in the chamber's lobby.

"If you look inside the rock well, you'll see it has a metal lid sealed with cement. We are the reason for that cover. Thirteen years ago, it wasn't so secure, and six preteen girls broke the old cover into the well."

"I can't picture you vandalizing anything." But he could picture Sunny doing that. When had she lost that carefree smile?

"We wanted to drink water from the well that Lavinia used to bathe Josiah Covington's wounds since it is supposed to be magic. That story is even sillier than you thinking the watch slows down time."

"So you're saying you used to believe in magic?"

"I wasn't even thirteen yet. I believed in a lot of things I don't know." Makenna rang up his purchase. "I hope you're using plastic. I've already made the deposit."

Quin held up his card. "I don't carry much cash. I'm curious. What don't you believe in now?"

Makenna shook her head. "Never mind me, I'm just feeling frustrated. It's hard to be my happy self."

"What's wrong?"

"I've been cataloguing the furniture I purchased today, and I don't know how I'll sell them. The pieces are only fifty years old—too new for most people to consider to be antique. A foolish purchase, but they were the first decent furniture pieces I've been able to pick up in weeks."

"Supposedly, I know something about marketing. May I look at them? I might have an idea in return. And maybe you'll have an idea for me."

"What do you need?"

"For First Night, I ordered six hundred children's New Year's party kits: paper hats, noisemakers, those confetti poppers. The shipment showed up, and it was wrong. Instead of six hundred kits, I have sixty kits for ten different holidays."

"Wow, it sounds like we both have problems. Come on back and look at the furniture."

Although the back storeroom wasn't as full as normal, it still resembled organized chaos. "This bedroom set and the desk are two of the pieces I purchased today. Then there's the hutch over there." Makenna pointed to a piece that only dated back to the 1960s. "I don't know what I was thinking when I purchased them. Vintage, yes; antique, not so much."

Quin circled the '60s era dining hutch. "This looks like the type of thing my sister-in-law would flip."

"Flip? Like in flipping a house?"

"Something like that. Drives my brother crazy. He hasn't parked in the garage for months, but she makes good money. She picks up furniture from garage sales, social media posts, and a few things off the curb on garbage day, paints them with some special paint, and sells them."

"Really?"

"Yeah. I think I have some photos from her online posts." Quin opened his phone and scrolled to a photo album. Photo after photo of before and after furniture painted in whites, creams, and blues filled the page.

"People buy this?"

"In California and Nevada, they do. She got one of my other sisters-in-law doing it now too."

Makenna read the descriptions. Chalk painting? Shabby chic? Words she'd seen occasionally on Pinterest but never paid attention to because they had nothing to do with real antiques. Usually with antiques, there were posts about repairing, and refinishing on occasion, but not repurposing them. Owners might do that but never dealers. "Hmmm. That china hutch might make a nice coffee bar like the one in this photo. I just don't know where to start." Or where to find the time to paint. If it worked to flip furniture, there was a vast supply of things she could flip. Like all the things she passed on at estate sales that went for a song.

"I can ask my sister-in-law for tips. Be warned. Once she starts talking about painting, she doesn't stop."

Makenna ran her hand over the desk. If there wasn't too much sanding involved, she could probably do it. The old carriage house had several pieces of not-quite-old-enough-to-be-antique furniture she could practice on. "I'd like to talk to her."

Quin took back his phone and tapped out a text. "Do you mind if I give her your number?"

"Go ahead."

"May I have your number?"

"Oh, sure." Makenna rattled off her cell number. It had been a long time since she'd given her phone number to a guy. Too bad this was business and not personal.

Quin finished the text and pocketed his phone. "Now, do you have any solutions to my problem?"

"It might help if I see what you are talking about." Makenna wasn't sure if she'd asked the question because she needed to see them or if it was because she enjoyed talking with Quin. She'd already talked to him more about her history than she had to Wendell in a month.

"Have you eaten?"

"Not yet."

"We can pick up Chinese from Lim's on the way over and I'll show you my dilemma."

A tingle of excitement shot through her. "Business dinner?" Makenna wasn't sure why she needed him to understand this wasn't a date.

"Something like that—only with spring rolls."

"I can do that." She wasn't cheating on Wendell. They'd only discussed business, some of which she may not have needed to disclose to Quin if Wendell had called her back about the email. She grabbed her coat and joined Quin without a twinge of guilt.

The twenty boxes looked more overwhelming the second time around. Quin cleared a section on the conference table to eat at.

"What holidays did you say you had decorations for?" Makenna opened her orange chicken.

"Valentine's, St. Pat's, Mardi Gras, Easter, Independence Day, Halloween, Thanksgiving, Christmas/Winter, and New Year's." Quin tipped the box of crab Rangoon her direction.

She shook her head. "I don't do fish. I don't think I'm allergic; I just can't stand the flavor." She opened the cardboard shipping box nearest her and pulled out a green bowler hat. "All the kits have hats?"

"Or something to wear on the head: bunny ears, Mardi Gras crowns."

"Josie told me a bit about the play they're doing for the children at First Night. I should have paid better attention. Something about Baby New Year being lost? Since she's five foot even in heels, Josie is Baby New Year. She was saying something about the bunny costume being more for older men than kids."

A lump of rice got stuck in his throat. This was supposed to be family-friendly, not racy. Maybe he should have read the entire play and not left it to others. He'd assumed with the church committee passing off on the content of the play, it was all good.

Using chopsticks, she poked at the food in her box. "Don't look so worried. She made them replace it."

After chasing the rice down with a drink of water, Quin answered. "I hadn't heard about the costume."

"Josie wouldn't have worn it." Her cousin was too self-conscious about her figure to wear anything form fitting.

"So, Baby New Year goes to all the holidays?"

"I think so. I should have paid more attention to Josie than I did to the taffy puller. That thing is mesmerizing. I can call her." Makenna pulled her phone out of her pocket.

"No need. They submitted a copy of the play." Quin dug through a stack of file folders. "Mrs. Zimmerman read it and pronounced it cute. Since she's a grandma, I never bothered reading the entire thing. Here it is." He handed a copy to Makenna and scanned through his own.

Makenna handed back her copy. "The only holiday I don't see in here was Mardi Gras. If you hand out the kits randomly to the kids after the play, then bunny ears or leprechaun hats will make sense." Quin stopped at the third page. "Wow, how did you read that fast?"

"Took speed reading my first year of college. Two thousand words a minute comes in handy sometimes."

"Wow, that is fast."

"A bit on the abnormal side. Anyway, you could use all the holidays except Mardi Gras."

"Mrs. Zimmerman ordered two hundred and fifty extra New Year's kits, so even with taking out Mardi Gras, we should have enough. Unless I miscalculated numbers."

"If we have a blizzard, you'll have too many." Her teasing smile warmed him.

"Please don't even think it."

"I'll hope this year's blizzard waits until mid-January. Is that better?"

"Marginally. The only one I remember from living here was the April Fool's Day blizzard and being without power for two days. I think that was what prompted the move to California."

"I don't remember that one. I was alive but too young to notice, I guess. Most years aren't bad. People think we have snow from December to March, but it isn't really true."

"I keep telling myself that. One reason we always visited my grandparents in the summer was because my dad didn't want to get stuck in an airport overnight."

Makenna closed her empty takeout box. "Why did you and your mom move back here?"

"Mom always missed her home—fall colors, seasons, you name it. After Grandma died, she wanted to be here for Pops and worked it out with her job to work remotely. The chamber job came open and coincided with my background, so I moved out here too." Quin's shortened version didn't cover any of the personal details. The not-so-single coworker who had made his job difficult by spreading lies, and the threats from said coworker's husband—both of which now made him question the wisdom of this semi-business dinner with a woman in a serious relationship.

"Walter suspects the real reason you moved here is so that your mom can spy on him."

"And to take away his candy." Quin gathered their empty boxes and threw them away. "May I walk you home?"

"My house isn't on your way. I'm sure I'll be fine."

"We may live in one of the safest towns in Massachusetts, but I'd feel better if you let me be the gentleman."

She used the end of her scarf like a whip. "You mean Walter would wallop you?"

"He hasn't done that since I was ten or twelve. But he might raise my rent."

Makenna buttoned her coat and pulled her gloves out of her pockets. "I wouldn't want you in trouble with Walter. Plus, I'd probably get a lecture too."

Quin laughed and turned out the lights in the conference room. "I need my bag from my office. Will you wait?"

When he came out of his office, he found Makenna eyeing the garland in the reception area warily. "There is no mistletoe. Mrs. Zimmerman agreed it was not appropriate for the office and took it home."

"You're sure she didn't just weave it in someplace?"

"Even if she did, I'm not the type of man who uses it as an excuse to kiss a woman without her permission." Quin held open the outer door.

"So you've never kissed under mistletoe before?"

"By mutual consent. And you?"

"Grandma Wilson always hung a mistletoe ball over the kitchen sink so that once a year people—meaning my grandpa—had to thank her properly for her hard work. I thought it was cute. Once I realized mistletoe was a tree-murdering parasite, I wasn't so enamored by the idea of being kissed under it."

They crossed the street at the corner by the bookstore. "So, no?"

Makenna laughed. "No. And thank you for not using it that day I accosted you at your office. I should apologize. I was a bit over the top with the whole 'Christmas was banned' thing. It turns out most of my friends didn't realize it either. It had been a long day, and I could have approached it differently."

"One of those last-straw things or another 'uneducated tourist' moment?"

"Maybe. I just want to apologize for not being very nice about it."

"I'm glad you called me out on the name. I'm sure some surrounding chambers would have mocked me, and I'm trying to do a good job." Quin turned down the alley leading to her house. "Is it always this dark back here?"

"No. I have a motion light—" Makenna waved her arm. A light attached to the back of the store burst to life, flooding the area with white light. "See, not dark at all."

They stopped at her gate. Quin reminded himself this was a business dinner. "Have a good evening, and don't let my sister-in-law take up all your time with her paint ideas."

"My phone has been buzzing with texts for the past half hour. I peeked, and it was her. I have a feeling I'll be watching lots of videos tonight."

Quin touched her arm. A handshake didn't fit the moment. "See you around."

"Thanks, Quin." Makenna ran up the front steps and unlocked her door.

He waited until the lights came on in one of the rooms before he left. If only she didn't have a boyfriend.

# CHAPTER 12

Somewhere between "Silver Bells" and "Rocking Around the Christmas Tree," the radio DJ reminded everyone that they were down to nine shopping days. Makenna double-checked her calendar before opening her email. Everything since Black Friday seemed like one long workday. For eight days in a row, Wendell hadn't answered her texts about the property purchase or anything else. Maybe *The Nutcracker* date was the end of their relationship. She was too busy to miss him. And then there were the brief visits from a watch-obsessed director of the chamber of commerce who'd caught her attention.

The song changed to Justin Bieber's "Mistletoe." Turning off the radio, Makenna pushed away all thoughts of Quin. She needed a distraction and breakfast. The store wasn't due to open for thirty minutes. Makenna hurried down the street to the café.

Overnight frost collected on a few of the windows she passed, sparkling in the pale sunshine. Snow was overdue this year. The warmth of the café steamed up her glasses when she stepped inside. Makenna cleared them before approaching the counter. "Morning, Keira."

"The usual?"

"Yes, please."

"Do you want to try one of my new scones?" asked Keira.

"Like the ones from Thanksgiving?"

Keira stared Makenna in the eyes and nodded.

*Magic.* The thought that food had magic was more than a bit terrifying considering the experiences she'd had selling furniture and Quin's insistence that the watch was magic.

What did this mean if there was something different about the scone? Would she have the same flavor as the one at Thanksgiving dinner, or would it be another? Or would it even work since she knew this time? Of course, if the scone gave her memories, then what did that mean for all the odd connections she was having in her own shop? "Sure, I'll try one."

Keira carefully wrapped a scone and put it in Makenna's takeout bag on top of her breakfast biscuit. "Do you want a caramel apple cider with that?"

"Not today." Makenna paid and hurried back to the antique store. Today was the first time that she'd have some shabby chic furniture for sale. Last night, she'd had the Monroe brothers rearrange one corner so she could put the refinished pieces in it. One of the sites she'd consulted said that painted furniture should cure for thirty days, but Makenna was too eager to see if they would sell. Another website said that if she used a special wax, they'd be ready now. Makenna would caution the buyers about using harsh cleaners and hope for the best.

She set her food on her desk in the back room and ate the breakfast sandwich as she checked the list of estate sales for the week. There were never many in the weeks leading up to Christmas. Only two looked like possibilities. One she would normally skip offered several non-antique pieces. She flagged it just in case the items she painted sold.

After taking a drink from her water bottle, Makenna picked up the scone. Would she have a memory this time? The implications of the possibility were overwhelming. Then it could only be magic. She closed her eyes and bit into the scone.

Watermelon.

Just like at the city Independence Day festival when she was thirteen. *She carried a slice of watermelon for Grandma Abigail on a thin paper plate. An older boy playing Frisbee ran into her, knocking her down. The watermelon splattered into mush on the sidewalk. Another boy yelled at her for getting in the way. The last one stopped and helped her up. Quin.*

*He scooped up the ruined watermelon and tossed it into a waste barrel, and then offered to get her another slice. Makenna couldn't find any words. He'd touched her hand, and her arm was all tingly. Stupidly, she'd shook her head. The other boys yelled at Quin to hurry. She finally mumbled that she was okay and that he should go play. Later, Liberty told her the tingly feeling was from the fall. Makenna thought it might have been love.*

Makenna sat down hard in the office chair she kept at the desk. Which was weirder—a watermelon-flavored scone or the memory? She hadn't thought of that incident in years. She'd been ignoring the same tingly feelings around Quin for weeks. One thing for sure, she hadn't fallen this time.

The bigger question was, was the scone magic? And were all the strange sales she'd had the last few weeks the same thing? Yesterday, it had been a box of useless gears that she marked down to $3.50 weeks ago. The man who purchased them was almost giddy as he related stories of his grandfather working as a machinist and had tipped her $31.50, insisting that the gears were worth ten times the price she'd charged.

Her phone alarm rang. Five minutes to opening. She was out of pondering time.

Grandpa sat with his buddies in the café's corner. Quin nodded as he walked by them to the counter.

"Hey, Quin, you need to buy one of those new scones so you can help solve an argument. These two don't think they taste like caramel apples." Grandpa held up his scone.

Quin didn't need this today. There was a letter to the editor decrying the ice carving contest allowing chainsaws. He still wasn't sure if noise pollution, safety concerns, or something else had upset the letter writer.

"I'll have whatever it is they are telling me to have and a sausage biscuit."

Keira put his order in a bag. Quin thanked her and headed for the door.

"Not so fast, kid. What does your scone taste like?"

Quin held up his bag. "I'm pretty sure it will taste like a scone."

"But what flavor?" asked Judge. "Blueberry?"

Gene held up his scone. "Key lime."

Quin opened his bag and pulled out his scone. There weren't any obvious colors or additions like berries or nuts.

"Hurry up and take a bite," said Pops.

Quin bit into the scone, not sure what to expect. The texture was right, but it tasted like the orange creamsicles—the kind that he used to buy from the ice cream vendor in the park on walks with Grandpa. *See that little girl over there? Here is a dollar. I want you to go buy her something.*

*"The little one with the yellow shirt?" He was sure he'd seen her at school. Maybe a first grader. She wasn't in third grade like him.*

"Yup."

"Why, Grandpa?"

"To help her be happy."

"Is she sad?"

"Her mom and dad were killed in a car accident and now she has to move away to live with her grandparents."

"Oh." Quin ran over to the little girl. Her blond hair was tied up in pigtails. "Do you want an ice cream?" He held out the dollar.

"Are you a stranger?"

"No, I'm Quin. Everyone says my older brother Carl is strange. He likes vegetables more than candy."

"Okay. My name is Sunny. I'd like some ice cream."

Blinking away the memory, Quin spoke. "It tastes like orange creamsicle."

Grandpa scowled. "You're sure?"

"Just like the ones you used to buy me from the ice cream cart."

The three old men looked at each other. "Well, whatever flavor they are, they aren't burned. I'm going to get another one." Judge pushed back his chair.

Quin took the opportunity to leave. The memory was one from the summer before he and his family had moved to California. The little girl had to be Makenna. He hadn't realized she'd been so young when her parents died. Maybe it was someone else. Next time he saw her, he'd ask.

A customer walked around the refurbished furniture again. "May I help you?"

"I love this piece." The woman ran her hand over the desk. "Do you have a matching bookshelf?"

"Not yet." Would the style need to match or just the colors? That was a good question for the internet.

"If you get a matching set in these colors, will you call me?" She pulled a business card out of her purse. "I'm redoing my office. Two bookshelves would be better."

"I'll see what I can find. What is more important to you—the colors or the style of furniture?"

"Colors. I love this combination of blue and white."

"And if the furniture styles were more eclectic than the same?"

The woman tapped her chin. "As long as they look like they go together and aren't some Scandinavian put-it-to-gether-yourself stuff."

"I'll check with my supplier." A.K.A. her new alter ego. Antique dealer by day, furniture flipper by night.

The woman wandered through the shop, choosing a pair of old bookends to purchase before she left.

Makenna checked the estate sale advertising the more modern furniture. Bingo, bookshelves and two desks. She texted Walter to see if he would work Thursday morning. This week, she wouldn't come back with an empty van.

A little after three, the bedroom set sold to a man in his early thirties. He asked if she could hold the furniture until Christmas Eve when he would pick it up. Makenna hung a sign on the dresser.

*Sold.*
*Ask if you are interested in our reclaimed furniture.*
*Custom orders accepted.*

A little before closing, Quin entered the store. As usual, he headed for the glass case where Makenna kept the watch.

"You should just give in and buy it." Makenna teased as she returned to her spot behind the counter.

"That isn't the best sales line I've heard. You know the chamber holds small business education courses. We could help with that sales pitch." Quin's dimple showed with the smile.

"What brings you in here then if not the watch?" As soon as she asked, she regretted it. She hadn't meant to flirt.

"Walter got an offer on the Abbott building."

The building now housing Lim's Chinese takeout sat on the southeast side of Makenna's house. Not that she would ever tell Walter, but it smelled better than his butcher shop had before he retired and leased it to Lim.

"An offer like mine? Doesn't that make him the last person?" Walter was also the person she was most likely to compare contracts with. Walter was also the most likely to be vocal about a sale. Both facts that Wendell had to know.

Quin nodded. "Could we compare contracts? I'm curious."

The bell over the door rang. "Wendell?" What was he doing here so early in the day? She whispered to Quin, "Don't leave."

Makenna didn't bother taking off her glasses. If not wearing her contacts really bothered him, that was his problem. Wendell strode to the counter, and Quin stepped away, looking at a display of old costume jewelry. There was no way this wouldn't be a train wreck.

"Wendell, I wasn't expecting you."

"You haven't returned the contract."

"I called you eight days ago and have left messages every weekday since."

"I've been busy."

"I don't think this is the time or place to discuss this." Makenna nodded in Quin's direction. "I have a customer."

"Wasn't he in here before?"

"Yes, Quin is the director of our chamber of commerce. Quin?"

Quin looked up.

"I'd like you to meet Wendell A. Smith III." Liberty was right—his name W.A.S. and should be past tense. Makenna suppressed a smile, or she'd start laughing from stress and both men would think she was insane. Quin probably would after this and then she'd have no chance..."And this is Quin Kayhill. He was in here on some chamber business. Unless you wanted to buy that necklace for your mother?"

"I'm still deciding." Quin turned away.

"The contract?" asked Wendell.

"Not now." Had he always been so focused on what he wanted? Makenna wasn't sure.

"Then I'll take you to dinner."

"I have plans." The lie slipped from her lips.

"What are you doing?"

"I'm meeting with Quin and others over a project." Over Wendell's shoulder, she caught Quin's questioning look.

"Move the meeting. This contract is important."

"It wasn't important enough for you to return my call. And I am not dropping everything because you drove out here. You can't expect me to be here at your convenience."

"Are you breaking up with me over me showing up unannounced?"

"Again, not a conversation for my place of business."

Wendell reached for her hand. Makenna stepped back.

"Babe, are you still mad—"

"Not, here."

"Then when?"

"I don't know. Let me see how long the meeting will go." Makenna left the safety of her counter so she wouldn't have Wendell between her and Quin. Part of her brain recognized that she was using Quin, but he'd wanted to compare contracts, so there could be a meeting. "The meeting with Walter, one hour, two?"

Quin searched her face and glanced at Wendell. "You know Walter, it could run longer than I plan."

*Thank you.* She hoped he could read her thoughts. "So I should plan on two hours." She turned to face Wendell. "It looks like I'd be available about eight."

"I have to be back in Boston by seven thirty."

"Then you can call me, and we'll talk."

"Fine." When Wendell leaned in, Makenna turned her face so his obligatory kiss landed on her cheek. Wendell glared at Quin before leaving. Makenna watched as he got into his car, noting that it was in the fire hydrant no-parking zone.

She turned to Quin. "Thanks. I don't want to discuss that contract with him until I know more about what is going on. I don't like it when he pressures me. I hope that wasn't too weird or that you don't feel like I was using you, though I probably am. I know, that's so rude." Makenna couldn't stop the words flying out of her mouth. Any chance of impressing Quin ever probably walked out the door with Wendell.

Quin held up his hand, his eyes kinder than usual. "We're good. You seem a little flustered."

"I'm fine. Things have just been weird the last few weeks with him, and—" She cleared her throat. "Sorry TMI personal life." Makenna went back around the counter, checking the watch as she went. The time seemed normal to her. "I do want a real meeting with Walter. Can we set it for tonight?"

"Are you okay with meeting at Walter's?"

"At 6:30? I can walk over after I make the deposit."

"I can stop by and walk with you."

Walk with him. Yes that would be great. Instead she said, "You don't need to do that. You've done so much already."

"I'll be here by 6:15 and walk you over to do the deposit too." He wasn't running after that display of awkwardness with Wendell. Business or personal.

Makenna wanted to see if he would stay longer. "I didn't have time to tell you—I sold out of the shabby chic furniture you suggested. Well, kind of. The bedroom set is sold, and another woman wants the desk if I have matching bookcases, and I had a couple of inquiries."

"That's great." Quin looked at the furniture that was still there.

"The bedroom set is being delivered on Christmas Eve. I left it up so that maybe I can get some other orders. I had the Monroe brothers help clear one side of the carriage house so I can paint."

"Isn't it cold out there?"

"Electric heater. The paint doesn't like to be cold any more than I do. I might move the painting into the house though. The heater only heats one corner. And yes, I'm careful with space heaters."

"I didn't say anything."

"But you thought it, right?"

"How did you know?"

"I remembered something earlier today you did when you were fifteen or sixteen and realized you're the kind of person who would think about how unsafe space heaters can be." *And worry about me.*

"What did you remember?"

"Promise, you won't laugh? I had a watermelon scone— don't ask me how Keira came up with *that* flavor—and remembered an Independence Day town picnic."

"You fell, and the watermelon splattered on the sidewalk."

"You remember too?"

"I hadn't thought of that in forever. I had an orange cream-sicle scone today and had an odd memory. How old were you when your parents died?"

"Six and a half."

"Do you remember a boy buying you ice cream?"

Makenna covered her mouth to keep from gasping. "That was you, wasn't it? Grandma was upset because I'd wandered off, and then when I couldn't remember your name... I looked for you every day that week but didn't see you."

110

"That was the summer we moved to California. I think it was the last outing Grandpa took me on. He gave me the dollar and told me to buy you an ice cream."

"That is just weird. We both eat odd-flavored scones..." More than weird, but no way would Makenna say the word *magic* out loud.

"No less weird than this watch. I swear it says only a minute has passed since Wendell left, but it feels like longer doesn't it?"

Oh, sweet broomsticks, he was right. Magic was returning to Hawthorne. Makenna could only nod.

# CHAPTER 13

**P**rinted copies of both buy offers lay across Walter's kitchen table. Quin used sticky notes to highlight areas. Unlike Makenna's, Walter's offer hadn't come from the law firm where Wendell worked. However, the firm was mentioned twice in sub-documents where the wording should have been more boilerplate. The real estate agent was the same. Quin pulled up the real estate website on his laptop. "This isn't the type of agency that deals with home sales. They specialize in acquisitions."

"What does that mean?" asked Walter.

"I think it means they convince people to sell properties where someone wants to purchase the land, like to build a mall or something."

Makenna pulled out a hand-drawn map of the block. "Has everyone gotten an offer then?"

Quin pulled out his pen and wrote "sold" through two boxes and drew question marks on two others. He pointed to the three properties to the west of Makenna. "These are the ones with contingencies about other properties selling."

Makenna traced the wedge-shaped block. "So someone wants the entire block? Why?"

"I don't know. Who is that buyer in Leeds?" asked Quin.

"I don't remember. They modified the contract since I first opened it."

"Wasn't it an email attachment like Grandpa's?"

"No, mine was on a cloud server with the law firm. I saw Leeds, England, and thought about Liberty blowing up if a Brit bought property in Hawthorne." Makenna looked at Walter.

Walter laughed. "The spirt of '76 lives on in that girl. Woe be it to anyone who tries to cancel a patriotic event."

"Noted—no canceling patriotic events." Quin placed his hand over his heart. "Independence Day and Patriots' Day are sacred."

Makenna swiped at his arm. "You make it sound like Covingtons retaliate or something."

"Careful, boy, they'll put a hex on you." Walter slapped Quin on his back.

Makenna stopped laughing.

Quin felt suddenly self-conscious. "Looking at this map, I wonder if we should have a meeting with those who have been approached about selling."

"Including the ones who sold?" asked Makenna.

Walter shook his head. "Old Monte Monroe is celebrating his hundredth birthday this next year. His kids probably took care of the sale without him even knowing. Linda Gee has had such a hard time these past few months with the cancer, I can't blame her for selling. I'm sure she thought it was God's tender mercies."

"The sales of the first two properties will have public documents; I'll check with the city recorder. I'll also check for permit enquiries." Quin stacked the contracts into piles. "Makenna, if you could learn about the Leeds thing from Wendell, it would be helpful."

"I'll ask." She checked her phone. "I should get home. Thanks for looking over these papers. I won't sign them anytime soon; I have too many questions. And even though learning to run the store has been difficult, I'm not ready to give up."

Quin handed Makenna her contract. "It looks like it's raining. Would you like me to drive you home?"

Makenna looked out the window. "If you don't mind. It isn't that far, but this skirt and rain don't mix well—the old wool smells rather old and wooly to be exact."

The kilt-style skirt looked too short to be warm even over her navy leggings. Knowing Makenna's preference for vintage clothing, it probably was an authentic kilt, and he bet she could tell him the history of the clan the tartan represented.

They dashed to his car parked at the curb. Despite the downpour, Quin held her door open before running around for his own door. "Do you often get rainstorms like this?"

"Sometimes. This late in December, we should just be glad it isn't colder. If it turns to snow, the ice underneath causes so many accidents."

"Your commute is pretty ideal then." He checked over his shoulder before pulling out onto the quiet street.

"In the wrong shoes, it could still be treacherous. I'm just not in danger of hitting someone else."

Quin turned the corner.

"What is he still doing here?"

From the tone of her voice, Quin guessed she meant Wendell.

She slumped down in her seat. "Can you drive me over to Covington House? Call me a chicken, but I'm not in a place to have a face to face with Wendell."

"I thought he said he had to be in Boston by now."

"Wendell says a lot of things," she muttered. "Sorry, that was rude."

"Are you avoiding your boyfriend?"

"Kind of. I'm trying to figure things out. Liberty says I should have ended the relationship already. I see her point, but…"

"I get it." If only their relationship was over. Quin looked for a road to turn left onto to get to the B&B. "Silly question—how do I get to Covington House from here?"

"Fast way? Make a U-turn. Or continue for another mile or so and take the scenic route."

"Do you mind the scenic route?"

"No, the rain is slowing. Just watch the puddles on the old bridge. They ice over. Sorry, you probably knew that. I get a bit paranoid about car accidents…" Her voice trailed off. Her parents' deaths had nothing to do with the weather, but it was understandable she'd fear accidents.

"Thanks for the warning." Quin wanted to ask about Wendell. Actually, he had an overwhelming urge to push him out of Makenna's life. Couldn't she see he treated her like dirt? They reached the bridge and Quin slowed down. "You're right; it is slippery."

"Most of the old bridges are. Have you driven much in snow and ice?"

"Not in California."

"The first snowfall, ask Walter to take you out for a snow course. And between now and April, never assume a puddle is just a puddle. Black ice is real. Turn at the next stop sign."

They passed several homes half concealed behind trees. Covington House twinkled with rows of tasteful white lights. Quin pulled into the parking lot. "Can you get home without walking in the rain?"

"Liberty will take me or I'll spend the night."

"What if she's full?"

Makenna laughed. "I'm family, extended as it may be. I stay in the family portion of the house over the kitchens."

"You and Liberty are close then?"

"We're second cousins, but neither of us have first cousins on the Covington side, so we've never let a little thing like an extra generation get in the way."

"I'm not even sure what second cousins are." He kept the engine running for the heat.

"First cousins, your parents are siblings; second cousins, your grandparents are siblings."

"How do you know that?"

Makenna shrugged. "I spent every summer of my life in an antique shop. History just rubbed off on me. That's probably why I am a certified genealogist."

"That makes sense." Quin studied the wreaths in the windows, trying to find something to make the moment last.

"Thanks again for the ride and the detour." She gripped the handle of the door.

"Makenna? If you end things with Wendell, will you let me know?"

Her eyes grew wide.

"I'd like to take you out, but I'll not ask if—"

"Oh."

"Sorry, awkward."

"No, I'm fairly sure we aren't exclusive. I thought we were—"

"I don't want to push you."

"You're not. I think it would be fun. It's just a little weird right now—" She bit her lip. "Can I take a rain check?"

The wipers squeaked on the window. "It's not raining anymore."

Makenna laughed.

"So a definite maybe on a date someday?"

"Definitely."

Her smile lit up his heart. Before he could get out of the car, she opened the door and ran for the side door of Covington House.

Quin watched until she entered safely. Instead of returning home directly, he retraced the scenic route. The BMW still sat near the alley to Makenna's house. Someone sat behind the wheel.

Maybe that date with Makenna would come sooner than later.

Liberty turned from the stove where she had a teapot heating. "What dragged you in?"

"Wendell is camped out at my place, and I don't want to be in my house alone with him."

"My special chamomile blend or apple and spice?" Liberty held up the tea bags. "Remember, you have a lot of explaining to do."

"Apple."

Liberty prepared the tea and led the way back to the family parlor. "Ok, spill. And don't worry, I'm the only one back here. Mom has front desk until ten, and Gramps is upstairs watching some old John Wayne movie."

"Well, *The Nutcracker* date was a disaster." Makenna filled Liberty in on the details. "After the ballet, he walked me back to my parking garage. No 'let's catch dessert.' No conversation. Usually he tries to get me to go back to his place, telling me it's too late to drive home, etc. Not a word. Just a kiss on the forehead. And don't even start your lectures."

"You mean like, 'You need to make Wendell A. Smith pasttense just like his monogram'?"

"I think you're right. I just feel like I'm giving up on someone who has been there for me. Wendell was there when I needed him."

"We all like having someone. But having the wrong someone isn't any good. Remember my junior year of college?"

"Am I that bad?" Makenna sipped her apple spice tea. She didn't need Liberty's nod to tell her what she already knew. The safety of having a boyfriend wasn't worth having one like Wendell. She'd known it for months. Breaking up meant being alone. At least now her social media said she was in a relationship. Even though it hadn't felt like much of one since August or September when more and more dates started getting canceled.

"We all want love. And there is nothing better than a good snuggle in front of a warm fire. But sometimes it isn't worth the cost."

"Eight point two million."

Liberty set down her tea so fast, it splashed out onto the saucer. "What?"

"Last week, Wendell, as a representative of his law firm and some estate agent, sent me an offer on the house and store for over eight million dollars. Today, he turned up at the shop asking why I hadn't signed it. Quin has found that everyone else on the block has received an offer this year. Only two have sold that we know about."

"We—Quin?"

"I tell you I have an eight million dollar offer and you ask about Quin?" Makenna bit her cheek hoping Liberty wouldn't see her smile.

"Your voice softened when you said his name."

"Did not."

"Whatever. Back to the eight million—we can discuss why you're blushing later." The annoying smile on Liberty's face disappeared behind the rim of her teacup.

"The steam from the tea is making my cheeks warm. Anyway, someone is trying to purchase all the original property that belonged to Hill house, and we think they are out of Leeds, England. Wendell's firm is involved in the legal end."

Liberty scooted forward in her chair. "You will not sell to the British."

"I don't intend to. I just think it is weird that Wendell's firm has been involved in buying up all that property and he never mentioned it. I asked him to call me after I got the contract, and instead of a call, he shows up days later demanding I sign it. He asked me to go to dinner, but Quin had already asked to compare my contract to Walter's, so I went to Walter's house. Wendell got all huffy and said he had to go back to town, but when Quin drove me home, Wendell's car was parked next to the alley. So I had Quin bring me here."

"Ignoring the Quin issue—which we will discuss—you need to dump Wendell. His relationship is looking more about the money than you."

"I know, but he can be so sweet." He could, even if it hadn't been often.

Liberty raised her brows. "Kissing someone else in the theater isn't sweet."

"I'm pathetic, aren't I? Don't answer." Unwanted tears pooled in her eyes. "I'm just so lonely. I know I have you, Aunt Lisa, and Grandpa Dean, but with my Wilson grandparents dead and Grandma Abigail gone, Wendell was there for me." She sighed. "I need to admit it was over months ago." Makenna set her tea down and swiped at her eyes. "I'm one of those women in books I want to yell at for being a world-class chowderhead."

Liberty swooped in for a hug. "And I'm always busy proving to Grandpa that a Covington daughter can inherit this old place."

"I know you're always here for me. That's why I came."

"No-Bake Cookies or Fondue?"

"Do you have any fruit?"

Liberty dropped her jaw. "I run a B&B. Of course I do."

"Fondue."

"Good. Let's go eat and solve the problems of the world."

"Easier said than done. I'm pretty sure Keira is right about magic being back. I think I've experienced it too."

Liberty ticked off items on her fingers. "Wendell. Eight million. Quin. Magic. I think we need a double batch. Someone has been holding out on me."

"Oh, and Grandma Tansy shoplifted the watch." Makenna filled Liberty in on everything but Quin. The potential future date was not something to bring up. Especially when Liberty had teased Makenna about the wish she'd made at the well all those years ago. Preteen Makenna believed kisses were the most magical things of all. Not once in her life had a kiss ever been like in the movies—even almost thirteen years later.

Liberty dunked a marshmallow in the pot of chocolate. "So, what are you going to do now?"

"One, end things with Wendell. You're right, I don't need him in my life. Two, I'm not signing the contract. Three, we need to talk to Claire, Keira, and Josie. Part of me hopes it is coincidence, but what if it isn't? Are we supposed to control the magic? Or is it so diluted that it only manifests in small ways? The thought of magic scares me. It is a huge responsibility."

"I don't have any idea. I don't think I've experienced anything out of the ordinary lately. We are coming up on the thirteenth anniversary of when we tried to become witches. Grandpa added checking the seal on the well to my to-do list."

Makenna finished her strawberry. "It's not like I do anything to cause mine. I just match people with stuff. Other than the watch. Quin's the only one who thinks it bends time or whatever squirrely thing he thinks is going on. I alternate between trying to joke about it with him and worrying that there *is* magic going on."

"An old spell, maybe? How old is the watch?"

"Early 1800s. I need to see if I can find anything in Abigail's files."

"I can't believe you don't already know that. You know every other historical detail about this town."

Makenna dunked a banana slice, achieving that perfect amount of coating. "Grandma and I never discussed much about the Hill side of things. And she never discussed Lavinia or magic except as stories—or maybe she meant them as histories? I don't know, I wish I could ask her."

"Grandma Tansy might know, but she hasn't been herself lately so who knows what she'll say. The whole claiming-she-knew-Lavinia at Thanksgiving still freaks me out. Have you ever seen Tansy's birth certificate?"

Makenna's phone rang. She held it up so Liberty could see Wendell's photo before she answered on speakerphone. The unmistakable hum of a car engine filled the background space. "Hi, Wendell."

"Why haven't you come home?"

"I am visiting a cousin." She didn't ask how he knew she wasn't home.

"Do you know how cold it is out here?"

"It was raining, so I assume somewhere above freezing?"

Liberty covered her mouth to keep from laughing.

"I waited for you."

Lying in wait like a lion for his prey. "Um, last you talked to me, you said you had to be back in Boston before eight o'clock. If you were waiting for me, you should have called or texted."

"I just wanted to see you."

Her lie radar went off.

Liberty pretended to bang on the table and mouthed, "Dump him. Dump him. WAS. WAS. WAS."

Makenna turned away to keep from laughing. "Wendell,

I don't want to see you. It's over. I think it has been for a while, and you know it. Otherwise you wouldn't have called me on Thanksgiving with such a lame excuse."

"But, baby."

"I'm not your baby."

"Can't we talk about this? Us?"

"We *are* talking."

"I mean in person. Come home and we can."

Liberty shook her head and pointed to the library. "Here."

"I'm over at Covington House. You are welcome to come here."

The car engine roared. "I'll be there in a minute."

The call ended.

"Do you want a room I can eavesdrop on?" Liberty led the way to the public areas.

"I can be strong without knowing you are judging my breakup efforts."

"Then use the library. No one is in there tonight, and the old bellpull still works if you need me."

Makenna rolled her eyes at Liberty at the same moment Wendell burst through the front door.

Liberty stepped forward and gestured to the book-filled room. "Mr. Smith, I was just telling Makenna you could use the library. Just a reminder, it is just past nine thirty, and we have quiet hours starting at ten."

Makenna chose one of the wingback chairs opposite of the couch Wendell sat on.

"Why don't you sit over here?" He patted the cushion next to him like he always did. The same way Grandma Wilson did to call her Boston terrier pup.

"Break-up session, not make-out session."

"I thought we were getting along so well."

"We were—a year and whatever ago. You were great through both of my grandmothers' funerals, but we never

123

moved forward with our relationship, and you don't seem to listen to me."

"I can be better."

"You need to do you, and I need to be me. You don't get to criticize my glasses or my lack of style and try to make me into a Boston socialite." *Like the woman you kissed.* Makenna wasn't going to bring her up, whomever she was. She wasn't the reason she was breaking up with Wendell.

"But with all that money—"

"As my boyfriend, you don't know about that money because I haven't told you. You are not my lawyer either, so the contract isn't part of this discussion. In fact, this isn't a discussion; there's nothing to discuss. I am out of this relationship."

"But, baby—"

"Not your baby." Makenna stood. "I assume you can find the front door?"

"What about the contract?" The hint of a whine in Wendell's voice didn't help his case.

"A year ago, a certain Boston lawyer advised me to never sign anything without thoroughly examining it and hiring an attorney. I'm following your advice. Since you already have something to do with the offering party, I am assuming consulting with you would put you in an ethical dilemma."

"But you can trust me. I'd never do anything to hurt you."

"If I can trust you, then why didn't you return my calls? Why didn't you tell me about the sale? And why did the contract change to not show the buyer is out of Leeds, England? Oh, and who were you kissing in the middle of our date?"

Wendell's face drained of color.

"If I can trust you, tell me who the mystery buyer is and why they want my home." She kept talking across the room.

"I can't. Client/attorney privilege."

Makenna paused in the doorway. "Then I think we are done."

"Makenna, wait." Wendell stood only inches from her. "I love you. Doesn't that mean anything?"

Makenna wished she'd asked for an eavesdropping room. She needed strength right now, and knowing Liberty could hear her would help. She could do this, there was no feeling behind the words he spoke. "Three little words as we break up doesn't change things. You've had months to say them. We both know I was stupid enough to say them once, but I don't love you anymore. I'm not sure I ever did. At the moment I don't even like you very much."

"Bradford-Stone Worldwide."

"What?"

"The name of the client."

"Thank you, Wendell, and goodbye." Makenna pushed through the employees-only door.

Liberty stood on the other side. "I'll make sure he leaves."

Makenna stood alone in the hallway, her heart considerably lighter. A stress she hadn't known she carried was gone. Breaking up wasn't half as bad as she'd feared.

# CHAPTER 11

The meeting with the women of the High Street Quilting Club took place in one of the senior center meeting rooms. Quin showed them the videos of ice sculptors using special chainsaws to create majestic features. The women *ooh*-ed and *ahh*-ed over the delicate creations.

"How will we know the children watching will be safe?" asked a woman in a lavender sweater.

"We're putting up a plastic fence barricade around the area." Quin found a slide of the obnoxious orange fencing.

"That's not enough. My twin grandsons can get into everything." The woman's face reddened to match her Christmas sweater.

The oldest woman in the group shook her head at the speaker. "Gail, your grandsons are seniors in high school. They should know better."

"Still, there needs to be more." Gail folded her arms.

"What would you suggest?" Quin hoped they could come up with something.

"Someone should stand there and watch?" said the lady in lavender.

"That's an excellent idea. The problem is who. The police are already doing rounds at the event. Several organizations have volunteered to host booths. Do you know of a group that might help us?"

The women looked from one to another.

Gail raised her hand. "We could, if we all took turns so we didn't get too cold."

"Our husbands can help too." The oldest woman leveled a glare at the other two women.

"Is there anything else we need to do to solve the issue with the chainsaws?"

Gail looked around sheepishly. "I probably should retract my letter to the editor."

Quin wouldn't breathe a sigh of relief until it was in print.

"I'll make sure she sends it today." The older woman kept her eyes focused on Gail.

"Thank you very much for your time. Is there anything *I* can help *you* with?"

They all shook their heads.

One more thing off his checklist. And he didn't feel the need for an antacid. With less than two weeks to go, he hoped there would be no more First Night opposition to quell. On his way back to work, he stopped at the café for lunch. Only Judge and Gene sat in their corner.

"Where's my grandpa?"

"He's working over at Abigail's. Makenna must have done well with the estate sales today. He's usually back by lunchtime."

"I should go check on him."

"Take him one of Keira's new cookies." Judge nodded at the bakery counter.

Quin added two cookies to his order.

The bell over the door rang as Quin entered Abigail's Antiques. Quin paused. Most of the stores used electric buzzers activated by a footpad. The bell gave a bit of old charm to the store.

Pops frowned behind the register.

"What's wrong?"

"Makenna sold my favorite toy truck. What am I supposed to do between customers if I can't remember all the good times with my brother?"

He traced the watch through the glass case as he always did. "Uncle Andrew? Why don't you tell me about him?" Quin hadn't known his uncle who'd died in Korea.

Pops launched into a story about building sailboats and racing them along the shores of the Misty Hollow Pond. "Andrew wanted to win so badly, but the old swan didn't want us anywhere near her babies. She chased him halfway back to town, honking and flapping her wings. He told me I couldn't count it as a win since his boat was gone. We never did find it. If they ever dredge the pond, I'm sure it will be there."

Quin checked his watch. As usual, time in the antique shop slowed down. He decided he could listen to another story and not be late to his next appointment. Halfway through the tale of rolling a giant snowball down the hill on Misty Hollow Road, Makenna came through the back door. Her cheeks were rosy from the cold.

"Hi, guys." She paused a step. "Are you two eating cookies at my counter?"

"A man gets hungry when he works." Walter took another bite out of his cookie.

Quin swept the crumbs into his hand and dropped them into the trash bin. "Oops, you caught us."

"Thanks for cleaning up your mess. Are those Keira's latest creations?"

"And they're good too." Walter finished his cookie.

Quin held out his half-eaten cookie. "Want a bite?"

Makenna pinched off a corner. "I wonder what these do."

"What was that?" asked Walter.

"Did you know that both Fig Newtons and Toll House chocolate chip cookies were invented in Massachusetts?" Makenna plopped the cookie piece into her mouth and turned away.

Walter finished his cookie. "Of course I know that. There was a big argument when those politicians decided on the state cookie. You two probably don't remember as you were so young. I still think Newtons should have won. At least they are named after a city."

"Did you find anything good at the sales?" asked Quin.

"Best Thursday in a long time. The estate sale hadn't been picked over, and besides having some pieces for me to repaint, there were some nice antiques for the store. I'm going to have to clear out more of the carriage house or use my dining room as a painting studio. I can't believe the number of orders I've gotten. I'm adding 'reclaimed furniture' to the store website. Quin, you're a genius."

Walter shook his head. "Don't go calling him that. He'll get a swelled head."

Makenna pointed at the tablet she used for a register. "Put your hours in the computer, Walter."

"Why? You know I don't cash any of your paychecks."

"Which is why your daughter set up direct deposit."

"Rebecca can't to do that!" Walter stomped from behind the counter.

"Actually, Pops, you put both of us on your account at the bank. Mom can."

"That wasn't why I put you two on my account. I'm going to give you a piece of my mind."

"Walter, it would be easier if you just faced the fact that I'm going to pay you to work here. I'd hate to hire someone else."

"You can't do that. No one else knows the store like I do."

"Then it's settled. I pay you." Makenna switched places behind the counter with Walter. "Since you are both here, I have some other news I meant to text you... The company in England is Bradford-Stone Worldwide."

Quin typed the name into his phone. A website popped up, but the content didn't make sense for a village like Hawthorne. "I can research. How did you find the name?"

He'd never seen Makenna smile so big. "I broke up with Wendell. He told me the name in hopes I'd change my mind."

Walter cheered. "About time. He was never good enough for you. I told Abigail that last year, but she didn't want me interfering."

Quin wanted to ask her out on the spot; however, there'd be no stopping his grandfather's interfering if he did.

"Thanks for watching the shop. I'll forgive the cookies this time. Next time eat in back."

"I'd better get over to the café. I've missed out on an entire morning of Sergeant Major." Walter put on his coat and left, the bell ringing overhead.

The air grew thick with anticipation. Quin cleared his throat as the bell rang again. It wasn't Walter. Instead, it was a group of laughing shoppers.

"Do you mind if I come by after work tonight?"

"Of course not. If I'm not here, I'll be back in the carriage house or maybe in the dining room. The house is easier to heat and freezing the paint isn't good for it."

"Excuse me? Can you tell us how much this quilt is?"

Makenna smiled at Quin and went to help her customer.

Quin whistled on his way back to the chamber. He kind of had a date for tonight.

The dining room won. The space was well lit, warm, and easily cleared of furniture Makenna didn't need. The Monroe brothers made quick work of moving her dining furniture out to the carriage house while she boxed up the china. Bringing the newly acquired pieces into the house was a bit trickier due to the narrow steps and doorways. No bones or bookcases were broken in the process, earning both boys a small bonus in their paychecks.

Makenna debated between painting and inventorying the other items she'd purchased that morning at two estate sales. The set of white glassware needed to go out on the floor, as did the spinning wheel.

The spinning wheel might have to go on her list of odd things. At the second sale, hidden in a back corner behind a large plant, it had called to her just as Sleeping Beauty's had to the fairytale princess. The urge to search it out had been unmistakable. There was, however, no sharp spindle waiting to prick Makenna.

The silver tea service she'd purchased sat locked away in the safe until she could clean it and identify any marks. Today's sale had been *Antiques Roadshow*-worthy as, nestled between relatively invaluable items, there were several marvelous pieces that, like the spinning wheel, dated over one hundred and fifty years old. She also picked up a few books for Claire's first-edition section. A signed book of poetry by Louise Chandler Moulton and another by Henry Wadsworth Longfellow would be worth one hundred times what she paid for it if they proved to be real.

Then there were the locked jewelry caskets. Neither looked especially valuable, but like the spinning wheel, they seemed to want her to buy them. If the magic was something real, then Makenna figured she should give it a chance and follow what could just as soon be foolish impulses.

Someone knocked on the front door. She checked through the window before opening it. He really came. "Quin, come in."

He looked her up and down. "I've never seen you in pants."

"It's impractical to paint in a dress, and don't worry, even Liberty does a double take when I'm in pants."

"I brought grinders. I didn't know which was your favorite—I got a roast beef, a melted cheddar and bacon with Russian dressing, and a ham, turkey, and Muenster with lettuce and tomatoes."

"From Mario's, right? Can't go wrong with anything there, though I've never tried the tuna. Come on back to the kitchen. I have milk, apple cider, and water. The cider is from Covington House. Liberty keeps me supplied, although I have to freeze it in quarts so I don't accidentally make my own hard cider."

"Experience?" He raised his brows.

"Not mine. Grandma's."

Quin set the takeout bags on the table. "I'll have water."

"Thanks for bringing dinner. Is this our date?" Makenna set two cups next to the bags.

"It could be a first one if you want it to be."

First implied a second. That tingly feeling was back. Liberty had definitely been wrong back when they were kids—this tingling had nothing to do with being hit on the head. "Let's see where this one is going, though I warn you, the activity part of this date could ruin your clothes if you choose to stay."

"I'll take my tie off then."

After dinner, Quin loosened his tie. "I have a T-shirt on underneath—do you mind if I take off my button-down?"

Makenna didn't expect him to ask. "You really want to help? I can find an apron if you want to protect your pants." She pulled out a pink gingham apron and a white canvas one that invited others to 'kiss the cook.' "Sorry, I have nothing else."

Quin took the canvas one. "Since I'm not cooking… but if you decide you want to, I wouldn't be opposed."

Makenna turned her back to hide the blush she knew was there. "Before we can paint anything, we need to remove the old gunk. You'll want some gloves."

As they cleaned, they talked about various topics such as why a grinder wasn't called a sub or a hoagie, and which band they would like to go hear the most. They both liked a cappella groups.

"I sang tenor in my high school choir but didn't continue in college."

"I manage a fair beatbox. Several of my friends and I sang at college for fun." Makenna demonstrated a *bop-bop-boom* rhythm.

When it was time for the first coat of paint, Quin reassured Makenna that he knew most of his sister-in-law's techniques. He started on one bookshelf and she started on the other. Not only did he finish first, but he also didn't have even a drop of paint on his gloves.

Makenna looked at her speckled arms. "How do you do that?"

"Do what?"

"You don't have a speck of paint anywhere."

"My mother calls it *naturally fastidious*, my brothers call it something else. How did you get paint on your cheek?"

Makenna touched her cheek with her gloved hand.

Quin laughed. "Now there is more. Where did those baby wipes go?" He found them on the worktable she'd set up in the corner. "Hold still."

His gentle touch sent a shiver down her spine. Makenna held her breath as their eyes met. "You're not wearing your glasses."

"After a conversation with my eye doctor, I broke down and ordered another contact. It finally came in yesterday. It's much easier to paint with them."

Quin dropped his hand from her face but didn't move away. "You got paint on your glasses?"

"How did you guess?"

He leaned in, looking from her mouth to her eyes. Makenna mimicked the movement.

A train whistle sounded.

Startled, Makenna jumped back, bumping her nearly empty paint can sitting on the bookcase shelf. Cold paint ran down her back.

Quin held up his phone. "I guess I need to change Pops's ringtone... Don't move. You'll drip on everything."

"Now I know what it feels like to be slimed on one of those kids' shows I used to watch."

"How can I help?" His dimple would be her downfall.

"I think leaving might help the most. I should get out of these clothes while I am standing on the drop cloth."

"Do you have a robe?" he asked.

"On the back of my bathroom door."

"I'll get it for you and disappear while you change. Then I can help clean this up before it ruins anything."

"I don't dare turn around to see the damage."

"Just stay there." Two steps out of the room, Quin stopped. "Where's your bathroom?"

"At the top of the stairs. It should be the only room with the door open." Makenna prayed she had nothing embarrassing sitting out.

Quin came back a moment later with her robe. He set it on the desk in front of her. "I'll be in the living room—I mean, parlor. Pops keeps telling me I use the wrong word."

Makenna unbuttoned the old plaid shirt she wore, glad that it didn't need to go over her head and that her hair was in a bun. Careful not to add paint to anything else, she stripped out of her jeans and set her clothing in a pile on the floor. The damage a cup of paint could do. She could only imagine what Liberty would say to this first date. Instead of a kiss, she got slimed. She wrapped the robe around her and raced up the stairs.

Dressed in a pair of sweats, she returned to the scene of her latest disaster. Quin's rolled-up pants showed off his bare feet. A trash can stood next to him, full of paint-covered paper towels. "I put your clothes in the kitchen sink. My sister-in-law says if you act fast, you can usually save your clothes."

"You didn't need to clean up after my clumsiness." She folded up the soiled plastic drop cloth.

"After hearing Pops's stories about working on the lines when he was barely out of high school, I changed his ringtone to a train whistle. It's my fault it startled you."

"Not your fault. Walter has many stories."

"I never knew he did, but ever since I bought that truck from you for his Christmas present, we've been talking every night." Quin deposited another paper towel into the trash can.

"What did Walter want?"

"He needed me to stop by Stop & Shop and get him a few things my mom didn't buy."

Makenna checked the grandfather clock in the hall. "Then you should go. Thanks for your help."

In the hall, he sat on the bench and put on his socks and shoes. "When can I take you out on a real, pre-planned date?"

Makenna bit her lip. With the furniture painting, spare time had become a luxury. "Sunday afternoon? Or next Wednesday? I am going to Red Leaves Books' Jólabókaflóðið celebration that Claire is holding on the twenty-third."

"I promised Grandpa I'd take him into Boston on Sunday. How about the Christmas Book Flood—because no, I am not even trying to pronounce an Icelandic word—and then dinner?"

"I'll try not to create another disaster that requires a change of clothes." Makenna clutched the bag of baby wipes to her chest as she showed him to the door, not sure if she should kiss his cheek. Trying to get the almost-kiss moment back would be too awkward.

Quin solved the problem by kissing *her* on the cheek before he left. For the first time in her adult life, Makenna wished for mistletoe.

# CHAPTER 15

Two days before Christmas and all was well. Check marks filled Quin's task list. Everything from mailing presents to his nieces and nephews, to handing out winter greetings to chamber members had been accomplished. First Night plans were all running smoothly, and the ten-day forecast showed promising weather. He hadn't had more than one antacid for days. Best of all, tonight he had a date with Makenna.

He'd stopped by the antique store daily since the night they'd painted. The few minutes he spent there lightened his spirits. Although it defied logic, he still had a nagging feeling that time inside the store ran on a slightly different schedule.

The cloud over everything was Bradford-Stone. According to his research, the only reason they would want prime real estate near the common would be for a hotel. Hawthorne needed a hotel like they needed an Elvis impersonator. According to Liberty, the bed and breakfast only reached one hundred percent capacity a few days a year. Hawthorne was too far from Boston to be convenient for tourists and too near to not be a day trip. No building applications had been turned in, and the entire block was in a city historic preservation district. A new hotel would have to be built in a style consistent with the 1820s Hill house and couldn't exceed forty feet in height.

He quietly communicated to the business owners that there would be a meeting to discuss their interests and that of the city of Hawthorne. With one exception, everyone had been happy about his announcement.

The train whistle sounded on his phone. "Hi, Pops."

"I wasn't fast enough again."

"On your email trip deal?" Quin sat back in his chair to listen.

"Yes."

"I'm sorry. How many times have you tried?"

"Over a hundred. I want to find a place we can go together."

"I'd love to go with you anyplace other than Siberia. The cold and I don't get along."

Walter laughed. "Deal. Nothing requiring furred coats."

"Sounds good. I'll see you tonight."

"Tonight." Pops's call disconnected.

Quin checked his watch. He was even running ahead of schedule. He whistled one of his favorite tunes as he left his office.

Mrs. Zimmerman looked up from her desk. "Someone's in the holiday spirit."

"Today feels like one of those rare, perfect days, and I am embracing it."

"More like the eye of a hurricane, if you ask me. However, the eye makes it possible to get through."

"I'm sure you're right. I expect the rest will hit next week, and we'll both want a holiday come January second."

"Speaking of which, the extra two hundred New Year's party kits showed up this morning. I checked the boxes myself. Oh, and this came for you." Mrs. Zimmerman held up a jar of Covington House cranberry sauce. "Liberty said she noticed you didn't order any for Christmas and wanted to make sure Walter had some."

"Walter and my mom leave for Rhode Island in the morning. I'll send it with them. Pops was hoping to get one of his vacations for Christmas, but it didn't happen, so he's going to his sister's house."

"You mean you'll be alone for Christmas? I'm making a huge dinner. You're always welcome to come over."

"Thank you for the invitation. I intend to sleep all day, if I can, and then read the rest of the time. I'm hoping to pick up something good tonight at the Jol-a-book-a—I'll never get that word right—Christmas Book Flood celebration."

"I wish I could get my family to celebrate Jólabókaflóðið. All night reading books sounds like the best Christmas ever." Mrs. Zimmerman closed her computer. "Thanks for letting me have Christmas Eve off. I still have a couple of things to do for the grandkids."

"See you Monday." Quin checked the boxes in the conference room. It was looking like a toy store. He locked up and went home to change into something less casual than his suit and snowflake tie.

The lights from the bookstore lit up the street. Through the window, Makenna laughed with her cousins. She'd changed her clothes too. The green velvet dress gave her the illusion of a Christmas sprite. Her hair swirled around her shoulders.

"Are you going in or just going to lurk?" asked Judge, his wife holding onto his arm.

"Give him a break, dear. It takes courage to talk to a girl that pretty. I remember you lurking often enough. I thought you'd never get the courage to come talk to me."

"I was just waiting for the right time." Judge gave his wife a peck on the cheek before entering the bookstore.

Quin followed. Stacks of books wrapped in green in the shape of mini trees decorated the room.

"Welcome to our Jólabókaflóðið, book flood, or Christmas Eve, Eve Sale, if your Icelandic is rusty." Claire handed him a flier and pointed out the discounts on several books. "Don't forget to put your name in the drawing."

Quin thanked her and made his way to Makenna's side. "You look like the spirit of Christmas tonight."

"Thank you. Your Christmas sweater is a bold choice. I'm impressed."

"I see you've already found some books." He nodded at the basket she carried.

She linked her free arm through his. "I've had my eye on this one for Liberty for a while. It is about making herbal teas. And this one is for me." She held up a historical romance. "Do you have anything in mind?"

"There's a true crime novel I've wanted for me and a small-portion cookbook for mom. She hasn't figured out how not to cook for a family of five teenage boys. Grandpa and I are ready to smuggle the leftovers to the homeless shelter."

They wandered around the shop, checking out various titles. Makenna found a New England history book with beautiful illustrations but refused to purchase it after noting it lacked several important details.

Grandma Tansy bumped into them near the bottom of the stairs. "Makenna, there is a book on New England antiques up in the used section that you should check out."

"Thanks, I will." Makenna nodded and passed over the next section of books.

Grandma Tansy tugged on Quin's arm. "She needs this book. Don't let it slip by." For a woman in her late seventies to mid-eighties, she was surprisingly strong as she pushed him toward the stairs.

Quin added Makenna's books to his own basket and escorted her up the stairs. "Has Grandma Tansy always been this—"

"Pushy? Nosey? Insistent? Not that I remember, but now that my grandmother has passed, Tansy seems to have added me to her list of people to watch over."

"So what book do you need?"

"Something to do with antiques. I have several books and mostly rely on websites for my valuations. I don't need another book. But if I don't find it, I'm afraid she'd 'borrow it' and make sure I get it." Makenna ran her finger along the shelves as she searched. She stopped at an old brown leather-bound book.

"Is that it?"

"No, it's a history of Hawthorne I've never seen. Claire usually tells me when she gets another one in." Makenna turned the pages. A loose one fell to the floor. Quin retrieved it for her, and she tipped it back in. "I don't see a price either. I hope it isn't too much. I want this one."

They continued along the shelves until they found a book laying on its side and sticking out. Makenna opened it. "Grandma Tansy is anything but subtle. I'm sure this book is the one she wanted me to find. It's got a bunch of handwritten notes in it. Claire doesn't usually have such desecrated books in her used section." She added it to the basket Quin carried.

"I'm surprised there aren't more people up here with as busy as the store is."

"We are the only ones, aren't we?" Makenna walked over to the railing. "Oh no, Grandma Tansy is shooing people away from the stairs. If we were in a historic romance, I'd think she was trying to ruin me by having us found alone."

"Is that all it took to be ruined?"

"According to the novelists. Kissing definitely."

"So If I kissed you right now and messed up your hair and you smeared lipstick on my face, we'd be engaged?"

"Something like that. We better hurry before she tries something." Makenna took Quin's hand.

They were halfway down the stairs when Grandma Tansy yelled. "Look who's under the mistletoe."

The entire room froze.

"There isn't any—" Claire's protest died as Keira pointed to the space above Quin's head.

Makenna looked above her. It was impossible not to miss the large kissing ball and its red ribbon. It hadn't been there when they went up the stairs. How had Grandma Tansy done it?

Quin squeezed her hand. She met his eye, and he raised a brow, silently asking for permission. He smiled just enough to show his dimple. If only she'd taken advantage of the privacy on the second floor and kissed him then. Makenna dipped her head ever so slightly and leaned in, meeting him halfway. The kiss wasn't much more than a brush of lips, a promise of something more. If the room hadn't erupted in cheers, she wouldn't have pulled back so quickly.

Quin supported Makenna's arm the rest of the way down as people continued to clap.

Grandma Tansy had her hands on her hips. "Youth is wasted on all the wrong people. Someone needs to teach you how to pucker."

The people closest to them laughed nervously.

Claire joined Grandma Tansy at the bottom of the stairs, a pair of scissors gripped in her hands. "I didn't put it there, I promise." Claire hurried up the stairs to the second level. She leaned over the railing to cut the ribbon holding the mistletoe.

"Wait!" Judge shouted. "I'd like to kiss my sweetheart too."

"Let her cut it down. You can kiss me anytime." His wife grabbed him by the collar and proved her point.

Quin led Makenna into a row of self-help books. They looked at each other, but neither spoke. He rubbed his thumb across her knuckles and warmth spread up her arm. Did he wish for privacy too?

The crowd booed as Claire's scissors cut through the ribbon.

Quin leaned closer. "Do you want to go to dinner now?"

"Yes. Let's escape before someone asks questions." Oh, the gossip that would come from this. No one other than Claire and Keira would have noticed if they were holding hands, but a kiss on the stairs witnessed by more than a hundred people. . . Yikes, it would have more people talking than a Hollywood gossip show. Last summer there had been a thread on the *Heard Around Hawthorne* social media page dedicated to Quin's arrival that speculated on how long he would be single—until the post was removed by the administrators.

The line at the counter was thankfully short.

Claire tucked the scissors into a drawer and waved Makenna over to her register. "I'm so sorry about that. I don't know what has gotten into Grandma Tansy lately. Can I give you an extra discount?"

"You don't need to do that, Claire. Both of us understand it wasn't you. I got suspicious when I realized we were the only ones upstairs." Makenna pulled her books from Quin's basket.

Quin set his books on the counter for Keira to check out.

"I don't know what we are going to do about her. I wish I knew how to get a hold of Eden. She isn't on social media. I've looked for years." Claire opened the Hawthorne history book. "Where did you find this?"

"Upstairs."

Claire opened a new screen on the computer she used for a checkout. "I don't have it in inventory, and I've never seen it. Did this book come from up there too?"

"The antique book is what Tansy sent me up to find."

Claire turned the books over and over. "I'm going to give you these along with the mistletoe ball and call it the Grandma Tansy discount." She put all three items in the bag with her other books. "You also owe me a bit of tea." Claire cast a side glance at Quin clearly indicating the tea was of the gossip type.

"Liberty wants to plan a tea party for after the holidays. All five of us." A party with lots of stories as well as food.

Claire's eyes widened. "Oh. Definitely."

Buttoning up her coat, she studied her other cousin. Keira's smile was missing something. Makenna leaned over the counter and whispered, "Is Keira ok?"

"Man problems." Claire handed Makenna the receipt. "More tea for after the holidays."

Quin held the door open for her. "I'm parked by the chamber. Do you want to take your books to your place first?"

An icy wind swirled around her ankles. The car was closer. "My books should be fine in your car."

She tucked her hand in his elbow and leaned into him for protection from the wind. Quin opened the car door for her and took her bag of books. "I'll put these in the trunk."

He hopped in and turned on the heater. "I'm still not used to the cold."

"No one is ever truly used to it. We just appreciate warmth more until August becomes unbearably humid."

Quin took Autumn Road, heading south. "There is this Italian place in Newton I've heard about or we can choose someplace else."

"Italian is great." She couldn't come up with anything else to say. Watching out the window, Makenna tried to think of anything other than that brush of a kiss that hinted at something more. Was there more? Could there be? If there was magic, it owed her more of a kiss, and she wanted it all. Technically,

Quin was a rebound relationship. Rebound relationships had a bad rap and people steered clear of them, yet she'd carried a secret crush for Quin for so long. Surely, the crush negated the rebound part. Makenna replayed the brief kiss in her mind.

She'd kissed Quin Kayhill! Her wish from thirteen years ago had come true. Wishes never came true. Granted, it was only a half wish or half kiss… Sweet Broomsticks.

She'd just gotten her wish, and Keira and Claire had witnessed it.

Although the headlights illuminated the road ahead perfectly, Quin couldn't focus. He'd never been one to leave things half done, and the kiss under the mistletoe wasn't finished. He glanced at the GPS. Twenty-two more minutes of driving this way could be hazardous to both of their health. Ahead was a lawn and garden store. The unilluminated business sign assured that the store was closed. Quin turned into the parking lot and parked, leaving the engine running. A streetlamp brightened the interior of the car enough that he could see Makenna's questioning eyes.

"I'm having problems focusing on the drive."

She looked down at her hands. "It's the mistletoe kiss, isn't it?"

"I feel like I started something I need to finish." Quin unbuckled his seatbelt. Makenna had released hers apparently just as eager as he was. She met him halfway. Her lips were warm and soft and hinted of apple cider. Quin ran his hand up her arm to rest behind her shoulder, pulling her closer. He ended the kiss and rested his forehead against hers. "That's what our first kiss should've been like."

"I'm sure that was our first kiss. The one under the mistletoe was like the little, teeny spoon they give you to taste ice cream when you're trying a new flavor at Baskin-Robbins. It didn't count at all."

"Even that little scoop has calories. It counted. Because if it hadn't happened, we wouldn't be sitting here now." He kissed the tip of her nose and sat back. "I would have waited until after dinner."

"I'll count it as a pre-kiss then."

Makenna's smile was so adorable, he nearly went in for the second kiss—or third, depending on who was counting. "I take it you didn't mind your first mistletoe kiss?"

"It was with the right person. Although I would've preferred the other hundred people hadn't been in the room."

Quin rubbed the back of his neck. "That *was* awkward. I had planned on finding a bunch of mistletoe and using it in a more private setting."

"You know, Claire gave me the ball of mistletoe."

Quin raised his eyebrows.

"We could use it later to practice. Grandma Tansy thought we didn't quite know how to do this. Of course, we should probably wait till after dinner. I don't usually kiss on the first date. And this feels like eating dessert first."

Double death by chocolate dessert. "This will be the third time we've had dinner together. We could always say it's the third date if that makes any difference."

Makenna buckled her seatbelt. "Third date will make it easier to explain."

Quin put his car in gear. "Explain what?"

"It's kind of a long story. Let's just say, thirteen years ago I made a wish when I was with a bunch of my cousins and two of them watched it come true tonight." Her voice sounded slightly hesitant.

"Are you trying to say that you wished to kiss me?" His chest swelled with a feeling he couldn't name. No wonder male peacocks strutted.

"Maybe?"

"Are you not sure about your wish or not sure about telling me?"

"Liberty won't let me forget about my wish. I was the only one of us who wished for a very specific person. You have to understand, it was one of those preteen things that girls do that guys think are totally weird."

That would have been the summer he spent so much time in the antique store. "On behalf of my teenage me, I'm very flattered. I hope I was worth the wish."

He turned onto the highway and the car picked up speed.

"It was everything my preteen heart expected." Her voice was so quiet he almost missed it.

Quin tried to wipe the funny grin off his face for the next fifteen miles. If the reflection he caught of himself in the rearview mirror at each stoplight was correct, he'd failed.

# CHAPTER 16

Ten minutes after the antique store opened, Liberty bounded in. "I expected a text last night."

Makenna rearranged a set of embroidered linen towels that was perfectly in order. "Why?"

Liberty held up her phone to the *Heard Around Hawthorne* social media page. "I'd thought there might be an explanation for this photo. And this photo, and this photo. Because if I'm not mistaken, it's you and Quin kissing inside the bookstore."

Makenna grabbed the phone from Liberty. "Oh, no. I just expected gossip. The short explanation is Grandma Tansy. The long explanation is Grandma Tansy."

"It doesn't look like you did anything to deter him. And this was the big wish come true. You're the first one to have their wish come true."

Makenna put a finger to her lips to quiet her cousin. "We don't know that for sure."

"I know I deserved a text."

"I was going to tell you tomorrow after Christmas dinner."

Liberty frowned. "I thought I was your best friend. I should've known first."

"Kind of hard to let you know first when there were a hundred witnesses. You could have been there."

Liberty picked up an old eggbeater. "I planned to be, but I had a guest coming. Leaving Grandpa in charge of the front desk is always iffy when I'm expecting guests. At least someone posted it in video."

Makenna gasped and covered her mouth with her hand. "Please tell me you're exaggerating."

"Would you like to see it?"

"I think I want a black hole to open up and swallow me."

"With or without Quin?"

Makenna slapped Liberty's arm, and chin pointed to the window. "Can we drop the subject now? I have customers coming in."

"As long as you promise to give me all the tea tomorrow."

"There's not much to give. My wish came true. There, you have the tea." Makenna plastered on her welcome-to-the-store smile and turned to greet her customers.

Mrs. Gail Monroe of the High Street Quilters led the group. "Is this you? Are you trying to give our town a bad name? I don't know if my grandsons should work here."

It was going to be an exceptionally long day.

Quin reached for the fountain pen under his desk. It slipped out of his fingers. He pushed his chair back and crawled under the desk. Above him, a train whistle sounded. Startled, Quin hit his head on the underside of the drawer. He forgot to change Pops's ringtone. That should have been on his task list.

"Hi, Pops."

"Don't you *Hi, Pops* me. Have you been kissing my little girl? Before you answer, Judge already sent me a photo. And while I was looking at it, the bargain vacation disappeared again." Too bad on the vacation. If Walter finally snagged one of the quick-sale deals to the Bahamas off the internet, he would be too happy to complain about anything for a week.

"I kissed Makenna under the mistletoe."

"For the entire town to see? I thought I taught you better than that."

"Makenna was fine with it. I didn't force her to."

"I have half a mind to come back up from Rhode Island and check on her."

"She's fine." Quin rubbed his head.

"You're sure? It's all over that book-face thing."

Oh, no. Not good. "I haven't spoken to her today. And no one has been into the office to complain." *Yet.* Someone was always in to complain.

"Well, I hope you know what you're doing. If you hurt my girl…"

"Pops, I thought I was your boy." He crawled back under the desk.

"Makenna doesn't have anyone in her corner. I've been watching over her from afar since she was old enough to sit behind Abigail's register. You got your mom and all your brothers, who else is going to fight for her?"

"All her Covington cousins?" Quin picked up the pen successfully this time.

"All the more reason to watch yourself. No one knows what the Covingtons are capable of."

"Seriously?"

"Just treat her right. I got to go. Your mama says it's impolite to be on my phone when we arrive at my sister's place."

"Merry Christmas, Pops."

Quin opened his browser to check on the page someone had dedicated to Hawthorne gossip. Sure enough, his kiss under the mistletoe had already garnered three hundred reactions—mostly likes and hearts. One commenter with the name of Cook59 cheered the new couple while BetPet expressed concern that the chamber might show Abigail's Antiques favoritism. Favoritism? Someone didn't understand the role of the chamber.

The office phone rang. "Hawthorne Chamber of Commerce."

"Quin, its me." He recognized Mrs. Zimmerman's voice. "Do you need me to come in? Are the phones ringing off the hook?"

"You and Walter are the only calls I've had this morning."

"You're sure you're fine?"

"Yes."

"For the record, I thought of mistletoe for the two of you first. I knew you'd be too cute together. Merry Christmas." Mrs. Zimmerman wisely hung up before Quin could respond.

On the bright side, no one was complaining about the noise the fireworks would make at First Night or asking why the music on the common was recorded instead of a live band playing at one of the indoor venues. There was a reason mothers warned their sons not to lick cold metal. The same held true for a cold trombone mouthpiece in sub-zero weather not to mention the damage caused to clarinets and other wood instruments.

Just before lunch, representatives from the High Street Quilt Club stormed the office, all speaking at once.

"What color should we make for your wedding quilt?"

"Why didn't you tell us you were dating? I asked my niece up for First Night to meet you."

"Such public displays of affection."

"I approve of Makenna."

"They say photos on the internet never die."

Quin plastered on his best smile. "Ladies, welcome to the chamber. How can I help your quilt club?"

"We don't need anything."

"Just wanted to speak our mind."

"It would be good for you to settle down here permanently."

The grin on his face was going to crack. "I'll consider your advice, ladies. You saved me an email. The ice carving will be from 2 p.m. to 6. Do you have your safety guard rotations worked out?"

"Four hours? It takes that long?" asked Gail Monroe.

Success. Quin got them to change topics. "It can take up to twelve hours, but we felt a four-hour window was better for the competition."

"And they use chainsaws. How long would it take with an ice pick?" asked a woman in a lavender knit cap.

Quin shook his head. "I have no idea."

"Don't worry, we have watching the area covered. That way you can have more time with your girl."

Pointing out that Abigail's Antiques would be open until the first fireworks wouldn't help, so Quin just smiled. "Happy Christmas and a Merry New Year." At the quilters' giggles, he thought about what he'd just said. "I mean, Merry Christmas and Happy New Year," he corrected, trying to keep from blushing.

By mid-afternoon, the flood of customers subsided. Most had been acquaintances curious about Makenna and Quin's photo. At least half purchased something. The odd pull to show a certain item to a customer occurred twice. Both times the customer purchased the item, but neither elaborated on why. Makenna noted that, other than the truck for Walter, she'd known none of the customers when 'the pull' happened.

An empty space sat where the bedroom set had been that morning. The Monroe brothers had loaded it up in the man's rented truck soon after she'd opened. Makenna would love to offer delivery; however, the boys were too young for that work. Even if she drove the van, she couldn't unload it herself. A problem for another day.

Another customer came in. Makenna dug her fingernails into her palm and smiled her fakest of smiles. "Bethany, how can I help you?"

"Wow, it really was you. With your hair down, I hardly recognized you."

"Can I show you anything? I have some lovely white milk glass—the kind your mother likes to collect. Did you need a Christmas present?"

"She has shelves full of the stuff. Do you have something else she might like?" Bethany checked her nails.

The pink daisy Pyrex came to mind. "I have something you might just want some day. It even matches your fingernails."

Bethany followed Makenna to where she kept the vintage kitchenware.

"Aren't those the cutest!" Bethany picked up a casserole with a lid. "But at this price? You've got to be kidding me."

"You'll find the same thing on eBay for twenty percent more."

"Really? They are cute enough, they even make me want to cook." Bethany inspected the dish from every angle.

"I think I would bake your meal in something else and transfer it to the casserole for presentation if you were going to use it."

"Is it microwave safe?"

Makenna shrugged. "In theory, since it is glass, but I wouldn't want to risk it."

"I'll get it, anyway. Mom will love it."

A half hour until closing time, Makenna still had customers

in the store and a dull throbbing in the back of her skull that was threatening to turn into a full headache. A delivery man entered with a huge bouquet of roses mixed with evergreens. He started to set them down on a hand-crafted table that dated to 1783. Makenna rushed to intercept him.

"Makenna Wilson?"

"Yes."

"These are for you. If you'll sign here."

Makenna signed with her left hand while balancing the vase against her right hip. Quin wasn't one of those huge display guys, was he? She excused herself and took the display to the workroom where she could set it on something stray water wouldn't ruin. A computer-printed card fell to the floor.

> *Merry Christmas.*
> *Love, Wendell*

*Rotten hawthorn berries.* What possessed him to send such a thing? She hadn't answered any of his calls or emails. Makenna took three cleansing breaths before returning to the store.

A few customers remained in Abigail's Antiques. Quin checked his watch. Makenna should have closed a minute ago. He caught her eye and pointed to the Open sign and mimed turning it. At her nod, he flipped to closed. The sign wouldn't keep a local out of the store with the lights on and the door unlocked, but no one passed by as he waited for the store to empty.

Makenna locked the door after the last customer exited. "I'm assuming that you aren't here to purchase anything?"

"No. I came to look at the watch and talk to the beautiful proprietress."

"If that watch stops time for you while you're in the store, please don't let it tonight. I need today to be over."

"Can I help with anything?"

Makenna pulled out her bank bag and counted money. "I just need to make the deposit."

"Big day?"

"I had more customers than usual and most wanted to talk about our kiss. Several were polite enough to purchase something." A faint blush colored her cheeks.

"Thanks to the famous photo, I presume?"

"Something like that. Did you get any complaints at the chamber?"

"Hard to tell if they were complaints or instructions on what I should do with my life. It never occurred to me that one kiss could make us local celebrities." No wonder movie stars wore baseball caps and sunglasses in public.

Makenna stopped counting and studied Quin for a moment. "This is going to sound weird. In the back room there is a box sitting on the left worktable—ignore the flowers—in the box is a drinking glass. You'll know it when you see it. Will you get it for me?"

"A drinking glass?"

"Yes, versus eyeglass."

The flower arrangement was too large to ignore. Quin settled on not snooping to see who it came from.

The only box on the table held several collectible Coca-Cola items. His next oldest brother, Jamison, would be in heaven if he saw the box. Quin found the only glass in the box. Twelve years ago, he would have given it to his brother for Christmas. That was the last year he gave anything to his brother. The fight the next day had been epic. Under the influence of who knew which drugs, Jamison had hit their mother and yelled the vilest things. It was all fifteen-year-old Quin could do to pull his brother off and hold him at bay while Mom called 911. The years since had been a roller coaster of rehab and recurrences. At some point, Jamison sold his entire Coca-Cola collection to feed his habit. Quin had avoided his brother as much as possible since.

If Makenna hadn't asked for the glass, Quin would have made an excuse and left—anything to stop thinking about reconciling with the brother closest to his age. He hurried to the front counter and set the glass down with more force than necessary. "Is this what you wanted?"

Makenna picked up the glass and studied it in the light, rotating it around. She shook her head. "I don't think it was as old as I'd hoped. Will you put it back, please?" She set the glass down and finished preparing the deposit. "Do you mind watching the store for me while I run over to make the deposit?"

She didn't give him time to react as she dashed out of the front of the store without a coat. Even native New Englanders had enough self-preservation skill to recognize it was literally freezing outside. What was wrong with Makenna tonight?

Quin set the glass back in the box, careful not to chip it. According to Mom, Jamison had been dry for a year now.

This time his curiosity won, and he looked for a card with the flowers. There wasn't one. He couldn't help looking at the box of collectables again, his brother on his mind. They had so many fun times before his brother became an addict. Jamison had been the brother to teach him how to surf. Maybe this year, he should answer Jamison's Christmas Day phone call.

By the time he finished reminiscing, Makenna was already turning off the lights in the front section of the store. "What are your plans for the evening?"

Reminisce about Jamison. "I hadn't planned much."

"I'm taking the floral arrangement over to the retirement center and picking up a pizza from Mario's."

"Pizza for Christmas?"

"It is a tradition my Mom started when I was little. She wanted to have a nice dinner, but I refused to eat turkey without saying gobble-gobble until everyone lost their appetite. She asked me what I wanted, and I told her 'pizza from the man at the front door.' So, she ordered pizza. Whichever grandparents I was with on Christmas continued the tradition. Then I'm going to celebrate Jólabókaflóðið and sleep in until I go to Liberty's for Christmas dinner. What about you?"

"Mom and Walter went to Rhode Island to my great-aunt's. I planned on spending the evening celebrating the Book Flood too."

"You aren't even going to try on that word, are you?"

"Been there, tried it. Nope." Quin rebuttoned his coat.

"I can see if they can add another pie to my order if you want to come over and eat with me."

"Everything pizza?" Quin helped Makenna on with her coat.

"Is one enough for you? I have to have leftovers for breakfast, so I'm not sharing." She activated the alarm system.

"I promise to leave you leftovers."

"Good. I'd hate to go all Grinchy on you." Makenna's laugh reminded him of silver bells. He couldn't imagine a better way to start out the holiday.

# CHAPTER 17

Mother Nature should know that December 25 means snow. This year, no one sent her the memo. Makenna wandered around the house. Her original plan to read her new romance book had been spoiled by eating pizza in front of the fire last night, discussing great and not-so-great fiction. Quin had declined her secondhand invitation to dinner at the B&B, saying he had something to do. Makenna wondered if it had anything to do with the Coca-Cola glass.

Her phone rang. An unknown Boston number came up on the screen.

"Hello?"

"Merry Christmas, baby. Did you get the flowers?"

Makenna sat in the closest chair and buried her head in her free hand. "Merry Christmas, Wendell. The receptionist at the retirement center took the flowers into the main dining area. She assured me the residents would love them. Have a lovely day. Goodbye."

Her phone rang again a few seconds later. Same number. Makenna blocked the number.

A text pinged from another unknown number.

*—This is Wendell, I'll be there in thirty minutes to pick you up for dinner.*

*No, thank you. I have other plans.* She sent the answer and blocked the newest number.

Dinner at Liberty's wouldn't be for another four hours. Going there this early would mean questions about Quin she wasn't ready to answer. The relationship was too new to discuss in the detail Liberty wanted. Yes, the entire town knew they kissed. That didn't mean she needed to tell how it made her tingle all the way to the toes. Or how she felt pretty every time Quin looked at her, hair up, glasses and all. Or that despite both of them being well read, they didn't agree that Jane Austen was superior to Dickens.

Above all, she wasn't ready to discuss the impression that sent Quin after a glass he didn't purchase. He'd been more contemplative all last night, yet she didn't want to ask him if it had to do with the glass. Or the vision—for lack of a better word.

The same thing happened earlier that day with a cameo and a woman dressed in designer clothes. With tears in her eyes, the woman purchased the cameo and left the shop on the phone with her grandmother whom she was going to visit that day. From the loud conversation, this change in plans didn't please her husband who trailed behind. Then there was the man she guided to a marble game to share with his grandchildren. More and more, she was convinced it couldn't be coincidences. Magic seemed like the wrong word too. Maybe magic didn't need spells to work.

Liberty's was not an option. Staying at home wasn't an option either if it meant facing Wendell. She didn't want to have a fight.

The store. Makenna tossed on a thick wool sweater and grabbed the books she'd purchased the other night. The good thing about no white Christmas was she wouldn't leave tracks to the back door of the store.

Looking over all the little things she'd left undone, she chose the project that promised the most fun. The two locked boxes she'd purchased at last week's estate sale would be fun to open. Unlike the Christmas gifts she'd wrapped for herself under the tree, she had no idea what she would find. Makenna searched for the lock-picking kit. She hadn't used it for almost a year. It wasn't in any of her desk drawers. Or in the toolbox.

Makenna checked to make sure the street was quiet before running out to the front desk and looking through the shelves under the counter. The dust tickled her nose. She hadn't cleaned the area since shortly after taking over the store…

*Achoo!*

Dusting under the counter needed to move up her priority list. On the bottom shelf she found an old cardboard box. Makenna dusted it off, sure it hadn't been there earlier. Inside the box was a small ledger. Another thing to enter into the computer. And a letter addressed to her.

*Makenna,*

*If you are reading this, I've been gone some time now. I asked Tansy to retrieve this box and give it to you when the time was right. I had hoped that I would live long enough to give it to you myself, but you aren't ready yet.*

*You may have discovered some things aren't business as usual about the store. I'm not sure if it's the store, the things I feel I should acquire, or the people that need them. Tansy says it is a Covington thing, that I attract objects* that are necessary and that are needed to make homes happier.

I asked my mother-in-law, Doris Hill, if she ever had items match to people. She laughed at me. Other than Tansy, I've never told another soul. Even with all our stories about Lavinia, I think my other cousins would laugh. We don't talk about magic being real. Well, other than Tansy. I don't know if this is magic. There aren't any spells. I can't do anything like cupcakes to calm a gaggle of irate bridesmaids or manipulate items. I can't heal bodies the way Tansy does, but I would like to say I can heal hearts. The truth of the matter is I just bring people and things together and hope it helps lives change for the better.

I started keeping a journal of items that matched themselves to people and asked Tansy to give it to you. I don't know if it will help other than to know that you are the same kind of crazy I am.

I love you and wish I could be there with you.

Always,

Grandma A

Makenna put the letter back in the box. If she had found this during the summer, she would have wondered if some of Grandma's medications had been off. But Grandma Tansy

164

hadn't given it to her either. How long had it sat under the counter collecting dust without her noticing? No telling what Grandma Tansy could have done.

Someone pounded on the front window. "Makenna! I know you're in there!"

*Rotten hawthorn berries.* Wendell.

There was no way he could see her from there.

*Bang. Bang. Bang!* "Makenna!" This time he rattled the door.

Makenna's phone buzzed in her pocket. Great. Wendell had set off the alarm. She pressed the number for the alarm company. "Hi. This is Makenna Wilson. 54389A34. It is a false—"

Police sirens drowned out her voice. Makenna stood and ran back to the workroom to disable the alarm and get her keys to the front door.

"Yes, it is a false alarm. My old boyfriend was trying to get my attention. An officer is on site." She hurried to the front door.

The operator on the other end ran through a list of questions and asked for Makenna's ID again before ending the call. A not-too-happy Wendell yelled at Officer Hastings on the sidewalk. Makenna unlocked the door.

"You called the police on me?" Wendell advanced a step, but the officer cut him off.

"No, you set off the alarm with all your pounding on the window and rattling the door." She turned to Officer Hastings and his partner. "I'm so sorry you had to come out."

"Most excitement we've had all morning." Officer Hastings watched Wendell without turning to her.

His partner grinned. "Other than the phone call about the reindeer tracks in the Warren's front yard."

Wendell tried to push Officer Hastings aside. "Why aren't you ready?"

"Wendell, I told you I had plans today. You and I aren't dating anymore."

Officer Hastings sidestepped closer to Makenna. "Is this man harassing you?"

"Careful. I'm a lawyer." Wendell puffed out his chest. He reminded Makenna of a dachshund taking on a German Shepard.

"No, he just needs to leave."

"You heard the lady, Mr.—?"

"Smith, Wendell A. Smith the Third."

"Mr. Smith, Ms. Wilson has asked you to leave. Makenna, go ahead and lock back up. I have nothing better to do for the next couple of hours but wait for him to leave. A slow shift."

"Thank you, officers."

Makenna watched through the door as the officers directed Wendell to his car. Maybe he'd get the picture now that their relationship was over. Still, it surprised her that just banging on the door set off the alarm. She checked the connector when she locked the front door. She'd call the alarm company on Monday to check the system.

Her phone rang. Another number she didn't recognize. "What part of broken up don't you get?"

"That was fast." The California accent was not Wendell's. "Quin?"

"Is there something I need to know?"

"Oops. Sorry. I didn't recognize the number. Wendell has taken to calling me from unknown numbers, and Greg—I mean Officer Hastings—just came out to the store."

"Are you alright?"

"I'm fine. Wendell set off the security alarm. So… starting over. Hi, Quin. Merry Christmas."

"Merry Christmas to you too. I'd ask if I caught you at a bad time, but I'll take it you're not at dinner yet."

"No, what's up?"

"You know the glass you had me get last night? The Coke one?" Quin held the phone to his ear and paced around his little kitchen.

"Yes."

"Will you reserve it and the contents of the box for me?"

"Sure. Not that I would have sold it today."

"I know the store isn't open, but you said you sometimes do online sales."

"The entire box is yours. May I ask why?"

"My brother. He collects Coca-Cola things. We talked this morning." The five minutes had been the longest conversation they'd had in years without anyone yelling or breaking something.

"And?"

"We haven't talked in years, and I called him because of that glass. How did you know I needed that glass?" He moved to the living area still unable to fully wrap his mind around the morning's call.

"I didn't."

"Makenna. Something is going on. I know you know it. You got this pensive look on your face. I've seen you get it with customers. You did it with the truck I gave Grandpa. Oh, he called this morning, and he loves it, by the way. How did you do it?" There had to be an explanation. "The drinking glass made me do it" was too lame a reason to reconcile with his brother.

"I didn't do anything."

"I don't get it. Why would seeing a bunch of old junk finally push me to reconcile with my brother?"

"I don't know." She sounded sincere, but she had to know something. "I have three hours before I go to dinner if you want to talk, and I know there would be enough food if you wanted to join us."

"No, thanks. Jamison is going to call back after his fiancé's family finishes with their presents so we can talk alone. Whatever you did, thank you."

"You're welcome."

"Maybe you can drop by after dinner. I want to spend time with you because I'm afraid this week will be insane. Not only that, but I'll be a lame date for New Year's since I'll be worried about the sound, and the fireworks, and the ice sculptures, and the weather, and everything, but I would really like you by my side at the stroke of midnight." Quin ran a hand through his hair.

"I'd love to be there. I won't get the store closed until about eight or nine that night, and then I'll come and find you. In the meantime, we can catch a minute here or there."

Quin thought about the watch. He could fully test the theory this week. "Thanks. And thanks for whatever you did."

"I didn't do anything."

"You did. Merry Christmas."

"Bye. Merry Christmas."

Quin stared at the phone for a moment. Part of him wanted to take Makenna's offer for dinner but missing his brother's call wasn't an option. Even if he couldn't find a rational explanation. Rational? Hadn't he just accused Makenna of doing something? Magic didn't exist, even in Hawthorne. It was nothing but a convenient crutch used to explain odd things—like Keira's scones and cookies. Or the watch. It was just the memory of his brother with the collection, and maybe Makenna had really needed that glass right then.

Now she probably doubted his sanity.

*He* doubted his sanity.

The busiest week in his life was about to kick off, and he was now balancing a girlfriend and a reconciliation. He was definitely the only crazy person in the room.

Liberty lay sprawled across her bed while Makenna curled up in the big comfy chair. "Best part of Christmas Day—the shop was closed."

"Lucky you. Try running a B&B. I'm never closed. In fact, we are full up this coming weekend thanks to your boyfriend and his First Night. Not that I'm complaining. It is a nice extra boost during our quiet months. December through February aren't peak tourist times."

"Ignoring the boyfriend remark."

Liberty leaned on one elbow and propped her chin up. "You promised you'd tell."

"It's still early. Not much to tell."

"Well, you kissed him."

"Under duress." Makenna tucked her feet under her.

"And you didn't kiss again? Oh, look at you blush!"

"Quin is a genuinely nice guy, and his kisses exceed my preteen wish. He also thinks I control magic."

Liberty sat up so fast the bed banged against the wall. "What?"

Makenna explained the watch and the cola glass and then told her about the ledger she'd found.

"So what was in the locked box?" Liberty moved to the edge of the bed.

"I don't know. I haven't found the lock-picking tools. I may have to order new ones. By the time the police escorted Wendell away, I forgot about looking."

"Wendell? Your storytelling skills are leaving a few gaps."

"Nothing to tell." More precisely nothing she wanted to tell. "He just doesn't take no as an answer. Either that or he has never been dumped before."

"That's hard to imagine."

Makenna laughed with Liberty.

Liberty gained her composure first. "So where are you going to go from here?"

"I don't know. It's a new year, full of possibilities." Makenna raised her teacup in a salute.

Liberty mimicked the gesture with her teacup. "I need some possibilities, too."

"Any possibilities in particular?"

"Not really. My chances of Grandpa handing Covington House to me hasn't changed. Since I'm his sole living descendant, it is either pass the B&B on to me or search for the next eligible Covington male."

"If it is of any worth, Uncle Dean hasn't asked me to shake the family tree."

"And I really want a boyfriend this year. And not another friend who happens to be male and tells me all about the women he's crushing on." Liberty set her empty cup down. "But those are the same things I wanted last year."

"Maybe this will be your year."

Liberty checked her watch. "I better go downstairs. I'm on desk duty."

"Surely you aren't expecting anyone on Christmas night."

"Officially, no. We get one or two people a year who need a room due to a holiday family fight."

"I need to get going, too." Makenna carried her cup and saucer to the kitchen.

"Where are you going?"

"Quin's."

"I thought you said he wasn't a boyfriend."

"Maybe I lied."

Liberty threw a dishtowel at Makenna who ducked out of the door fast enough to avoid being hit. "Merry Christmas!"

# CHAPTER 18

Santa may have had a list and checked it twice, but he had nothing on the lists in the chamber's conference room. Everything from power cords to back-up plans to the cost of roasted chestnuts was triple checked, color coded, and checked again. That was—everything but the weather.

The brown Christmas had given Quin a false sense of hope. Now with less than twenty-four hours to go, the weather forecasters spoke the four-letter word Quin didn't want to hear: s-n-o-w. For the first time in days, Quin reached for his bottle of antacid.

Mrs. Zimmerman waved a dismissive hand at Channel 25. "He isn't saying it's a nor'easter, and it isn't the tail end of a hurricane. Stop borrowing trouble. Not a single station is mentioning the years 1978, 1997, 2005, 2015, because it is just your normal old December snowstorm. Mark my words, no more than five inches. The city will have the streets clear and everything will look fine."

"But look at that storm system."

"Are you a meteorologist?"

"No?"

"When is the last time you spent a winter in the commonwealth?"

"When I was fourteen and it didn't snow."

"This will bring just enough snow to sled and build a small snowman. If school was in session, the busses would be right on time in the morning. You've got to stop worrying."

"But I can't!"

"Go to the café get yourself a cup of hot cider or one of those coconut cupcakes. Then ask Judge, Gene, and your grandfather about the snow. They'll tell you it isn't worth the ulcer you're giving yourself." Mrs. Zimmerman pushed him out of the room.

In the corner of the café, the daily game of Sergeant Major was in full swing. Until the game was over, asking questions would be met by a glare from whomever was losing. He stood in line to place his order and a cider for Makenna. Since Christmas, they'd only managed a few stolen moments here and there. He had too many things to worry about and the watch only stopped time for fifteen minutes at the most, usually less. His phone vibrated in his pocket. He looked at the out-of-state number. This could only be another thing to add to his worries. Without ordering, Quin left the line and the café.

The days after Christmas were always slow. Makenna didn't mind. Wandering through the store gave her a chance to check on her inventory. She refolded a seventy-year-old blue and green quilt. Who had made it? How had they used it? Such thoughts often came to mind when she pondered her antiques. Most items had a history that she would never know.

The saddest were the old photographs dating back to the 1870s and sometimes earlier. Faces of unknown men, women, and children stared out of them. Their names and their lives forgotten, their images filed away in a box and sold for a dollar.

A delivery man entered the shop. "Just one today." He handed Makenna the small brown box and the tracking device for her to sign. Her new lock-picking tools.

"Thanks. Have a Happy New Year."

As he exited, a customer entered. Makenna slipped the package under the counter. "May I help you?"

The woman shook her hatted head and meandered around the store. Makenna resisted the urge to open her new tools and pick the locks of the two boxes sitting in the safe in the back room.

Josie entered the store. "I need a fantastic dish to display my newest creation. What do you have?"

"It depends if it is on top of the counter or in your glass case."

"That depends on if you charge me full price or give me a family discount." Josie poked through the kitchenware.

"I don't have a family discount. Do you know how many people in this town would try to claim it?"

Josie stood on her tiptoes and peered into the cabinets where Makenna kept the more expensive and breakable pieces. "You should. By the way, I saw your new shabby chic pieces. I would like a hutch in a French blue and either brown or black. It needs to fit on the north wall near the door where the baker's rack is. It would look much better there." She tapped on the glass. "The cake stand with the blue flowers, please."

Makenna unlocked the cabinet. "That is definitely an in-the-glass-case piece."

"It is the perfect shade of blue. Do you suppose anyone will carve ice flowers tomorrow? I want this creative ice vibe for my January decor."

"I haven't thought about it much." At the dinging of the bell, Makenna looked over her shoulder. The browsing customer left, patting her oversized purse. Not another shoplifter. "Josie, have you had any problems with shoplifters?"

"Just the occasional kid trying to steal candy. I filled the display-only candy with a Vegemite filling, and I don't have any problems anymore. Why?"

"I've had several minor items go missing. Grandma Tansy returned the only valuable one, but that woman who was just in here made me wonder if she took something."

Josie pointed to one camera. "Maybe you caught her on camera."

"Even if I did, it won't do much good unless she stole something valuable. I'm not going to have the police investigate a small item."

"You should. Officer Hastings needs something to do other than snoop into my life."

"What?"

"Ever since Emily's wedding, he's been checking up on me. Drives me crazy." For years Emily Hastings and Josie had been inseparable—until Emily was swept off her feet and left with her handsome prince in a swirl of white satin and tulle this past summer.

"He's just concerned for his little sister's friend." Makenna put the cake plate in a box and wrapped tissue paper around it.

Josie ran her credit card through the reader. "You really do need a family discount."

"What do you think the ten percent off was?"

"The friend's discount."

"You're a third cousin, do you really expect to get more off of a sale?"

174

"No, but I can try. Do I get it on my hutch too?"

"Were you always this pesky?"

"Aunt Abigail called me her little tornado, so probably."

"She called you a dust devil."

"Little tornado sounds better."

Makenna dropped a pen on the floor behind the counter. The empty space where her package had been caught her eye. "I think that woman took my package. I hadn't even opened it."

"Do you know what it was?"

"Lock-picking tools." So much for opening the boxes tonight.

"That should be an interesting police report. Why did you need them?"

"I can't find Grandma's, and I purchased some old, locked boxes I need to open."

"I locked myself out of my shop last year. Aunt Abigail got the set from the letter desk in your parlor. Did you check there?"

"No, I'd only ever seen them here."

"Maybe she had more than one set." Josie picked up the box. "I'd better get back, before my new employee starts to sample the candy. If she finds the Vegemite ones, I'll be employee hunting again."

Another customer wandered in. Tourist. They wanted something made by Paul Revere. Makenna smiled and explained that most of the known authentic pieces were in either museums or private collections. A single Revere spoon could easily fetch fifteen to twenty thousand dollars at auction. Despite her calm explanation, the customer left grumbling under their breath. They hadn't even looked at the carved ship she'd suggested.

She checked the text that came in while she'd talked. It was from Quin.

*—I was hoping to see you today, but disaster after disaster. Driving out to Springfield. See you tomorrow.*

He'd been true to his word about being busy this week. Hopefully, Quin could rest on January second. Since Keira's original recipes had appeared online and not tasting the same as they did at the café, the mistletoe kiss was no longer the talk of town. Although her heart ached for Keira, Makenna liked having her privacy back. She didn't want people speculating if she and Quin were still dating since they hadn't been together for more than a few minutes at a time all week. She'd moved the cola memorabilia to the house so no one would sell it until Quin went through the box.

As soon as the store was empty, Makenna brought up the camera feeds. The only thing the woman took was the package. Under the hat, she'd tied a scarf. According to the marks on the doorframe the woman was nearly five and a half feet tall. Too tall to be Grandma Tansy. Makenna dialed the police station.

# CHAPTER 19

Tiny white missiles hit Quin's windshield. Twenty miles from Hawthorne, he slowed down and turned on the wipers. They mocked him as they swished right to left and back. Snow-ing, snow-ing. Having a December without the average ten inches of snow was a good thing. Unless Mother Nature dropped all ten tonight. The extra rain early in the month made up for the lack of frozen precipitation. Arguing with the snow pelting his car would not make it stop.

Waiting at a stop sign, he noticed the snow fell almost straight down. Good. No wind. Wind meant blizzards. A light snow could be good. According to locals, snow would mean it warmed up and a few inches wouldn't stop anyone from coming if the temperature remained in the high twenties. He'd much preferred anything that started with twenty degrees ended with Celsius.

Soon the road was white with two tracks to follow. At least he wasn't the only person driving around. When he parked in the driveway, it took a moment to unclench his hands from the steering wheel. Driving I-5 during rush hour never prepared him for back roads in a snowstorm.

As Mrs. Zimmerman predicted, only four inches of snow covered Quin's car in the morning.

Grandpa stood near the front window. "Looks like a perfect day for First Night. The temperature is up, and everything looks prettier with a blanket of snow."

"I wish I could be as optimistic."

"This time tomorrow it will all be over, no matter what else happens. So, enjoy the day."

Considering he'd already taken two aspirin, Quin didn't know if he'd make it twenty-four hours. "Easier to say than do."

"You need to relax. Take time for the important things. Did you see Makenna yesterday?"

"I texted her." He wanted to see her and, it turned out he could have before he left for Springfield since he'd had to wait twenty minutes for the order he'd needed. He should've called her instead of triple checking his to-do list on his app.

Walter glared over the top of his reading glasses. "Not good enough." He took a ten out of his wallet. "Go take her some of that cider you both like and take a moment before the day gets away from you."

"Keep your money, Pops. I can pay."

"This is my treat."

Quin took the money and headed out into the winter wonder nightmare.

Makenna was still at the house. An odd disappointment filled him. He would have more time with her in the store because of the watch. Ugh, he needed more sleep. Time didn't really stop; it was just some illusion. She answered before he knocked.

"Come in. Don't worry about the snow, it is perfect. Today will be perfect."

Her comments warmed him like the non-existent sunshine. "How did you know?"

"I notice little things, like you obsessing over the weather app on your phone all month." Makenna took her cup of cider.

"I got muffins today. I didn't realize the town even had their own berries." Quin set the bakery bag on the kitchen table.

"Hawthorn—no E—berries grow all over the world. We do have a particular variety in this area. There are trees all over town. The berries are loaded with antioxidants and may help lower blood pressure. Some say they lessen anxiety." Makenna studied him from head to toe. "Do you need mine too?"

"Are you saying I am anxious?"

"You seem more stressed than usual today."

"I'm usually stressed? I thought I was getting better. I used to go through six or eight antacids a day. I haven't taken any in the past two days."

"Quin, I don't mean it like that." Makenna sat at the table. "Today is a monumental day for you. Anyone would be stressed."

He sat opposite her. "I just want First Night to turn out and help the town." *And not be the ruination of my career.*

"I know you do." She reached across the table and held his hand. "You've got this. Some little things will go wrong today—they always do. That will be the key. No one but you will ever know about them. The big things will be right: the music, the play, the fireworks. I'll come find you about ten. If you need a minute, come to the shop. Remember, you have friends."

"Thanks. I just can't help wanting things to be perfect."

"You don't want them too perfect or next year it will have to be bigger and better than perfect, and that is way too much stress."

Next year? Quin saw the time on the kitchen clock. "I'd better go." He kissed the top of Makenna's head.

"See you tonight at ten. And save your New Year's kiss for me."

She followed him to the door. "It has your name on it. I could give you a preview now."

"Hmm. That would lower my stress considerably."

Makenna wrapped her arms around his neck. She was the perfect height for him. Their lips met. This could never get old. Quin angled his head and pulled her closer. Too soon Makenna ended the kiss. "I said preview. Not the entire show."

"Are you telling me I have to go to work?"

"Yes." She opened the door and pointed out into the cold.

Quin leaned over and stole another quick kiss.

"Stop procrastinating. You have an amazing day ahead. She gave him a playful push out the door.

He paused at the bottom step. "Midnight: you, me, the whole show."

"You got it."

Officer Hastings found the empty delivery box in a dumpster in the alley next to the café. "Sorry, Makenna, it looks like your lockpicks are gone."

"I feel like I just enabled a thief."

"Nothing else was missing?"

Makenna shook her head. "I don't get it. Of all the things to steal, the box that just arrived with a twenty-five-dollar lock-picking set is so random. And she had to reach behind the counter to do it."

"You didn't recognize her?"

"No, she kept her hat on and tucked her scarf under her chin. The coat was a long wool dress coat. Generic. I have one almost exactly like it."

"May I see the video again?"

Makenna brought up the footage on her laptop and turned it so Officer Hastings could see.

He stopped the video. "Squint at the video. And tell me who she reminds you of."

It couldn't be. The woman was four inches taller than Grandma Tansy.

"Look at those boots. They have a two-inch base. If she stuffed them inside, it could be."

Makenna rubbed her temples. "It can't be Grandma Tansy. She isn't shuffling. Of course, she didn't speak to me, but Josie was here too. How did neither of us recognize her?" *Magic. No way.* "I'm sorry. I should have recognized her and not taken your time."

"Do you want me to talk with her? We could be wrong."

"No. I'll talk to the cousins. I just don't understand what she is doing."

"Everyone loves Grandma Tansy. We're all keeping an extra eye on her."

"I should be happy she was dressed for the weather this time. Thanks, officer. Now to order another set of lockpicks. It will be easier than getting her to give them back."

"Do I need to know what you are doing with lockpicks?"

Makenna pointed to an old desk. "Sometimes I buy stuff like that desk that have a locked drawer and no key. Believe me, I'm only breaking into stuff I own."

Officer Hastings put his gloves back on. "Happy New Year and good luck with Grandma Tansy."

As dusk fell, the blocked-off street filled with people. A few came into the store and browsed or thawed out. The Monroe brothers came by with their girlfriends to show them where they worked and point out the huge and heavy furniture they moved. Soon after, she heard the fireworks for the children's show. She locked up the store and watched them through the front window. With less than a hundred in cash sales, there was no point in trying to get to the bank through the crowd. She dropped the window covers and put the items that belonged in the safe away.

She changed into warmer clothes before wandering around the common. The ice sculptures were amazing. Mrs. Gail Monroe proudly proclaimed that there had been no incidents despite the sculptors using real chainsaws. The ballerina dancing with a flowing scarf only deserved second place because the dragon fighting the knight looked like he breathed fire and not frozen water.

Teens and adults danced to the recorded music coming from the gazebo. A few young children wearing bunny ears, leprechaun hats, and tricornes trailed along after parents. A young witch waved a wand at Makenna and shouted, "Happy New Year."

She followed a sign to the library where a brass quartet played in the large central lobby. Returning to the common, she saw Keira and Brant and waved. She needed to compliment Brant on his amazing fireworks show. She checked her phone, still a half hour before it was time to locate Quin.

Bethany rushed up and grabbed Makenna's mittened hand. "There you are. I've been looking for you all over. You've got to come see this."

Makenna had little choice but to follow Bethany across the lawn to the ice sculptures. They stopped at a sculpture of doves inside of what looked like two wedding rings—not at all in line with the theme of First Night. Wendell stepped out from behind the sculpture with a microphone connected to a speaker. He raised the microphone to his lips. *Rotten hawthorn berries.* Bethany held tight to Makenna's arm.

"Let me go."

"Just hear him out."

"Makenna Wilson." Wendell went down on one knee.

"Stop." Makenna covered her mouth to hold in the scream that would attract more attention.

"Over this past year and a half, we have had some ups and downs, some misunderstandings and fights. But I've concluded that you are the only one for me. Marry me, Makenna, and make me the happiest man in Boston."

The crowd that gathered around them started cheering.

"No!" Makenna yanked her arm out of Bethany's grasp and pushed her way out of the crowd. She bumped into someone and dropped her phone on the sidewalk. She reached to get it, only to have someone sidestep on top of it. "Excuse me, my phone."

The shattered screen blinked once and faded. Only two hours left in this year, but Makenna wanted it to end now.

Quin checked his phone again. Makenna hadn't called or texted and was now three minutes late to find him. Three minutes wasn't a big deal; not everyone ran on the same strict time code he did.

Carrying a cup of hot chocolate, Bethany stopped him on his way down the sidewalk. "Hey, Quin. Grand celebration. Too bad about Makenna."

"What about Makenna?" Quin used his business smile. Two brief dates with Bethany when he first moved to Hawthorne made him careful not to encourage her.

"Haven't you heard about Wendell's proposal? It's all over social media."

The cold that hadn't bothered him all day seeped into every bone in his body. "Proposal?"

"See for yourself." Bethany showed him a photo of Wendell kneeling in front of Makenna near one of the ice sculptures. Makenna's hand covered her mouth.

That explained why she hadn't been answering his texts. Quin clenched his jaw and tried to smile. No matter how briefly he dated Bethany, he would not give her any satisfaction in his reaction. "I must congratulate her when I see her. If you'll excuse me, I was on the way to the senior center. They're having difficulty with the microphones."

By the time he arrived, a technician had already solved the problem. Quin searched for a place where he could have a quiet moment. There wasn't one. His phone pinged.

—*Police responded to a disturbance near the ice sculptures. Situation under control.*

Not much he could do there but follow up later.

Ping.

—*Child ill near gazebo. Requesting clean up.*

—*The park grounds crew replied they were on their way.*

Ping.

—*Last showing of play starts in 10 minutes. Do you know where the ASL Interpreter is?*

—*Oh and Baby New Year. We can't find Josie.*

Quin jogged over to the church, not sure he could help with either situation. He hadn't seen Josie or the interpreter since the last performance.

Ping.

—*Baby New Year found. Josie says Quin needs to check second-to-last box pew on south side of church.*

—*Sign language interpreter here.*

—*There was a hot chocolate incident. Solved.*

According to the brochure in the chamber lobby, one hundred years ago, when the parishioners had added a heating system to the church, they voted to keep the original high box-style pews along the south side of the church primary for young families. For tonight's performance, the section of box pews had been closed off for public access. Quin unhooked the guide rope and let himself into the enclosed area. When someone tried to follow him, Quin pointed to his badge and gestured to the empty standard row of pews in the center of the sanctuary.

He looked over the gate before opening it. Makenna sat on the floor. She looked up with tear-filled eyes at the click of the latch.

Quin sat on the bench close to the door. He bent forward, elbows on his knees so he couldn't easily be seen. "What are you doing here?"

"Hiding." Makenna held up her destroyed phone. Chunks of missing glass exposed the film underneath. There was no ring on her left finger.

"You're not engaged?"

Her eyes narrowed. "You thought I was?"

"I wasn't sure what to think when Bethany showed me the photo."

Makenna leaned her head back against the pew wall. "Really? You didn't notice her holding me there?"

"I was shocked. And then things started happening. A sound system down, the police dealing with a disturbance—"

"Wendell."

Which probably explained why her cousin had disappeared before the play and then sent him here. "I understand now why you didn't return my texts. But why are you hiding here?"

"I needed to get away from the crowd. This was close by."

A gong sounded from the front of the room. "Welcome to the Adventures of Baby New Year..."

Quin slid off the pew and joined Makenna on the floor. He slipped an arm around her back and pulled her into a hug. They snuck out of the building when Baby New Year was stuck in Valentine's Day trying to explain she wasn't Cupid.

"I wanted to see all of her play; I'm just not up to having people stare at me right now."

"What can I do?"

"I just need to go home. You need to focus on this." She nodded to the common. "I'll see you tomorrow. Happy New Year."

The kiss on the cheek was a poor substitute for the New Year's kiss he'd anticipated.

# CHAPTER 20

A wise business owner would have closed for New Year's Day. Makenna didn't count herself as being wise on many levels. Her only customer of the morning had been after gossip, not an antique. The Hawthorne Happenings page was full of news from First Night, including eyewitnesses of her proposal and Wendell being escorted away by the police. His use of private sound equipment violated some local statute.

Under the photo posted by BetPet announcing the engagement, Makenna added the comment, "I said no" using her AntiqueGirl login ID.

By the light of day, the proposal didn't seem nearly as embarrassing as it had last night. She contemplated sending Wendell the phone repair bill. According to the man in the repair shop, the phone only needed a new screen. Still, it would be a couple hundred dollars she hadn't budgeted in her personal expenses. Thankfully, her December revenue was higher than she'd expected, thanks to the flipped furniture, so she could pay herself a full wage as well as the money she'd shorted her pay in November.

With no one in the shop, she pulled out the antique book Grandma Tansy had recommended. Absently, she flipped through the pages of grainy black-and-white photographs of various antiques. Many of the values had more than doubled since the book's printing. Here and there, a handwritten note had been added. The book owner had obtained and resold several pieces. Makenna detected a theme. Halfway through, she turned back, in search of a preface. As she suspected, this book only dealt with goods manufactured in Massachusetts, Maine, New Hampshire, and Vermont. It detailed several small family-run businesses. Knowing her Great-Grandfather Wilson had been part of a multigenerational furniture making family, Makenna searched for Wilson and Sons in the Haverhill area and turned to page 279, where a section on the furniture makers started. On page 293, she paused, set down the book, and ran into the workroom. She brought out one of the two locked boxes and compared it to the photo. The box was an exact duplicate down to the hand-carved scrollwork. She needed those lockpicking tools. Makenna looked closer at the photo and saw the key sitting next to the box. She'd seen that key before... but where?

The pounding on his apartment door matched the pounding in his head. Quin squinted at his phone. He'd slept well past lunchtime. Not surprising, since he didn't get home until nearly three in the morning.

The pounding started again.

Quin stumbled across the apartment and opened the door wide enough to let Walter in.

"Did I wake you?"

"Not yet." Quin slumped onto his couch.

"Then I'll try harder." Pops took the seat next to him.

"Why?"

"Because that lawyer is all over the innerwebs saying he's engaged to your girl." Pops held out his phone.

Quin blinked several times before the photo Bethany showed him came into focus. "I talked with Makenna last night. They aren't engaged."

"I know that. Makenna posted that in the comments. But she needs to know you still care. Have you talked to her today?"

"Not yet." A yawn escaped Quin's mouth. "I figured I'd call when I woke up."

"Well, you're up now."

"Up and coherent," he clarified.

"Being awake is highly overrated." Pops slapped him on the back. "You best get yourself over to the store and have some one on one time with your girl."

"I need a shower." And a moment to clear his foggy brain. And maybe some ibuprofen.

"I'm not stopping you. I'll even make you some eggs."

"You cook?"

"How do you think I survived for the last three years? Any butcher worth his salt can cook meat, and I can't eat every meal at the café. And sandwiches get old fast. You haven't eaten an omelet until I make you one." Pops took Quin's offered hand and stood.

"Okay, I'll go shower."

"Don't worry, I'll go light on the onions."

Quin stood in the hot water for a full minute before the significance of few onions registered.

One hundred and fourteen antique keys lay on the sales counter. Makenna found them in an old coffee can used to prop open the back-office door. From the amount of duct tape on the top of the can, no one had opened it for years. New keys were added through a slit in the lid. On the counter, she sorted them by size and assumed age. She'd narrowed her choices down to three that matched the photograph.

Her favorite customer entered. "Quin, I thought you'd still be sleeping. Your goodnight text was sent after 3 AM."

"Pops kicked me out of bed." He looked around them. "The store is quiet today."

"Probably not worth the three customers I've had to keep it open."

Quin rearranged the keys so he could see the watch. "I don't have any appointments today. I wonder if the watch will still work."

Makenna pondered her answer. Denying there was something magical about the watch was almost as bad as admitting that she believed. "Why do you think it gives you time?"

"Maybe because I'm always in a hurry and it wants me to slow down, stop and smell the roses—or in my case, your perfume."

"I don't wear perfume. It's an oil blend that Grandma Tansy makes. So roses might be more accurate."

"How long until you close?"

Makenna checked the time on the register. "How about now? I doubt anyone else will come, and I want to see if any of these keys work."

"On your locked boxes?"

"Technically they are jewelry caskets. They could contain anything from rubies to rubble. I'm dying to see inside." Makenna flipped the sign to Closed and locked the front door and closed the blinds. "Which key should we try first?"

Quin held up a small iron key. "My guess."

Makenna tried it on both locks.

They repeated the process twice before the lock turned and clicked inside the lock on the box made of hickory. "According to the book that I found at Red Leaves the night of the Jólabókaflóðið sale—"

"—the night of our first kiss..."

Makenna rolled her eyes. "That too. Focus so I can finish, then we can... Anyway, Wilson and Sons in Haverhill made this box."

"Wilson? Relatives of yours?"

"Direct line. I looked it up this morning after reading the description." She'd also found a brief life sketch of her eighth- and ninth-great-grandfathers. "This design was one the family used for personal gifts. It wasn't sold to anyone. There are only ten caskets like this known in existence. If this one is authentic—" She cut herself off. "Too much talking. Ready?" Makenna slowly opened the lid. A folded paper lay on top of a silver-handled hairbrush. Underneath was a stack of papers tied with a string. "Oh my, oh my, oh my."

"What?"

"I think this is one of the authentic Wilson boxes. I was reading about this tradition they had of the husband brushing the wife's hair. For their weddings, they started giving the wives silver-handled brushes in a box. This could date back to the early 1800s."

Makenna picked up the brush. Her father used to brush her mom's hair. In her mind, she saw them laughing in front of a vanity desk mirror—only, that brush had a wood handle, not a silver one. Makenna was sure it wasn't a memory. The image faded into one of her grandparents and then their parents, whom she'd only ever seen in photos. Then she pictured a couple she'd never seen but their clothing was Civil War era. She dropped the brush back into the box.

"Makenna?"

"Sorry, what?"

"You zoned out. Like you didn't even hear me."

"Just a daydream. Picturing my ancestors with the hair-brushing tradition. I like to imagine what the people were like who first owned an item." The explanation was as close to the truth as she dared explain.

"Interesting tradition. I wonder if anyone still carries it on." Quin inspected the brush.

"Maybe. Not as many women have long hair or brush it one hundred strokes a day. That sort of thing isn't really in fashion anymore."

"How long would it take to brush one hundred times?" He pulled the pen holding her bun in place out of her hair. And ran his fingers through to loosen the twist.

Hair follicles she didn't know existed tingled on her scalp. So that was the attraction of a man brushing a wife's hair. "Maybe ten minutes."

"This brush doesn't look like it is up to the task anymore."

"The bristles are a natural fiber of some sort. I'm afraid they might break if I tried to brush my hair with it."

He turned the brush over and traced the floral design. "Kind of cool if you think about it. It gave the couple ten minutes every night to decompress and talk." He set the brush down. And took her hand. With his other hand he tucked a strand of hair behind her ear. "I've never brushed anyone's hair before."

Makenna leaned into his touch. "My mom used to brush mine when I was little. I liked it."

"Maybe sometime we—?"

Makenna broke eye contact. "The tradition was only for married couples."

"Oh, so what about the letters?"

Makenna unfolded the top one.

192

*I cannot brush my hair. I've tried every night since my dearest Samuel passed. Am I silly? I cut off over two feet of it today. It is still long enough I can put it up. My daughters would be shocked if they knew. I miss him so much. I'm locking this up until I am braver.*

*L*

"I think this must be in one of the oldest boxes. Makenna pulled up her family history app. "See, this Samuel Wilson married a Lucy. He was the son of the first cabinetmaker in the family, Thomas, but it was Samuel who started Wilson and Sons. They didn't have a son named Samuel, but there are some grandsons."

"Maybe the other letters will give you a clue."

Makenna slid the top one out of the ribbon.

*Christmas Eve, 1837*

*My dearest Lucy –*

"It *is* them. Look at that date."

"What does the rest say?"

"It's a love letter on their fortieth anniversary." Makenna folded it back up. "I feel like I'm invading their privacy." She checked the phone app. "Look, he died later that year."

Reverently, she closed the box. "Let's see what's in box number two."

Five keys later, the box popped open. Dozens of scraps of paper spilled out. Makenna picked up the closest one.

March 8 - I saw L talk to a dry cow. The cow gave milk the next day.

Quin read the next one.

> May 15 - L and her daughter planted eggs in their garden.
> No new chickens.

He set it next to the lid. "What is this?"

"I have no idea, but they all seem to be in the same hand-writing. Listen to this one—"

> August 2 - L's windows always gleam. I asked her what she
> used. She lied. Water doesn't clean windows that well.

> October 2 - Bought a potion from L. Still have wart.

> July 4 - Every well in vicinity frozen over except L's.

Makenna paused at that one. "I bet that was 1816. That year had wicked weird weather. They called it the year without a summer. It snowed or froze over every month."

Quin read through several more. "Whoever wrote these didn't like L very much."

"What about this?" Quin held up a larger scrap.

> L made scones. Everyone loves them and all their interesting
> flavors. I think they taste like dust.

"Doesn't Keira make scones like that?"

Makenna sorted through the ones they'd read. Scones? Perhaps she'd better read the rest of these in private. She put them back in the box. "I'm hungry. Let's go find some dinner."

"Mom made a ham for New Year's. She is saving dinner for us."

"Beats the microwaveable meals in my freezer." The unused keys clanked as she dropped them back into the old coffee can.

He helped her put things away. Makenna kept sneaking glances at him. If only she had the mistletoe now.

She paused before setting the alarm and turned to face him. "Before we go, I still have my first kiss of the new year to give to you."

Sweet broomsticks, his lips were warm and moved over hers, returning the kiss that should have been theirs hours ago. Makenna ran her fingers through the hair at the nape of his neck. She pulled back. "Sorry that was a few hours late. I should have come back out and not hidden away." She kissed him again.

Quin trailed kisses along her jaw to her ear. "You know what they say, better late than never."

# Chapter 21

After the month's preparation for First Night, the chamber seemed too quiet. For the last two days, the phone hadn't rung more than a handful of times. Quin put all the non-digital information from the New Year's event into a folder and set it on Mrs. Zimmerman's desk to file. He could have filed it himself, however Mrs. Zimmerman had less to do than he did.

Walter burst through the front door, a half-crumpled letter in hand. "Look at this!"

Quin took the paper his grandpa thrust at him. "Notice of inspection? I don't understand."

"Me either, which is why I came to the chamber."

"This company is out of Essex county. I'm sure the city has nothing to do with them. They aren't in my files."

"I knew it was something shady. Do you have that meeting planned yet for all the business owners on that block?"

"No, I could calendar it for tomorrow night in the conference room."

"I'm going to go see if anyone else got this letter." Walter turned to the door and stopped. "What time is the meeting? I'll spread the word."

"Everyone is closed up by six, right?" Quin started typing on his phone calendar.

"Not Mario's Pizza or Lim's Chinese place."

"Right. Let's make it for eight. They should be past their rush hours."

"Or make it a breakfast meeting at 7 a.m."

Quin moved the blue square on his calendar. "Good idea. We should invite Linda Gee and a representative of the Monroe family."

"Should I stop by the café and make an order?" Walter's eyes twinkled.

"Promoting the café? Or you just want free food?" Quin laughed. "Mrs. Zimmerman will take care of the order, Pops."

Quin gave Mrs. Zimmerman the numbers he expected and returned to his office to text Makenna.

*Did you get a letter about a building inspection?*

*—No, but I got an email from Wendell. Something about breach of promise and embarrassment, and he'll make it all go away if I sell.*

*I didn't think breach of promise was a thing.*

*—According to my internet search, it isn't. He didn't even give me a ring, which apparently, I would have to give back. And I didn't make any promises. Grr... What's up with the inspection?*

*Not sure. Meeting tomorrow here at 7 a.m. Walter is out knocking on doors now.*

*—That must be why he just walked in. Bye.*

Quin called Ms. Conley, the city planner, and left a message with the receptionist. Maybe this week wouldn't be slow after all. Which wasn't necessarily a good thing.

Makenna leaned into Quin's shoulder and watched the TV. She was supposed to be painting. A yawn escaped her lips.

"Am I boring you?"

"No. I just have the strangest feeling like I could fall asleep."

"So I *am* boring you."

"I don't sleep, at least not much. Perpetual insomnia. It's gotten worse over the past year. The idea that I could fall asleep here in your arms is the most amazing thought."

Quin adjusted his hold so she could use his chest as a pillow. "You don't look as tired the last couple of weeks as when you stormed into my office in November."

Makenna hid another yawn behind her hand. "I've been sleeping better since Christmas."

"Christmas or our first kiss?" There was a teasing tone to Quin's voice that made her smile.

"Definitely first kiss. You are the anti-Prince Charming. Instead of waking a woman up, you put her to sleep." She yawned again.

Quin smoothed her hair down and took off her glasses. "Sleep. I'll wake you up at ten and go home."

"Really? What will you do?"

"Listen to a few chapters of the audiobook I got from the library."

Makenna relaxed. The steady *thump-thump* of his heartbeat echoed in her head.

The last gong of the grandfather clock was fading when Quin woke her. "Your clocks say it's time for me to leave, sleepyhead."

Makenna sat up. "I really slept, didn't I?"

"Unless that was someone else drooling on me."

"I did?" She inspected his shirt but didn't find a damp spot.

"No. You didn't. I'm happy you got some sleep." He helped her to stand. "Show me to the door and lock up."

At the door he hugged her. "Go to sleep. I'll see you in the morning." His kiss was light as if he was trying not to wake her completely.

Makenna closed the door behind him and locked it. For the first night in months, she slept until her alarm went off the next morning.

# CHAPTER 22

The chamber conference room was already crowded when Makenna arrived. She greeted her neighbors as she walked around the room to an empty chair. Walter stood at the head of the table. Makenna patted his shoulder as she passed.

Walter stopped her. "I may not be able to work for you next week. I'm feeling lucky, and I know I'll grab one of those vacations this time."

Makenna nodded. She'd heard the same thing every other week since October.

Quin greeted each business owner, including the two who'd already sold, and then started the meeting precisely at seven. "Thank you for coming. One purpose of the chamber is to help businesses communicate with each other. Every single business owner on your block has received a significant buy-out offer in the past few months."

Nods and assenting murmurs filled the space.

"Those of you who have sold, this meeting is not to blame or shame you. It is merely to see if we can understand what is going on in our little town. I spoke with the city planner, Ms. Conley, and she was unaware of any building proposals or future plans for that area. According to her, the fact that the Hill house may fall under historic preservation lines could complicate this beyond the historic preservation district rules. Those rules allow for new builds as long as they blend in with the existing styles. Miss Wilson, do you know if papers have ever been turned in to apply for historic preservation status on the house?"

"No. It isn't like it's Covington House. It's just another old building. I definitely don't want tourists back there, and I don't think anyone else here would either." With so many old buildings in town, it never occurred to her to seek any historic status on the house. A sign declaring "In 1857 nothing happened here" would be accurate.

Quin looked at his written notes. He'd learned people perceived a notepad as more businesslike than using his phone. "I'll leave that as an option if this thing, whatever it is, gets worse. Ms. Conley was of the opinion that the house could easily qualify. Next, several questions have come up, and because of the size of our group, if you could initially answer by raise of hands."

In a sucession of questions, they learned several things. All the offers were for more than known fair market value. Quin didn't ask for the exact dollar amount. Over three-quarters of the contracts had come through Wendell Smith or the law firm he represented. In four cases, including the two that sold, they'd been told that Makenna had already agreed to sell. The last three contracts had clauses tying them to sales of other properties. The only business that hadn't had an offer was the law office. One attorney pointed out the obvious: that they would have been the first to be suspicious. The name Bradford-Stone appeared on only two contracts.

Quin flipped over his page. "This is where I am confused. Last spring, Bradford-Stone Worldwide announced their intention to expand their luxury hotel line, yet nothing shows that Hawthorne would be a good choice. Covington House Bed and Breakfast only reaches full capacity three or four weeks out of the year. Most of the time, they hover around seventy percent occupancy, most of that to repeat customers. The Bradford-Stone website shows their smallest hotels with fifty rooms. The B&B has twelve with an option of converting two more."

Murmurs filled the room.

"What about the inspection notices we've received?" asked the owner of the hair salon.

"According to the city, the letter Walter Abbott received had no validity from a governmental level. I assume the rest of the letters are the same, but I would need to see them. I believe it is a scare tactic. Those of you who haven't sold need to decide what to do."

"I'm not selling so some Brit can build a hotel. They'll probably build a high rise and ruin the view." Walter looked around the table before snagging another Danish.

"What about me? I already sold." The woman who spoke hadn't removed her coat and hat. It was common knowledge that Linda Gee's battle with cancer was not going well.

"I think I can speak for everyone here that the money was a godsend in your situation and neither of you who sold had any way to know what was going to happen. We are just hoping you can shed some light on these mysterious offers." Quin made eye contact with every building owner around the table. This fight was not between Hawthorne residents. "The rest of you need to take a united stand. There may be more dirty tricks like these letters. The city planner is aware. If anyone gets a visit from an inspector you don't recognize, call her and the police department."

"Shouldn't we vote on this?" asked the owner of the beauty salon. "I don't want to stand up if everyone else is selling out. This is a lot of money."

The shoe repairman raised his hand. "What about Makenna? She's dating this lawyer guy. What if she sells out?"

Makenna leaned forward. "I am *not* dating Wendell Smith. We broke up several weeks ago. And I refused his much-publicized proposal on New Year's. I love Hawthorne and its history. There's no way someone is going to tear down Hill House." Makenna paused, a new thought occurring to her. "For the past several months, I've had difficulty buying new merchandise. Quin helped me figure out an alternative source of revenue, which just may save my business. He has Hawthorne's and our best interests in mind."

Walter raised his coffee mug. "I say we vote to reject the sales offers as a group. We are all in this together or we're not. If Quin is right and things get worse, we can face this like our ancestors did. The British are not coming to Hawthorne."

They met his speech with cheers and a unanimous vote. Everyone filed out, chatting with one neighbor or another, leaving Makenna alone in the conference room with Quin.

Makenna swept the crumbs off the table. "Do you really think things will get worse?"

"I think we should be prepared. I'm going to write a letter to Bradford-Stone and see if I can get them to look elsewhere. I want to know if this underhandedness is from them or their U.S. legal representation."

"You think it might all be Wendell?" She dumped used paper goods into the corner trash can.

Quin caught her hand and backstepped her to the wall. He put his hands on either side of her waist. "I'm not ruling him out. I found a video of his proposal. It was the most self-centered proposal I've ever heard."

"Really?"

"Not once did he say how wonderful you are or how much he loved you." His thumbs rubbed below her ribs, sending delightful tingles up her spine.

"I didn't really listen. I just wanted out of there so badly."

Quin lowered his head. "He didn't compliment your eyes or the way you smile. Or how determined you are to make your store run. How random bits of history pop out of your mouth. Or how—" Whatever he intended to say next was silenced when his lips touched hers.

This kiss held an intensity previous ones lacked. Makenna returned the kiss, pulling him closer. Wendell never kissed like this.

Quin stepped back, a lopsided grin on his face.

"Oops." Makenna grabbed an unused napkin. "You're wearing my lipstick." She erased the extra part of his smile. "I need to get over to the store. See you later?"

"Definitely."

Quin worked with the city planner, Ms. Conley, to draft a letter to Bradford-Stone. They sent it to several people— from the CEO to the vice-president over North American operations. Digging through an online directory, they found an address for an acquisitions and mergers division. A newspaper article about the announced expansion of the hotel division also led them to a Mr. O. Bradford.

The city manager hit send. "I hope someone in that group will listen to us. Hawthorne doesn't need a hotel."

According to the app on Quin's phone, it should only be 4 p.m. in Leeds. "If we're lucky, someone will read it today. Thanks for all your help."

On the way back to the chamber office, Quin stopped by Red Leaves Books to pick up the thriller he didn't buy the night of the book flood sale. He stopped at the café, but they were out of the new fortune cookies he'd heard about, so he settled on a muffin.

Pops wasn't at his usual table with Judge and Gene. Gene answered before Quin could answer. "He's minding the antique store."

Quin changed directions and crossed the street to Makenna's shop.

"She isn't here." Walter glared across the counter.

"I came looking for you. That was a nice speech you made this morning."

"Wasn't a speech. It was how I felt."

"Where did Makenna go?"

"Don't know. She got a call about an early estate sale. Took off like a rocket about an hour ago. Said she'd be back before close."

Curious, Quin stepped to the counter and traced the pocket watch through the glass. Would time expand or whatever it did with his Pops again? "Has it been quiet here then?"

"Yup. The only thing anyone wants is some of that painted furniture. Or to talk to her personally."

"Maybe you shouldn't frown at all the customers."

"I don't frown at the customers—just you." Walter turned over a card in a game of solitaire.

"Why do you frown at me?" Quin snuck a peek at his phone. The minute hadn't changed yet.

"Habit, I guess."

"I caused the least trouble of all of your grandkids."

"That's because I always frowned at you, and you didn't dare try anything."

"So frowning at me is a preemptive device to ensure exemplary behavior?"

"It's worked for twenty-seven years." Walter grinned.

Quin checked his phone again.

"Stop checking your phone. Didn't anyone tell you that was rude?"

Quin set his phone on top of the solitary cards. "Pops, how long have we been talking?"

"Maybe five minutes."

"I was checking the clock in my phone. I don't know why, but if I come in here and look at this watch, time stops."

"You're addled."

"No, it keeps happening. I've never once been late for an appointment after being here, although I feel like I'm here forever."

Walter rubbed his jaw. "That's awful strange, even for a place like Hawthorne."

"Makenna doesn't believe me either."

His grandfather raised a brow. "Interesting. Strange things going on around here. First Keira's baking. Now time stands still."

"That's not all. Makenna has a way with things."

"What do you mean?" Walter leaned back on his stool, arms crossed.

"She matches people to stuff and the things change them."

"Go on." Walter collected his cards into a pile.

"Like the toy truck candy dish I gave you for Christmas. Because of it, you've told me stories about your brother. And I don't want to ignore your phone calls anymore, they don't bother me."

"I knew you were ignoring them. Are you saying I'm a bother?"

"Until the truck, I thought so, but now, it's changed. *I've* changed. I want to spend time with you. I can't wait for you to finally get one of those vacation deals so we can have a week together. Like all the Coca-Cola memorabilia. Makenna sent me after a glass on Christmas Eve. When I saw it, I thought about how much Jamison would like it, and then I ended up calling him on Christmas. I haven't talked to him on Christmas since the big fight. I forgave him. I still don't understand him, but I don't hate him anymore. Not that I'm going to hop the next plane to LA to see him. I just feel different."

"And you think this is the stuff?"

Quin held up his phone still on the same time. "I do. Either that or it's Makenna, and she's not here."

"Who's not here?" Makenna's voice came from the work-room.

Walter jumped away from the counter. "Good, you're back. I can go to an early dinner."

"Clock out first, Walter. I'm paying you, like it or not." Makenna's hair was back up in its usual bun, a pen with the Red Leaves Books logo holding it in place.

"Slave driver." Walter logged his hours. "Just watch. This will be the week I'm fast enough to get one of the last-minute vacations. Then you won't have anyone to fill in for you."

"Then I'll hope they let me look at the estate sales the night before." Makenna switched places with Walter behind the counter.

"Was your search successful?" asked Quin.

"Marginally. I gleaned more information than goods. Some-one has been paying the auction houses and estate sale mangers to exclude me from sales—which proved what I thought this morning. It started the week after Grandma died." Makenna took the seat behind the desk. "According to the man I talked to this morning, they've now been asked not to give me the discount that Abigail negotiated with them. The man felt it terribly unfair and told me he would not abide by it anymore."

"That's good news, isn't it?" Quin frowned at his phone. Time marched on again.

"Is something wrong?"

"It's time for me to go. What are you doing tonight?"

"Girls' night with my cousins."

"And after?"

"I'll text you to say good night."

Quin tapped on the glass case once before leaving the antique shop.

# CHAPTER 23

Claire, Keira, Josie, and Liberty all sat in Makenna's parlor. They piled the coffee table high with snacks, both healthy and not so healthy.

Makenna pulled out her boxes and books. "I'm not sure how to start this. Liberty knows some of it... There is magic in the antique shop." She held up Grandma Abigail's ledger. "Grandma wrote it down every time she saw it happen. I've started writing it down too. I don't control it. I don't think she did either. Sometimes when I'm at an estate sale or even bidding online, I just know something needs to come to the shop. I've only had a few items I've purchased find new owners—"

"What do you mean, find new owners?" asked Claire.

"It's like some things are supposed to go to certain people. I don't know why, but I think it is about family connections. Don't laugh—it isn't like geneal-ogy. It's teenage boys putting their phones away, asking their mom to play a game and pop popcorn. People call-ing relatives they haven't talked to. People finding their family."

Keira set her soda on the table. "When did this start?"

"Right before Thanksgiving. That's why when you told us after dinner that there was magic, I pushed so hard saying there wasn't any."

Josie crossed her arms. "Are you sure? People find things they like all the time in antique shops."

Makenna opened the ornate box and pulled out the brush. She handed it to Liberty. "Pass it around and tell me if you feel or see anything."

The women passed it around, and either shook their heads or shrugged.

"When I first picked up this brush, I saw my father brushing my mother's hair. It isn't a memory; I'm sure I never saw him do that. Then I saw my grandparents and my great-grandparents." Makenna related all she knew about the Wilson tradition of the husband brushing the wife's hair one hundred strokes every night. "This brush belonged to Samuel and Lucy Wilson when they were married in 1797. I am a direct descendant of them. I think I've even seen them in a vision in a log cabin, but I'm not sure since there aren't any paintings of them. And I know *vision* is an odd word, but I don't know how to explain it."

The only sound in the room was the ticking of the clocks. Liberty broke the silence. "Tell them about the watch."

"You know the old watch, the one Grandma Tansy borrowed and returned?"

Claire groaned. "I can't believe she did that."

"Quin swears it stops time for him. I came in today when he was explaining it to Walter. I'm not sure Walter believes him. Walter said something about the bakery items doing weird things. Quin also told him his experience with some items in the store. Yes, I was eavesdropping." Makenna let her cousins digest news. "I think there's more."

"Like you have a flying broomstick? That would be cool."

Josie dipped a stick of celery in spinach-avocado dip and flew it to her mouth.

Makenna and the others laughed. "I purchased another box at the same time as this one. No, let me start someplace else. The night of Jólabókaflóðið when Grandma Tansy sent me upstairs, I found two books. One is a catalog of New England antiques, the other is a history of Hawthorne. It differed from some of the other histories of the town. According to the new book, in 1823 someone attempted to put Lavinia on trial for witchcraft, but the townspeople wouldn't have it. I think this other box contains the notes from the woman who accused her."

"Why did it show up now?" asked Keira.

"I don't know. But it was one of the things I knew I needed to buy. I didn't see or feel anything when I opened the box. As we were reading the papers, I realized what it must be."

"We?" Josie leaned forward.

"Quin was there when I found the key to open the box."

"Exactly how much is Quin around? We all know your wish came true," said Keira.

"The question is, did yours? Is Brant the one?" Makenna ate a large bite out of the nearest cookie to avoid talking for a moment.

Keira blushed. "You mean did I know true love when I saw it—as obvious as fireworks in the night sky?"

Josie gasped. "I totally forgot the fireworks part. Like really a pyrotechnician doesn't get much more like fireworks."

The cousins asked questions about Brant.

Liberty picked up a 'misfortune' cookie and turned it over and over in her hands. "If I understand this correctly, Makenna has magic happening round her she doesn't control, kind of like a conduit. And Keira, you are able to control the effect of your baked goods to an extent?"

Makenna and Keira nodded.

"And this also happened in conjunction with your wishes coming true?"

"I hadn't made that connection," said Keira.

"Well, it's obvious it isn't by age as Keira is the second youngest and Makenna is third oldest. This does mark thirteen years since we tried to become like Lavinia..."

"So we will all find magical powers this year?" asked Josie.

Claire swirled the ice in her empty glass. "If our wishes have to come true first, it might not happen this year."

"I started feeling the magic over a month before Quin kissed me. And he'd been in town for six months, so I don't think it relates," said Makenna.

"You were dating Wendell then so there wasn't any romance," said Liberty. "Did it start before or after the day with Mrs. Zimmerman's near-miss with the mistletoe?"

"After?" Makenna squeezed her eyes shut. "I think after."

"So after you started thinking of Quin as potentially more than the director of the chamber?" asked Claire.

"You're trying to put words in my mouth." Makenna stuck her tongue out at her cousin and tossed a piece of popcorn at her.

Josie's plate clattered to the floor. "Well, if romance is part of it, I'll never get any magic."

"You and me both." Claire picked up the dropped plate and set it on the table.

Liberty flipped through the book on antiques. "Me, three. I kind of hope my theory is wrong on that part. It would still be cool to have magic, but I burned all my bridges that would make my wish come true. Every guy friend I have ever had has married someone else. And I'm not some sort of a person who would break up a marriage or wish for a wife's death."

"Didn't you wish for a friend to be your boyfriend?" asked Josie.

Liberty didn't look up from her book. "Yup, that wish died at college. Friends don't date friends. They date their roommates."

Makenna sorted through the evidence papers in the box, looking for other potential types of magic they could experience. "I thought you wished for something else."

"It was a joke. Or a handsome prince to come sweep me off my feet was pretty much a joke. Not that many princes in the world." Liberty turned the book around. "Isn't this the watch you have in the store?"

Makenna read from the page. "The first American watch manufacturer: Luthor Goddard. Luthor Goddard opened a watch factory in Shrewsbury during the trade embargo under President Thomas Jefferson. After the War of 1812, cheaper import watches were again available, and his sons moved to Worcester. He was the first watchmaker to serialize or number his time pieces. At the time of his death, he'd produced almost six hundred timepieces." She set the book in her lap. "If my watch is a Goddard, one, I am way underpriced, and two, I think I should try to sell it to a museum."

"What about Quin and stopping time?" asked Claire.

"I don't know. Grandma said the watch kept coming back to the store. Maybe it hasn't found where it belongs. Quin doesn't want to buy it, and I don't feel he needs it. I know that sounds weird... the Coke glasses were something I knew he needed. Not so much on the watch."

Josie started giggling. "So, if I have this right, we may have magic, but it may require fulfilling our wishes. And Grandma Tansy stole a watch worth thousands of dollars. And I still can't drink hawthorn berry tea without looking for chunks in the bottom of my cup."

"If anyone heard us, they would think we were insane." Keira joined in the laugher.

Someone rang the doorbell. Makenna answered the door. Grandma Tansy stepped in, bringing a small whirl of snow. "You had a party and didn't invite me?"

"It was just a girls' night." Makenna followed Grandma Tansy into the parlor.

"Well, ladies, it looks like you are one short." Grandma Tansy sat in the wooden rocking chair. "There were six of you when this started, and that's the way it needs to be."

Claire offered Grandma Tansy a plate. "None of us have heard from Eden in years."

Grandma Tansy nibbled on the corner of a scone and nodded her head.

Makenna bit her lip. Now was probably the best time to ask a question. "Grandma Tansy, why did you take, I mean *borrow*, the watch from the shop?"

"To keep you from selling it, of course. I assume you found it in that book I had you find."

"Yes, I did. I'm wondering what I should do with it."

"The time museum in Grafton already has one." Grandma Tansy tried one of the cookies.

Everyone waited for her to say more.

"The Hawthorne Historical Museum doesn't have one yet." Grandma Tansy raised her brow. "They received an endowment to purchase things too. Now has anyone seen my cat?"

"You don't have a cat," said Keira.

"If you don't know where she is, I'd better get going."

"We were just getting ready to leave. I'll drive you, Grandma Tansy." Liberty held up her keys.

Within minutes, they left Makenna alone. After emptying the garbage and tidying up, she went to put her books away. They were missing. She searched the room and came up with the only logical conclusion—Grandma Tansy had borrowed them.

Makenna's text came a few minutes before ten. *Did you have a good day?*

— *Yes. I got a lot done. Things I'd been putting off that would bore you to sleep. Call?*

His phone rang the clock chimes he used for her ringtone.

She didn't bother with hello. "You didn't bore me to sleep. More like lulled me. It was a good thing. I slept so well last night."

"Glad to be of service."

Makenna laughed. "New subject. Did you hear anything from the people in Leeds?"

"No, but I saw something weird." Quin fluffed his pillow and laid on the bed.

"Weirder than Grandma Tansy showing up to a party she wasn't invited to looking for a cat she doesn't own?"

"Maybe. I think I saw Bethany get into Wendell's car after work. I didn't think he'd come back to town."

"That isn't that odd; I win for weirdest."

"Bethany and Wendell isn't weirdest?"

"When we first started dating, she tried to flirt with him. Considering New Year's Eve, I think they must talk some. Although I am surprised he drove out here." Makenna yawned.

"Sounds like I am boring you to sleep again."

"I don't think it is boring. I think it is comfortable. I can relax around you—that's a compliment in case my voice is too sleepy to make sense."

"Good night, Sunny."

"What did you call me?"

"Sunny. I'm sorry if—"

"Don't be. No one has called me that since Grandma Abigail died. I miss the name."

"It fits. You are a ray of sunshine."

"Thanks, Quin. Goodnight."

"Night, Sunny."

# CHAPTER 21

Few things could bring the game of Sergeant Major to a halt once it started. Friday morning at just after half past ten, Quin witnessed such a moment. He'd stopped by the café to confirm he understood Pops's text about leaving for Nassau in the morning. Pops had finally snagged one of the last-minute deal trips he always tried for—flight and hotel for a week. Quin had the vacation time and only needed to move a few appointments, yet he wanted verification because the price of the entire vacation was less than a normal plane ticket.

As Quin waited for the game to end, all three men laid their cards on the table and peered out the window. It took him a moment to see what they stared at. The entire block catty-corner to the café had gone dark.

"Have you ever seen a single block have a blackout, Gene?" asked Judge.

"Nope. Have you, Walter?"

"Can't say I have. I guess I'd better see what's going on since one of those buildings is mine." Walter stood and pulled his coat off the back of his chair.

Quin finished his drink and held the door open for Walter.

"Think this is part of those desperate measures?" asked Walter.

"Not sure. We can't see the blocks to the west or south. It may just have started here." Cutting off power to one block shouldn't be possible. There must be another explanation. At the corner, Walter and Quin split up. Walter went straight to his building, Lin's Chinese Restaurant, and Quin passed the beauty salon. A woman sat in a chair with a towel wrapped around her head. Another sat near the window as the stylist continued to color and wrap her hair in foil.

Makenna turned her sign to Closed and was talking on the phone. Her waving hands emphasized her words. Quin made the universal call me sign and walked on. He turned the corner and a blast of wind caught him in the face.

One lawyer waved him into his office. "I've been on the phone with the power company. They insist we didn't pay our last bill, but I have the e-confirmation."

"The entire block seems to be out. I'm checking now." Quin waved to the building across the street, which had power.

The attorney frowned. "I'll keep calling. Someone will listen."

"Thanks. I'll let you know if I learn anything." None of the businesses Quin passed had power. He turned the next corner. The lights across the street were on while the lights on his side remained dark. He continued on and met Walter coming out of his building. "They claim I didn't pay the electricity. Ben Tills next door is my CPA, and he has the receipt. Of course, it's on his computer which he can't turn on because there is no power in my building."

"The entire block didn't miss paying this month. I'm going to go talk to all the owners about their payments."

"Did you notice those two buildings have power?" Walter pointed to the ones Quin hadn't passed yet. The only two buildings with electricity were the two purchased by the company in Leeds.

As the sun sank behind the leafless trees, the power to Makenna's block was restored. According to the electric company, a computer glitch was responsible for the error which left the block in the dark for most of the day. Not one building owner believed it.

Makenna turned her sign to Open, hoping that the last two hours of the business day would bring in some customers. Instead, her neighbors filed in to complain.

The first was the cosmetologist. "I can't do this again. If Sarah over at the Do-Up Salon hadn't let me go finish Mrs. Johnson's hair at her place, I could have been sued. You have no idea the damage that red hair dye can do if left on for hours. I had to reschedule a full day of appointments. Some women don't like to have to reschedule their Friday appointments. Next Friday, I have an entire bridal party coming in. Can you imagine what would happen if I had to cancel on a bride?"

All Makenna could do was listen and nod.

Ben, her accountant, came over with paper copies of the bill payments for power, water, sewer, and every other recurring expense. He printed them out for all his clients on the block.

Everyone asked a version of the question she did. "What next?"

The Monroe boys came in for their afterschool shifts. Leaving Kent at the counter, Makenna took the opportunity to run over and ask Quin what he knew. So help the Brits if they ordered this white-collar warfare.

Quin checked his email. So far there wasn't a response from Bradford-Stone. Any company who tried underhanded tricks like turning off the power didn't deserve a place in his town. He emailed the city manager to let her know what had happened and to ask if she'd heard anything.

Mrs. Zimmerman's voice carried into his office through his partially closed door. She was trying to convince someone to set up an appointment for the week after next.

Quin checked his calendar. Was it really the best time for him to take a vacation? Pops had been looking forward to going south for months. If Quin backed out now, his mother would have his head. Plus, the last-minute ticket was non-transferable and non-refundable.

"Don't tell me he doesn't have time." Bethany strode through his door without knocking. "See, he's right here."

"Miss Peterson, how can the chamber help you?"

"Keira suggested that the chamber might need a social media specialist to promote Hawthorne. Maybe even a travel blog."

A social media specialist wasn't a half bad idea. Hiring Bethany as that specialist had disaster written all over it. "The chamber isn't hiring at the moment."

She walked around to his side of the desk and sat on the edge inches away from Quin. "But you need me."

Nope. Not once had he ever needed her—not now, not ever. The two dates they'd been on were a mistake. Working with Bethany was out. "Another position isn't in the budget. If you want to start your own travel blog, there is nothing to stop you."

"But I want to work here." She leaned forward.

Quin pushed his seat back to distance himself. "If we were to hire someone, we would open up the position to the entire community."

Bethany slipped off the desk and plopped herself into

his lap, wrapping her arms around him. He tried to push her off so he could stand. "Please move."

"But Quin—"

A gasp from the doorway interrupted Bethany. Makenna stood with her hand over her mouth. She blinked twice before she turned and ran out of the office.

"Makenna." He pushed his still-shocked, want-to-be seductress away and ran after the woman he wanted to be with. "Makenna!"

Makenna stopped, her hand on the front door. "I came to find out what happened today with the power. Obviously, I came at an inconvenient time."

"I can explain." Before he took another step, Bethany emerged from his office and wrapped her arm around his.

Head held high, Makenna left the office.

Quin shook Bethany off. "Miss Peterson, there is no position available. Please leave."

"Quinten, you don't need to be like that."

"Yes, I do." Quin took another step away from her.

Mrs. Zimmerman emerged from the conference room and moved between Quin and Bethany. "As I said, Mr. Kayhill is very busy today." The wily woman crowded Bethany, forcing her to step away.

"You can't throw me out of here."

Mrs. Zimmerman waved behind her back for Quin to return to his office. "Mr. Kayhill has a phone call he needs to make. His next available appointment is a week from Tuesday."

Quin took the hint, returned to his office, and locked the door. The only call he wanted to make went straight to Makenna's voice mail. He looked at his list of things that had to be done before his early morning flight. If he hurried, he could finish everything before six when Makenna closed the shop. Then he could talk to her privately.

Automatically he reached for the bottle of antacid. His hand hovered over the half-full bottle. His stomach wasn't burning, he didn't need them. He set the bottle back in the drawer next to the sealed one he purchased the first of December. For the past year or more, he'd averaged a bottle a month. December should have been his most stressful since leaving California. Adding a girlfriend to his life should have made things more hectic. Either Makenna, the watch, or both had done something good to his system.

By 6:10, Quin completed his list and was ready to leave on vacation. Only the most important item remained—talking with Makenna about Bethany, and telling her about the vacation.

# CHAPTER 25

The comfort of an old-fashioned, claw-footed tub could not be underestimated, especially with a bath bomb from Grandma Tansy's shop. Yet it was not enough to soothe the parts of Makenna that hurt most. The long cord from the hall landline phone reached just far enough for Makenna to get a pep talk from Liberty.

"Bethany is a flirt who's tried to interfere with relationships before." Liberty tried to console her. Neither mentioned Josie's high school crush as evidence. "Keira explained how Bethany stole her recipes. I think the girl needs a good dose of integrity. I wonder if Keira can cook that up."

"But I know what I saw."

"Did he have his arms around her?"

Makenna brought the image of Bethany in his lap to mind. "Not exactly. I'm not sure how to describe what he was doing, but it wasn't an embrace."

"Remember our senior year in the cafeteria when the quarterback was getting up to leave with his teammates and Bethany sat on his lap?"

"Who can forget? The Friday night game was missing half the cheerleaders because they were suspended for the fight that followed."

Liberty laughed. "They weren't suspended for the game. They were too embarrassed to be seen with their black eyes. The principal only gave them each a day. I know; I was working in the office during the period after lunch. But my point is, what if in the last eight years, Bethany has perfected the sit-in-the-lap move?"

"Okay. But I still hurt, and I want to yell at him." Makenna squished a handful of scented bubbles into oblivion.

"Don't do anything tonight. Put your phone in a drawer and tomorrow you can talk to him. By then you'll be calm, and he'll be ready to talk."

"You're sure?"

"Yes. Put the cell in a drawer downstairs and go to bed." After another round of goodbyes, Liberty ended the call.

While Makenna's mind could wrap itself around the argument, her heart still hurt...

After her bath, she tucked her cellphone into a drawer without reading or listening to any of Quin's messages.

The next morning, she retrieved the phone to find another voicemail and several texts. The last text sat on her lock screen. The time stamp showed it was sent an hour ago.

*—Landed in Dulles. Please call. Flight to Nassau in thirty minutes.*

Dulles? As in D.C. airport? What was Quin doing going to Nassau? Walter must have gotten the last-minute deal tickets he'd been trying to get forever. Neither of them said anything about leaving to her yesterday. But with trying to deal with the power outage, there wasn't a time for it to come up. She hadn't given Quin the chance to explain last night or checked his messages. Makenna pressed play on the first message.

"There isn't a rational explanation for what you saw because Bethany isn't rational. I did not invite her to sit on my lap and I was trying to extricate her when you came in. Believe me, if a man were free to claim harassment..."

anyway, not the point. There is nothing between Bethany and me other than her refusal to believe that after two dates last summer, I have no desire to see her as anything other than an acquaintance. I'd usually say friend, but even that would be too much encouragement for her. I'll come by after work and we can talk. I'm leaving in the morning with Pops. That last-minute deal he wanted came through. I'll be back next Friday."

The second message was sent at twenty minutes after six. She'd closed in record time and had already left the store. She would have been at Mario's getting a grinder and a pint of gelato from his secret stash.

"Please let me in the store. I need to talk to you. I don't want to leave with things this way. I don't know how to make a choice between you and Pops because I love you both. I need to go with him. Our relationship has grown so much in the past couple of months, and I see him getting older. If I don't go with him, I'm afraid I'll never have the chance again. Please call me."

She replayed the message. Love? That could mean a lot of things in this context. There was no way she could fault him for choosing to spend time with Walter. If she had a chance to vacation one more time with her grandparents, she would have taken it too. The rest of the messages and texts were basically repeats of the voicemails, with flight numbers and times included. The word 'love' wasn't used again.

Makenna left a message on Quin's voicemail. "I hope you have fun with Walter. I can't say I am not upset about what I saw, but Bethany does have a reputation. And I should have given you a chance last night to talk to me. When you return, we can have a long face to face. I don't want you to have to do it over the phone on your vacation, though I do want to work through this. Bon Voyage."

In a week, Liberty would have talked her completely down. It was just so hard when her eyes saw something that logic told her not to believe, and her heart couldn't decide who was right.

Liberty's concluding question from last night echoed in her mind. "Can you try to trust Quin long enough to hear his side?"

Yes, yes, she could.

Blue ocean, warm weather, and a mind 1,250 miles away. One of those things was making it impossible to enjoy Nassau. Quin kept his smile in place as they traveled to see the famous swimming pigs.

Pops slapped his knee. "I never thought I'd see a pig fly, but swimming pigs has got to be close. Do you think it will be like the photos where they come right up to us?"

"Maybe." It better be. A ticket on the powerboat tour taking them to see pigs cost more than the flight and hotel. Had they not gotten such a great flight deal, he couldn't have afforded the excursion without a major budget overhaul. Swimming pigs better be worth it. On the bright side, all that time in the sea meant the pigs should be clean.

The boat bounced along the waves. Quin searched for signs that they were close to the bay. In his mind, he replayed Makenna's message. Should he have hope? He'd tried to call, but she'd answered with a text that she wanted to talk in person and that he should have fun. There was a smiley face emoji at the end. A smile was a good thing, right?

Pops pointed at a dolphin jumping over the waves. Quin looked at his watch. Time wouldn't be pausing for him this week. Pops was here. Quin snapped a photo of his grandpa's smile. Maybe he should follow the gazillion pieces of advice he'd received on enjoying the moment and trust that Makenna would talk with him when he got back. The boat slowed as it approached the island.

When they were still yards from shore, a large black-and-white pig swam out to greet them. The passengers joined the pigs in the clear water. Quin took a video of Walter petting a pig.

"Hey, Judge and Gene! See what you are missing! Jealous of my grandson yet?" Walter helped the pig wave at the camera.

Walter's enthusiasm was addictive. Quin grabbed a selfie with a pink piglet and Pops. The wild pigs were as tame as labradoodle puppies. They swam from visitor to visitor and ran along the shore with a pair of eight- or nine-year-old siblings. All too soon, their boat captain called them back to continue the excursion.

Later that night, Quin shared the videos with Walter.

"Look at us. I should have come to the Bahamas years ago with your grandma, but I could never find the time to get away from the butcher shop. Of course, after playing with the pigs today, I would have had to find a new career when I got back home. I'm glad you took the time to come with me."

Quin replayed the video of Pops petting the pig before sending it to Makenna. She answered with a smiley face and a pig emoji.

As Quin set his alarm that night, he realized he hadn't looked at his watch since the ride out to see the pigs. It was an outrageously freeing thought.

# Chapter 26

Taped to Walters's normal chair at Sweet Memories Café was a photo of him and Quin and a baby pig. It was a toss-up for which of the three subjects was more interesting. Makenna had already looked at the surfer body way too much over the weekend, so she tried to focus on the pig and Walter's huge grin.

"Care to vote?" Judge's question pulled Makenna out of her thoughts.

"Vote?"

"Most eligible bachelor: Walter, Quin, or the pig. Each vote is a dollar, and the money goes to the meals program at the senior center."

"What does the winner get?"

"The unofficial title of Hawthorne Most Eligible Bachelor," answered Gene. "We thought about a date, but so far the pig is winning."

Makenna took a dollar out of her phone wallet. "The pig has my vote."

"Of course, he does. Who would vote for that two-timing surfer?" Bethany interrupted the conversation. "Have you ever searched our chamber director? Our man has quite a history... married women... I don't want to see you hurt again so soon after Wendell. I thought you wanted to marry him."

Since the non-engagement photo on *Heard Around Hawthorne* disappeared, Makenna took the statement as an apology. The married woman thing didn't seem like Quin, but she didn't know him that well.

Judge scowled at the woman standing behind Makenna. "Some people need to check their facts. Not everything you read online is true."

"Of course it is. Just this morning I read about the Martians landing on Wrigley Field. Those Cubs will do anything to beat the Sox." Gene's scowl matched Judge's.

Ginger called out Makenna's name.

"That's me. See you around." Makenna avoided looking Bethany in the face as she stepped around her to get her order.

Ginger handed her the takeout bag and smiled conspiratorially. "I put one of Keira's latest creations in there. Let us know what you think."

Makenna peeked in the bag. A yellow frosted cookie sat on top of her breakfast sandwich. Idly, she wondered if Keira could formulate something to make Bethany disappear or for Makenna to forget the seed of doubt that Bethany had placed about Quin and a married woman. She hurried back to Abigail's Antiques to try the new cookie in private. With her luck, the cookie would have some spell that made her gush out her true feelings. After three days, she missed Quin. From Judge's reaction to Bethany's warning, Makenna assumed Judge knew something about what happened from Walter. Maybe the cookie could help her see truth. A lie detector cookie would be immensely helpful.

Ten minutes after her shop opened, Wendell parked in front of the store in the fire hydrant space. He walked around the car and helped a woman carrying a large black bag and camera around her neck. Whatever he had planned, she would not let him take photos of her or the store. If only she'd filed that restraining order.

Makenna met them at the door, blocking their path in. "May I help you?"

Wendell tried to push past her. "We just wanted a few photos of the store and the surrounding property."

Makenna stood her ground. "That will not be possible today."

The photographer took an uncertain step back.

"Don't be like this, Makenna." Wendell's attempt at sweet talk made her more determined to keep him out.

"Mr. Smith, shall I call the police?" Out of the corner of her eye, she saw Judge and Gene exit the café. The photographer now stood by the car.

"Be reasonable. We just need some photos."

Makenna pulled out her phone and placed her thumb over the nine. "No photography."

Wendell reached for her hand. "Babe—"

She slapped his hand away. Judge and Gene were less than twenty feet away now. Makenna searched her memory. Did Wendell know that Judge had never been a Judge? She hoped not. "Judge, how nice to see you. Do you know when my restraining order will be signed?"

Wendell took two quick steps back and raised his hands. "No need to get the law involved."

On cue, a police car pulled up beside Wendell's BMW. Makenna had seen the officer with Greg before but couldn't place her name. The officer spoke into her handheld radio before exiting the car. "Mr. Smith, I thought you never wanted to come to Hawthorne again. Maybe I misunderstood you?" The officer stepped between Wendell and Makenna. "Is this man disturbing you, Miss Wilson?"

"He brought a photographer. I was just informing them that I do not give permission to have a photo shoot here today."

Another black-and-white pulled up. Officer Hastings exited the passenger side of the vehicle. He immediately started writing a parking ticket.

"Wait, you can't give me a ticket." Wendell ran to his BMW.

The photographer stepped away from the car. Makenna felt for the woman, whoever she was.

The photographer removed the camera from around her neck and put it in the large black bag. "I was told this was a straightforward real estate photo shoot. I don't want any part of whatever's going on."

The female officer studied the photographer. "Do you mind telling me why you were hired?"

"To take photos of an antique shop. I was supposed to get a lot of background shots—the front of the building, cute displays, etcetera. May I go? Is there a commuter rail?"

The officer took the photographer's contact information. Gene offered to walk the woman to the MBTA rail stop three blocks away.

All the while, Wendell continued to yell at Officer Hastings.

Judge joined Makenna in the doorway. "You know we all love you, Makenna, but we don't understand why you ever dated him."

"I don't either. I made a huge mistake." Mistakes and men. Quin wasn't a mistake. She'd been sure about that this morning.

Judge opened the door and ushered Makenna into her own shop. "Don't make another one—what Bethany said about Quin and a married woman? The story on the internet about Quin and a married woman is as true as that UFO in Wriggly field. Promise me you'll ask Quin before you read whatever the innerwebs have to tell you."

They watched the officers deal with Wendell through the window.

Makenna bit her lip. She'd dated Wendell for so long and been blind to his true self. What if she was blinding herself about Quin too? A thirteen-year long crush could color things. "You think she is wrong?"

"I know she is wrong. But it isn't my story to tell."

"The three of you gossip about everything. And you won't tell me this?"

"We don't gossip, we inform. And in this case, you need to trust your heart. What is it telling you?"

"It's telling me to trust Quin, but I think I might love him so I could be wrong." Makenna barely heard her own whispered answer, but from Judge's nod she knew he heard.

The female officer pulled the handcuffs off her belt.

Makenna watched the arrest with morbid fascination. "How did I not see this side of Wendell for a year and half? I don't want to be wrong about Quin too."

"I've known Quin since the day he was born. He doesn't have a hidden side." Judge nodded at the window. "Some people are good at hiding their true selves. I'm just lucky to be an excellent judge of character."

"Is that where your nickname comes from?"

Judge chuckled. "Maybe. By the way, you might want a real restraining order from a real judge. Now what do you have for me to purchase today?"

"Have you considered a spinning wheel? I found one a couple of weeks ago that I think your wife would love..." Makenna allowed the impression to flow through her without fighting or questioning it.

A Segway tour of an island had never crossed Quin's mind as an option. For Pops, it was the perfect alternative to hiking. From the shore, they watched dolphins play, and viewed nurse sharks and stingrays. The tour guide added in enough fun historical facts to delight everyone. Quin couldn't help wondering if Makenna would be begging for more history.

Something burned under his watch. Quin checked his wrist, only to remember he'd left it in his hotel room. In its place was a pink circle. Sunblock would have been a wise choice. So far, the sunburn was the only thing he regretted about his decision to leave his watch off for the past three days.

"When we get home, I think I want one of these things." Walter patted the Segway he'd been using.

"I think they have Segway tours in Boston."

"I want to use it around Hawthorne."

"Then you'll be giving up all of that exercise you get, going to Sweet Memories every day, not to mention that the cobblestone sidewalks could be hard on your back."

"Way to ruin an old man's dreams. Who asked your opinion, anyway?" Walter sped up as Quin laughed.

Quin snapped a few more photos.

That evening over a leisurely dinner, Pops told Quin about learning to swim out in the old pond. "I was about six. One day after school, my friends and I started bragging how well we swam. One thing led to another and soon we were out at Misty Hollow Pond stripped down to our underthings. No one wanted to admit we couldn't do more than doggy paddle, and that water was cold as this glass of tonic." Walter pointed to his lemon-lime soda. "Somehow, I made it across without drowning. We all did. That fall, our teacher gave us a swim test at the high school pool. Every one of us boys ended up in the beginner class. Which is how we found out we had all bragged ourselves into a dangerous dare."

Walter's phone chimed, and he read the text.

"Anything interesting?" Quin asked.

"Not sure. Did you hear from Makenna today?"

"Just a smiley face after I sent her a photo of you on the Segway."

"Then my text wasn't very interesting." Walter put his phone away.

Curiosity ate at Quin, but Pops wouldn't give him a hint. After Walter went to bed early, Quin texted Makenna.

*How is your day? Anything interesting happen?*

*—Wendell finally got a parking ticket. I'll tell you more when you get back.*

*Are you ok?*

*—Yup. Enjoy your vacation.*

Quin stared at his phone for a moment before putting it away. Obviously, there was more to the story, but he couldn't do anything from the Bahamas. Even if he could, Makenna had it handled.

# CHAPTER 27

Makenna yawned and checked the clock. Multiple furniture orders kept her up late since Quin had left. She also wasn't sleeping as well either as when they talked each day. The texts and photos weren't enough to bring the calm his presence brought her. It didn't help that she kept analyzing where she'd gone wrong with Wendell and trying to overanalyze her relationship with Quin. Other than lack of sleep, the week turned out surprisingly well after Wendell's arrest.

At the Wednesday night's early estate sales, she'd picked up several non-antique pieces that could be flipped and sold, as well as a few antique pieces for the store. With Aunt Linda minding the store in Walter's absence this morning, she found several more pieces. It was her best Thursday shopping estate sale yet.

She'd found a cute headboard-baseboard combination she wanted to try to turn into a bench. The Monroe brothers put it in the carriage house along with the other furniture she intended to flip. Several of her grandfather's old power tools still worked, so she didn't need to purchase a saw—assuming she got up the courage to turn it on.

Almost as scary as using the saw was the thought the relationship with Quin was different than every boyfriend she'd ever had. Only it was the excited sort of scary like the first day of school when you got the teacher everyone raved about. Or getting your driver's license and merging onto the freeway for the first time as the only person in the car and realizing you did it safely.

The grandfather clock gonged. Friday. Quin was coming home today.

Standing back, she surveyed her work. After touching up a small spot near the base of a bookshelf, Makenna went into the kitchen to rinse her brushes in a bucket she'd kept for cleaning them, trying to be as environmentally friendly as possible. A light snow fell. Through the window over the sink, Makenna watched the flakes fall. The peaceful snow hush she loved filled her soul. A light flickered in the carriage house window. Makenna searched for the source of the light as it grew brighter.

Whirling, she pulled the receiver from the kitchen wall phone and dialed.

"911 operator. What's your emergency?"

Walter received a text from Judge about the fire twenty minutes before Quin's phone chimed with a text.

—*Arsonist tried to burn down the carriage house. No one hurt. Will contact Ms. Conley.*

Walter leaned over Quin's shoulder. "She doesn't put in much detail, does she?"

"She probably doesn't want me to worry." Of course, her text had the opposite effect, even with the knowledge from Judge's text to Walter that the fire had been quickly contained.

"Not much you can do until we get back. May as well enjoy our last morning on the beach. My tan needs some work, don't you think?" Walter held his leg for Quin's inspection, showing several inches of tanned skin between the hem of the Bermuda shorts and the top of the white compression knee socks.

Quin ran his hand through his hair. The few days he'd been on the beach had replenished his highlights. The combination of sun and surf always did that. What would Makenna say? May as well get a few more hours of beach in before returning to the land of icy winds and snow.

"I want to stop at a couple of gift stores this morning. I need to find Makenna something more than that Bahamian doll."

"I still say that you should get her the T-shirt." Walter pulled his socks up.

"That would be as bad as getting her fish scale jewelry. I can't imagine that a woman who hates fish would wear it."

"Some of that shell jewelry is pretty, and it isn't exactly fishy." Walter held the door open. "Come on, you're burning daylight."

Quin laughed and followed his grandpa to the last of their adventures together.

Ice covered the ground around the still-standing carriage house. The early morning light didn't lessen the damage. The blackened south wall suffered most. Makenna watched the fire inspector poke at a spot near the open double doors. A chill unrelated to the wintery morning ran through her.

Claire joined Makenna, bringing a large cup of hot caramel apple cider. "Have they said anything yet?"

"Other than I was lucky that I spotted it when I did? No. I'm glad they contained it so it didn't spread to any other buildings. The insurance inspector politely informed me it could take weeks for my claim to come through."

"Did you have much in there for the store?"

"About a thousand dollars' worth of furniture to flip. Grandma had some items that needed repaired in there, but I'd never gotten around to it. Most of it was tools and my car."

"Is your car covered?"

"Thankfully, yes. I don't know the damage to the car. I had visions of it going up in flames like on TV. Other buildings could have been affected." Makenna pointed to the three-story building behind her. "There is a cute couple that lives on the third floor. She's expecting in April. The woman who lives below them is hard of hearing. I was so afraid there might be an explosion. Apparently that big of an explosion is a Hollywood thing. If I had gasoline in the tank there might have been more damage to the carriage house, but they would have been safe."

"What were you doing up at one in the morning, anyway?"

"Painting." And thinking. Lots and lots of thinking.

"I liked the bookcase you had on display last week. Maybe I should have you do something to brighten up the bookstore."

Makenna wasn't sure if Claire was serious or if she was trying to keep her mind off the fire inspector and police chief's tête-à-tête. "Sure. Do you want me to paint something you have or a new one?"

The fire chief and inspector came over. "Arson. Two things in your favor: they used a timer device to start the fire, and the arsonist didn't count on the precipitation. Snow stopped one of the two ignition mechanisms. You must have seen the fire within the first two to three minutes. The accelerant wasn't on the inside of the building. Since this side of the carriage house didn't have as many things stacked along the walls, the fire didn't move as fast as it could have. If the other fire had started, it would have reached your car before we arrived."

Minor miracles that added up to something less than a disaster. Makenna wavered between being relieved and annoyed. "Thank you for responding so quickly."

"That's our job. We will be out here for a while collecting evidence. If we need you, where will you be?" The fire chief's dismissal was clear.

"In the house for a few minutes, then the shop."

"The structure is still sound. One or both of us will take you through when it is safe to assess the damage. We'll get you a report for the insurance company."

A lump settled in Makenna's throat. Claire took her by the elbow and started her toward the house. "I'm staying with you today. I wish I'd realized last night when I heard the sirens, I would have come over then."

"I'm fine. You need to take care of Red Leaves."

"One of my employees is taking care of opening, so don't worry about my bookstore. Do you know who would do this?"

"The same person who wants me to sell the house and the shop." On the back porch, Makenna turned to look at the carriage house. From this side, the smoky windows were the only evidence that something was wrong.

"Someone wants you to sell?"

"That someone seems to be trying to purchase the entire block. We think it's a company out of England and that they want to build a hotel." Makenna took off her coat and laid it over a chair. "I should let Ms. Conley and Quin know about this."

"Where is Quin? I haven't seen him for a few days. Usually he walks from his office to your store a couple times a day."

"He's with Walter in Nassau."

"Did Walter finally get one of those deals? I want to know if they found a roach motel or a decent one."

"Quin hasn't said."

"When will they be back?"

"Quin said he'd be back Friday. Today is Friday, right?" Makenna finished the cider and tossed the cup in the barrel. "You don't need to stay with me."

"You're kidding, right? Someone tried to set fire to your carriage house. You think Keira and I would leave you to face this alone?"

Makenna stopped at the bottom of the stairs. "I'm assuming your questions are rhetorical?"

Claire rolled her eyes.

"I'll be down in a minute then."

Once she was safely in her locked bedroom, Makenna sunk onto her bed and allowed emotions to flow over her. For the first time in years, fear caused her tears. At the same time, she was proud that she was doing this alone. As much as she wanted a hug, she didn't need it. She'd been too afraid to go through the aftermath of Grandma Abigail's death alone. Looking back, she could have done it. Her cousins would have been there if she needed them.

Makenna marched to her closet and pulled out her favorite blue cable-knit sweater. Armed with its warmth, she could face anything.

# CHAPTER 28

*A* few minutes after midnight, Quin pulled into the alley behind the antique store. Like Walter, he wanted to see the damage. Motion sensor lights came on as they parked. Despite the late hour, lights glowed from several of Makenna's windows. Quin texted her so she wouldn't report them as prowlers.

*Pops and I are back and stopped by to see the carriage house.*

*—Just cleaning up. Be out in a second. Watch for ice.*

*—And don't let Walter fall.*

"You tell her I've been walking for eighty years."

Quin didn't relay the message. In the dark, the damage to the carriage house didn't look as extensive as the reports from Gene and Judge had led them to believe. The real question was how much damage was inside. The boarded-up windows yielded no clue. They'd finished their circuit of the carriage house when the back door of Makenna's house banged shut.

"Come on in and I'll get you some hot chocolate."

Quin assumed hot chocolate meant they were still on speaking terms. He followed Walter into the kitchen and sat at the kitchen table.

Makenna heated the milk on the stove as she described what happened. "I've never been thankful for insomnia in my life before."

"Any idea who was responsible?"

"According to Ms. Conley, it isn't the Brits. She had a long conversation with someone this morning. They'd been looking at the area but seemed to have some inaccurate information about their prospects. The Brits were 'properly appalled—'" Makenna used air quotes. "—over the incidents with the power outage and the arson."

Quin added whipped cream to the mugs of chocolate. "Are they going to withdraw their offers?"

"I'm not sure. To be honest, I was not paying as much attention as I should have." Makenna unwrapped a candy cane and stirred her drink.

Walter frowned. "Do you think Wendell is doing this on his own?"

"I did an internet search on the firm he works for. Before I was born, they defended some shady characters with possible Mob connections. I thought that happened only in the movies."

"Like *The Godfather*?" asked Quin.

Walter grunted.

Makenna shrugged. "I'm not sure. The whole thing with Wendell makes me feel a bit stupid."

Using his spoon, Walter pointed at her. "You aren't the first woman to fall for the wrong guy because he said all the right things."

This conversation would go so much better without Pops helping. Couldn't Pops see he was embarrassing Makenna?

"Looks can be deceiving," Quin said.

From the raise of her brows, Quin knew she understood he wasn't discussing Wendell.

"They can be. Sometimes people end up in very awkward positions that are difficult to explain." She ducked her head and sipped her hot chocolate. The corner of her mouth lifted in a smile.

Walter looked from one to another. "Are you two discussing Mr. Smith or the lovers' spat that kept Quin from enjoying the beach?"

"From the looks of his hair, he enjoyed it plenty." Makenna's full smile melted his heart.

"It would have been more fun if I could have called you, or if you had been there."

Walter harrumphed. "I'll be in the parlor so you two can kiss and make up."

Makenna joined Quin's laughter as they watched Walter leave the room.

"How did she end up in your lap? Liberty and I tried to come up with ways."

"She came around my side of the desk. I scooted back to put some distance between us." Quin pushed back from the table to demonstrate.

"I see." Makenna stood and circled the table. "You left your lap unguarded." She sat in his lap and wrapped one arm around his neck. "And knowing you, pushing her to the floor wasn't an option."

He curled her waist with his arm, pinning her gently in place. "Lawsuits over that sort of thing are rather tricky."

"How long did you two date?"

"We went on two dates. We weren't dating officially. Ten minutes into the second one and I was ready to bail. Unfortunately, we were at Tanglewood, and I didn't think I should leave her there. I wished I could have explained to you before I left."

"I wasn't ready to hear it. Liberty talked me down. I still want to slap Bethany, and I'm not sure about you. It's hard

247

when you see one thing and try to believe another. Bethany also said something about a married woman?" Makenna implied the question more than asked as she stood from his lap and returned to her seat.

"Two years ago, a coworker asked me out. We went on several dates before I discovered that she was married. Her husband was deployed. Long story short, I ended things. She spread rumors, her husband threatened me, she spread more rumors…"

Quin put his cup in the sink and walked around the table. He pulled Makenna to her feet. "Thank you for wanting to believe in me. I wish I'd done things differently." What else could he say to heal the breach? No words came to mind as he tucked a lock of Makenna's hair behind her ear. Any excuse to touch her.

She tipped her head and studied his eyes. "I suggest you make an extra effort not to be alone with Bethany."

"Noted—have you with me at all times to protect me from conniving women."

Makenna laughed and stepped closer.

Quin leaned in to meet her for a kiss.

A crash came from the parlor.

They ran down the hall and found Walter sprawled on the floor.

*Never trust an antique to hold your weight unless it's been thoroughly tested*, Makenna wanted to tell Walter. She'd tested the matching footstool to the wingback chair, and it could only support feet if the user were sitting in the chair, not using it as a step stool. Makenna stepped over the remains of the stool, mentally ruling out a heart attack for Walter.

"Pops?"

Walter pushed himself up. "Nothing hurt but my pride." He gasped. "And maybe my knee."

"Walter, stay on the floor. Is it just your knee or your hip too?"

"My hip doesn't feel so good either."

Makenna exchanged a look with Quin, who was already holding his phone to his ear. At least this wasn't sabotage.

Driving Quin's car, Makenna followed the ambulance to the hospital. One benefit of a small town was Quin didn't need to give her address to the 911 operator and the EMTs knew not to look for the house on the street where the address wouldn't be found.

After the first half hour of sitting in plastic chairs holding hands, Quin was called back to Walter's room. Once again, insomnia was Makenna's friend as she read a book on her phone, ignoring the infomercials playing on the waiting room TV. If only Walter could have waited a few more minutes until he fell. She'd really wanted that kiss. From her experience, kissing in a hospital while a grandparent was under medical care was poor timing—something Wendell hadn't understood. She'd need to wait until Quin was in a better place.

Two hours later, the doctors gave them the news that Walter hadn't broken anything, but they would keep him through the night to make sure the bruises didn't turn into clots.

Quin drove back to Hawthorne, yawning the entire way. Makenna kissed him on the cheek before hopping out of his car. Anything more seemed too much for an early morning such as this.

# CHAPTER 29

One night turned in to two. Monday morning, after spending much of the weekend at the hospital, Rebecca raged at Quin for letting Walter fall.

Quin tried to get some breakfast down between defending himself. "How do you keep Pops from doing something he's set his mind to?"

"Why was he on the stool anyway?"

"I don't know. Maybe you can ask him when you pick him up from the hospital this morning."

"I can't do that alone."

"Sure, you can. You know as well as I do, he'll have every doctor and nurse eating out of his hand. They'll have a parade in his honor, escorting him home."

Rebecca pursed her lips. "Fine. I'll go get him, but if I need you, you'll hurry home from the office, deal?"

"Deal. I'd better get going." Quin kissed his mom on the cheek and hurried out the door.

Only a couple dozen messages lay on Quin's desk thanks to Mrs. Zimmerman's excellent care of the office. The most important was an invitation to a video conference with a Mr. Oliver Bradford of Bradford-Stone. Quin called Ms. Conley to catch up on the situation. She didn't tell him much that he hadn't learned from Makenna. Today's call should fill in the blanks.

He cleared off half of the items on his desk before going to city hall.

Ms. Conley took him to a conference room with a large screen monitor. "I'm not sure what to expect, so be on your toes."

The face of a man about Quin's age filled the screen. "If you don't mind waiting a moment, the CEO would like to join us."

"Not a problem," answered Ms. Conley.

An older man bearing a familial resemblance to the younger took a seat. "I'm Malcom Bradford, and on behalf of Bradford-Stone, I apologize for the trouble you have had over our attempted land purchase. This morning, we cut ties with our Boston-based representative, and we are searching for another location for our hotel. I am told that our representatives intimidated some sellers. Bradford-Stone doesn't work this way. What can we do to correct the situation?"

Quin looked at the camera lens instead of the screen so the men would know he was looking them in the eye. "Most of the owners lost a day of work due to a targeted power outage, and the arson fire caused several thousand dollars in damage. I am not sure where the owner's insurance agency is on the claim."

The older Mr. Bradford spoke. "If you will get us a list of the businesses that had their electricity cut, we will compensate them. As for the fire, please allow us to take care of the matter so that the owner's business insurance premiums are not affected."

"The structure was a carriage house and part of a residence. I believe it is under a homeowner's policy."

"They targeted a home?" The older looked to the younger for confirmation. Again, the younger showed him a paper that looked to be a map. "Was anyone injured?"

"No. Miss Wilson's carriage house was used for storage. The fire damaged several items inside and the structure. She was lucky to discover the fire early enough that the firefighters stopped the flames from spreading to other buildings. The carriage house is in the center of the block."

"I see that from the map. Unusually situated, isn't it? Since it was a residence, we want to cover all the repairs and the replacement of any damaged items. Is it appropriate to compensate your firefighters?"

"A general grant to the fire department charity might be best," said Ms. Conley.

The older Bradford turned to the younger, nodding once. The younger one took over. "Do you have questions for us?"

Ms. Conley flipped a page on her empty notepad. "I believe only two owners sold to you, and they were quite happy to do so for various reasons. What are you planning to do with those properties?"

"According to what you said yesterday, those sales didn't have any irregularities, correct?"

"No. Both owners were satisfied with the transactions, but we would hate to see those buildings torn down."

The younger Mr. Bradford showed something to the older. "These two properties are on opposite sides of the block. Currently we are renting them out. We will most likely sell them off. I'm assuming you can help us with an honest real estate agent?"

"Trina Hughes," Ms. Conley and Quin answered in unison.

The older Bradford closed a folder. "Please forward me her information. Again, we are terribly sorry for any trouble caused. They had assured us this was an easy sale that would be embraced by your town."

Quin bit his cheek not to laugh. The statue of Lavinia Hawthorne Covington was on every city website and brochure. The idea that the block facing the south side of her statue would be an easy sale to anyone from England struck him as funny. Bradford-Stone representatives should visit on Independence Day—or better yet, on Patriots' Day. This coming Patriots' Day, the female descendants of Lavinia Hawthorne Covington would be holding a reunion. If witches actually existed, the Brits would be in for a shock.

Ms. Conley cleared her throat. "I am sorry you were misled, and we thank you for taking care of this. It will go a long way toward smoothing things over."

When the call ended, Ms. Conley burst out laughing. "I'm a descendant of Lavinia's brother Thomas Hawthorne who died in the War of 1812. It was all I could do not to lecture them on exactly how unwelcome a company from Leeds would be as a competitor to Liberty's B&B. She might start another revolution."

"Can you picture Liberty leading the picket line with DAR members with her?" asked Quin.

"She'd invite every Daughter of the American Revolution in all of Middlesex County."

"Not to mention the reenactors..." Quin stood. "Thank you for helping solve this. I'm glad it ended well."

Closing her notepad, Ms. Conley tapped her pen on the table. "I hope it's over. Someone just lost a big contract worth a million or so in commission. That type of loss is hard to accept."

Quin paused at the door. "I'll make sure everyone knows not to let their guard down." Especially Makenna. Assuming Wendell was behind the fire, he may retaliate further.

While checking out, a customer looked through her phone. "Did you see we are in for a blizzard?"

"No, I hadn't looked yet."

The woman put her phone away and took her purchase. "I better get to the grocery store. The kids will want milk."

Makenna verified her weather app against the local television websites. Everyone agreed the nor'easter coming in would cause a blizzard with snow starting in the late afternoon. She needed milk too, but by the time she could get to a store, they'd be sold out. Yay, for instant hot chocolate. She had enough of the other essentials to survive two or three days.

Shortly after noon, Quin stopped by. "Pops is home. Mom asked me to pick up a few things from the store. Do you need anything?"

Makenna wiped down the counter in preparation for closing early. "The only thing I could think of was milk, but I don't need it the way someone with kids does."

Quin peered into the display case. "Where's the watch?"

"I moved it over to the bank while I wait for a new appraisal."

His face fell. "Why do you need an appraisal?"

"Turns out it may be a museum piece worth several times what I thought it was. It will help my bottom line so much, and it needs to be in the Hawthorne Museum."

"You can't do that. The watch stops—" He didn't finish his thought.

"Only for you. I don't understand it, but you're the only one who has ever said anything about it. Can you imagine how exhausted I'd be if it stopped time for every customer?"

Quin rubbed the back of his neck. "That would be a long day. What I liked was it gave me extra time to feel like I could talk and not run."

"You haven't looked at your watch once since you came in. Do you feel like you need to leave in a hurry?"

He looked around the store. "Actually, no. Though that may change the next time Mom texts an addition to my grocery list."

Makenna laughed. "Are you learning to slow down? Because you should hurry out to make sure Walter has whatever delicacy he's decided he needs."

"Since I met you, my antacid usage has declined significantly." Quin's phone pinged.

"Go. I'll talk to you later."

After no more customers came in for the next hour, Makenna closed the store. She cleaned up quickly and left the water dripping in the workroom sink. Preventing a pipe from bursting was about the only thing she could do to protect the store from the storm. If the power went out, there would be no heat. Even if the battery backup in the alarm system worked, responding to a robbery was a lower priority than if lives were in danger.

The Hill house had weathered many a blizzard. The biggest problem was that the water heater installed ten years ago needed electricity to run. The old radiator system had also been upgraded, relying on electric power. Makenna brought in several armfuls of wood in case she needed to use the fireplace, and checked the cellar to make sure there was no draft. Charging her phone and other electronics and backup batteries was a new item added to her checklist of putting flashlights and batteries in strategic locations. Then, like every other New Englander, she kept the weather on in the background, made dinner, and watched the snow fall.

# CHAPTER 30

Judging the depth of the snow from his third-story window was nearly impossible since all he could see were more heavy white flakes falling into what appeared to be an abyss. The thought was equally fascinating and frightening. According to the news Pops had on downstairs, the snow would continue for another five to six hours. Quin remembered a few blizzards from his youth. The anticipation of closing school. Power outages and tent cities in the living room. Building snow mazes, houses, men, and anything else they could. Shoveling walkways—that one wasn't so fun, even if it helped make bigger snow forts. As an adult he didn't see much fun in it at all.

He texted Makenna. *How are things going?*

*—Fine. Reading a book and drinking some hot chocolate. The powdered mix isn't as bad as I thought it would be.*

*Didn't realize you were a cocoa snob.*

*—Sometimes old-fashioned is best.*

*When it comes to hot chocolate, I agree.*

*—How's Walter?*

*Grumpy. Says the weather is making his bones ache.*

*—Probably true.*

*I should have asked you to stay over here.*
*—You wait until we're in whiteout conditions and then ask? LOL.*
*I wasn't thinking about it earlier. Pops had me running around checking flashlights.*
*—Good excuse. I'll be fine.*
*Promise to call or text if anything happens.*
*—I will. Have a good night.*
*G 'night.*

Quin returned to the main floor and Pops' parlor where the news still played. The dog lay curled up next to the recliner waiting for his master to move.

"Why are you still watching the weather?" asked Quin.

"Habit. I got stuck in my car in '78. They say the April Fool's Day storm of '97 was worse, but the city was better prepared. I'm more concerned this will be like the back-to-back ones of 2015. Every weekend until we had over fifty inches of snow. There was no place to put it."

"If you can't change it, why worry?"

"Look who is talking. Mr. Worry Wart himself."

Quin sat on the end of the couch nearest the recliner. "Apparently, it's genetic."

Walter laughed until he coughed. "Glad you met Makenna then. She seems to have taken some of that impatience away. And don't go saying it's that watch. I was daft to believe it, even for a moment."

Believing in a watch was irrational, no matter how he looked at it. Something about the watch was special. "Why were you standing on the footrest, anyway?"

"I thought I saw a red-light flash on the mantelpiece."

"A reflection of the mirror?"

"Nope. It was in the wrong place."

"Then what?"

"Reminded me of a camera. Like one of her security cameras. I wondered why Makenna put one in the house."

"She doesn't have one in the house." At least not that she'd mentioned.

"I'm pretty sure that's what I saw."

"Where exactly was it?"

"Next to that candlestick thingy." Walter changed the channel to another weather report.

Quin unlocked his phone and sent a text to Makenna.

*Do you have a security camera in the house?*

*— The one at the back of the store sees the front door.*

*Not one in the house?*

*— No, why?*

*Pops thought that there was one —* Quin accidentally hit send as the lights flickered out and the TV faded to black.

"The power went out early," grumbled Pops in the dark. "Flashlight is in the end table."

Quin found the flashlight and turned it on. He finished his text. *Sorry, power out. One on the mantel near the candles.*

*— Power out here too.*

*Are you okay?*

Quin waited impatiently for a reply.

*— Sorry needed to light the lantern. I'm fine. I have the fire going. I'll check on the camera and let you know. Keep warm!*

The footrest of the recliner popped closed. "Help me to bed. You may as well stay down here on the couch. It will be warmer since the attic is drafty and the radiator is the furthest from the cellar."

Quin had planned on staying down here in case Pops needed him during the night.

The halo of a flashlight showed from the doorway. "I'm here with extra blankets. Quin, will you close all the doors upstairs?"

In his apartment, Quin grabbed the backup battery for his phone from his bedroom and hoped they didn't have to wait more than a day for the power to come back on.

Light streamed in through the parlor windows. Eighteen inches of newly fallen snow obliterated all the stains of the world. Beyond the view of Makenna's world, snow blowers roared. No one had come up the alley to clear a path for her yet. Someone would soon. Sometimes she wondered if Mario and Ben had a competition to see who could reach her door first.

Makenna searched the mantel for the camera Walter saw. Nothing but a single red die. Which she didn't remember putting there. She picked it up to put back with the board games. It was heavier than it should have been. Upon closer examination, the single dot wasn't a dot but a glass lens. Wendell could have done this. The other possibilities were her cousins, Quin, and Walter. Grandma Tansy wasn't well versed in any computer usage. Quin and Walter were unlikely suspects, as were her cousins.

How many other cameras were in the house, and why? She dropped the die in the old copper teapot. The pot was the first antique she ever purchased with her own money, partly a consequence of stealing it from Abigail's shop to make tea with her cousins so many Aprils ago. The teapot was a good place to put mini cameras. After the hectic part of the storm was over, she'd let the police know. This wasn't a safety priority.

Grabbing a package of baby wipes she'd warmed on the hearth, Makenna ran upstairs to wash and change for the day. Before changing, she searched every inch of the bathroom for anything that could be a camera. Nothing appeared to be unusual or out of place.

A baby wipe shower wasn't the most pleasant way to greet a morning, but it was better than utilizing the cold water that she had dripping in her sink to keep the pipes from freezing.

Downstairs, someone pounded on her door. Makenna wrapped the elastic around the end of her braid as she raced down the stairs to answer the door.

"Open up! I know you're in there!"

Makenna slid to a stop inches from the door. Wendell? Not one part of hearing him at the door made sense. Who went anywhere they didn't need to in a blizzard? Even if Mass Pike were cleared, the secondary roads wouldn't be yet. Kudos to Mass DOT, but that efficiency was beyond any department of transportation. The drive from his downtown apartment shouldn't be possible.

"Makenna! Answer the door." He pounded harder.

Makenna pressed her back to the wall and scooted back to the stairway.

*Bang!*

Something harder than a fist hit the door. Makenna pulled out her phone. She didn't want to endanger lives by calling 911, so she dialed Quin instead.

"Hey. How are you doing?"

"Can you see from your house if they've cleared the roads?" Makenna wished she'd pulled out her boots last night. They were up in her bedroom closet. Going upstairs would cut off her only escape route through the back door. The cellar doors would be too hard to open from the inside with a foot and a half of snow on top.

"I heard a plow earlier. I think Maple might be. Why? Do you need something?" asked Quin. *Bang!* "What was that?"

"Wendell is pounding on my front door." Makenna slid along the wall to the kitchen. Her only escape was blocked by the snow. With no coat or boots, she wouldn't get too far before he could catch up to her.

"How did he get out here?"

"No idea."

*Bang!*

"Was that him?"

"Yes. Banging on the door." The top of the doorframe cracked. "Breaking down the door."

"Can you get out of there?"

"Back door through the snow. No boots. I don't know that I can outrun—"

*Bang! Crack!*

"Maybe I should have called 911."

"Pops is dialing now. Hide."

Makenna winced at the thought of the best place. But if it were a choice between spiders and an irate Wendell, she'd face arachnids. "Stay on the phone with me."

"I will."

The grandfather clock had stood in the same place for generations. Makenna opened the door and stopped the pendulum and then pushed on the back panel. It popped open into a two-and-a-half by eight-foot closet once used to hide great grandfather's wine collection during Prohibition. Holding the weights and pendulum to the side and stepping through the door wasn't as easy as it was when she was a child and could duck under the weights. Makenna closed the clock's glass door and set the pendulum back in its normal tick-tock pattern. She then closed the door to the back of the clock all but the last half inch. Unless someone looked directly at the clock, they wouldn't see her.

*Bang! Crack! Bam!*

The door banged against the inside wall. Wendell burst into the house. "I know you're here. Scared to face me after losing me nearly a million dollars? You'd better hide."

He searched in the parlor, disappearing from view. "A fire. I know you're here."

He ran to the kitchen. "No footprints outside of the back door. Come out, Makenna. I'll go easier on you. I can't believe I wasted over a year trying to woo you. You don't even know how much money you're sitting on?" He passed by the clock and stood at the base of the stairs. "I saw it the first time you brought me to this old crumbling-down house. All I had do to was find the right developer. Then you had the nerve to dump me. Do you know what that new boyfriend of yours did? He cost me my job, my career, and my money. Someone has got to pay—"

He stomped up the stairs and out of hearing. Items fell against the floor. Makenna weighed her options. "Quin." She whispered, hoping for a response.

"Still here." His voice sounded garbled.

"I'm going to run for it. I don't want to be trapped in the house with him. I need to hang up."

A garbled response came as she shut off her phone. Slowly she opened the secret door and stopped the pendulum. From the thumps on the ceiling above, Wendell was in the furthest room from the stairs. Makenna pushed open the case door and ran. She followed the trail Wendell had forged through the snow to the street.

Officer Hastings caught her as she flew around the corner. "Whoa, there. What's going on?"

"It's Wendell Smith. He broke into my house and is looking for me."

Someone threw a blanket around her shoulders.

"Go with the EMT. We'll check out your house."

Shivers took over as Makenna became aware of the cold. They helped her into the same ambulance that Walter had been in only days ago. They wrapped another blanket around her.

"We're going to take these wet socks off of you and warm up your feet."

The heat packs felt like fire on her toes. Makenna tried to pull away. "It burns."

"Don't worry, they aren't hot enough to burn, and the fact that you can feel your feet is a good thing."

"I wasn't out that long. I only ran from my front door."

A commotion had them all looking out of the rear window. Wendell yelled a string of profanities and struggled against his handcuffs as the officers took him to their patrol car.

"You'd think a lawyer would be silent when the police arrested him," said Makenna.

"What was that Miss?"

"Nothing."

Officer Hastings knocked on the ambulance door. "We have him. There's a big mess in there. You might want to wait until the power is on to clean up."

"We also advise wearing shoes when you do." One of the EMT's checked her feet. He turned to the police officer. "She is good to go if she wants. Only we can't let her out in the cold like this."

"I have a fireplace. I'll be fine."

"And a broken front door jamb."

A man in a faux fur-lined parka joined the officer. "May I help?"

"Quin? How did you get here?" He came. She hadn't even wished for such an impossible thing. Three blocks in the snow. As soon as she saw him, she knew how much she needed him. Not that she couldn't have solved things, but to have someone care enough to come, especially a California Boy, meant the world.

He pulled back his hood. "I walked fast."

"If you can figure out how to get Miss Wilson back into the house without her freezing her toes off, she's good to go."

Makenna waved an arm to get their attention. "I'm right here. If I could borrow a blanket for a moment and—"

"I'll give her a piggyback," offered Quin.

Officer Hastings closed the door behind Quin who eased Makenna to the floor. The damage was worse than Quin had imagined.

"I'm going to go through the house and take some photos for evidence, if you don't mind," said the other officer.

"For the record, it is usually much cleaner in here." Makenna stood in front of the fire. "I also found a hidden camera this morning." Makenna took the die out of the kettle. "I suspect it is Wendell's. I don't know if there are any more in the house."

"Once the power is on, the detective will come back and do a full sweep. If you find any more, take a photo of them and use a sandwich bag to pick it up and put them in a container."

While Officer Hastings took Makenna's statement, Quin inspected the damage to the doorframe. He wasn't much of a carpenter, but he could tell the door wouldn't stay shut in a spring breeze. Makenna could have been hurt. The same surge of protectiveness that caused him to run three blocks in knee-deep snow swelled again. This was more than just protectiveness. He'd known it for days now, sorted it out between the swimming pigs and the worries of if she would have him back—Makenna wasn't just another girlfriend. She was the last one he ever wanted to have.

Officer Hastings joined him at the door. "Block off the door with anything you can find and insulate it with a blanket. You probably won't be able to find someone to fix it for a few days. There are a few trees through roofs that will take priority." He turned to Makenna. "Best guess is he'll be out on bail in twenty-four hours or as soon as the judge holds a hearing. This time, get a restraining order filed and don't stay alone here until we repair the door."

Quin shut the door after the police officers left. He used a kitchen chair loaded with a set of 1969 encyclopedias to brace the door.

"And I told Grandma those old encyclopedias were worthless."

"Brant, the pyrotechnic guy, is remodeling the old gas station. I bet he can fix this doorframe. Do you want me to call him?"

"Sure. If you can't reach him, I'll call Keira."

"The baker? She can fix this?"

"No, she's dating Brant. My guess is they're together keeping warm someplace." Makenna flipped the wingback chair right side up. "I wonder if he could fix it today?"

"Might need to wait until you have power again. I assume he uses modern power tools." Quin stuffed a plastic garbage bag in the gap between the splintered doorframe and the door and filled the bag with newspaper. "Toss some things in a suitcase and come over to my place. We have room, and Pops will make sure you are well chaperoned."

"I wasn't too worried about the chaperone part." Makenna looked around the room. "I don't want to leave, but you are right. Can you put out the fire?" She ran up the stairs.

Using a poker, Quin separated the logs. She hadn't built up the fire much that morning. By the time Makenna returned, only glowing coals remained.

Sitting on the couch, she laced up a pair of knee-high boots. "By the way, snow is really cold without boots."

"Where were you hiding when he came in?"

"Inside the clock. The grandfather in the hallway has a door behind it. Go look. There is a flashlight on the kitchen counter."

Quin found the light and inspected the clock. "How do you get back there?"

Makenna reached around him and unhooked a weight.

"My grandpa would unhook the weights and the pendulum. I just moved around them." She unhooked them. "Be my guest."

Quin walked through the clock and stepped back in time. The shelves in the narrow room still held a few wine bottles. And old books. "Books?"

"*Modern Mechanics* published in 1920. Not old enough to be valuable, and not new enough to be useful."

A small leather case sat on a shelf at Quin's eye level. Unlike the surrounding shelf, it wasn't covered in dust. "Is this your missing lockpick kit?"

Makenna opened it under the beam of the flashlight. "No, but it is a nice one. How did it end up in here?"

"How many people know about this place?"

"I showed Liberty when we were about nine. But the room has been here for over a hundred years, so anyone could know about it."

"Another day, we should explore. Right now, I want to find a warm place."

Her breath clouded around her face. "You're right, this room is colder than the rest of the house. I didn't notice earlier." Makenna walked out of the clock, and he followed.

Quin waited while she put it back together. "So I'm the only person you've shown that to besides Liberty?"

"Yes."

"Why?"

Makenna rubbed fingerprints off the glass with her shirtsleeve and turned to him. "Because I trust you."

"Really?" Even after the Bethany mess? Quin didn't ask the last part because he didn't want to bring it up.

"You came for me." She stepped closer and lay her hand over his heart.

"Of course I did. Dispatch wasn't sure how soon the police could get here."

Makenna stood on her toes and kissed him. Warmth filled him, which also made him realize how cold he was. He pulled back. "We can do more of this when we're some-place warm."

With a saucy wink, Makenna stepped out of his arms. "I thought you said we'd have chaperones."

Quin pulled on his coat. "I'm sure we can figure out a way to get a few minutes alone."

# CHAPTER 31

Makenna squinted her eyes against the light and buried her head into her warm pillow. Her pillow groaned and moved. Quin. No wonder she'd been sleeping so soundly. Dreams of him did that.

"Turn off the light. I can't get any sleep." Walter's voice chased away the remnants of her dream.

The movement of her pillow forced her to open her eyes. Quin helped her move off his chest. "I'll get the light, Pops."

"Good. With the power on, I can get these two lovebirds off my couch." Walter directed his comment to Rebecca who walked into the room.

Makenna stretched her back. "I thought you enjoyed having me here."

"I do, but I don't like all that kissing stuff." Walter popped the lever on his recliner and brought it into a sitting position. "Every time I leave the room, all I hear is silence. I know what you two have been doing for the past two days."

Walter's assessment wasn't exactly true. There had been several times he left the room where they hadn't kissed at all. Going from a conversation with Quin's grandfather about the best seasons of the Red Sox to romance in ten seconds wasn't exactly her style. And the longer stretches of time he'd leave the room still weren't long enough to recapture the mood. Or the dog would come lay his head in her lap when they tried to kiss which was a total mood killer.

Leaving a lamp on in the corner, Quin sat back down on the couch. Makenna spread the quilt over his legs and snuggled back into his side.

Rebecca fussed over Walter. "I just came down to check on you." She turned to Quin and Makenna. "Don't go back home until you have that door fixed, no matter what Dad says."

Makenna nodded. They had given her the couch in Rebecca's apartment as her 'bed' but she fell asleep on Walter's couch with Quin and never made it upstairs. Not that she minded the situation at all.

Walter scuffled across the floor. "Are you two going to stay on that couch all night?"

"No, Pops. I'll walk Makenna up in a few minutes."

Walter stopped at his bedroom door, the dog at his heels. "Sure, you will, right after you lock lips again. Careful they don't freeze that way." The door shut with a click.

Quin put his arms around her. "I could think of worse fates than having my lips freeze while kissing you."

"It would be an interesting way to die."

"Die?"

"Without food or water, eve—"

Quin cut off the rest of her thoughts with a kiss.

Sweet broomsticks, it would be a pleasant way to die. She couldn't be in love this fast, could she?

# CHAPTER 32

Only a few snow hills remained where the plows piled the snow to clear the roads. Ice melt dotted cleared spots on the sidewalks, crunching under his feet. Quin couldn't believe that in a week everything was back to business as normal. If the common wasn't covered with snow, he might not believe that there had been a blizzard.

A pale green bookcase stood in the window of Abigail's Antiques. A small sold sign sat on the second shelf. Less than a day. Her reclaimed furniture was a tremendous hit.

Quin walked past the door and circled the block, checking on other businesses. A contractor truck sat in the south alley near the carriage house. The report of a nail gun echoed against the brick walls of the buildings flanking the alley. Quin cut through the center of the block, staying clear of the workers. He stopped to examine the repaired front door. If it didn't need a coat of paint, it would be impossible to see the repairs.

He circled to the front of the store and entered under the ringing bell. "Brant did a marvelous job on your front door."

"He wouldn't let me pay him other than reimbursement for the lumber." Makenna pulled a wooden box from under the counter. "Would you like to see this once more? I'm going to drive it over to the museum on my way to a preview of an estate sale."

Although he was loath to part with the watch, he understood Makenna's reasons for selling it to the Hawthorne Museum. Ten thousand dollars was more than any of her customers could afford. And like her, he wanted it to stay in the community.

The gold pocket watch looked rather ordinary against the black felt of the box. Quin opened it and watched the second hand make its way around the face.

The minute hand moved. "Did you see that? The time changed."

"That's what it is supposed to do."

"Not usually, not for me. It always gives me more time." He turned over the watch, making sure it was the same one.

"Maybe you don't need the watch anymore. You aren't the same frantic person you used to be."

"Or maybe I've run out of time."

Her quiet laugh made him smile. She walked around the counter and took the watch and box from him. "I don't think you were ever out of time. You just tried to control it too much."

Quin glanced around the store, making sure that no one else was around before taking Makenna's free hand. "I've learned I enjoy spending time with people I love. If the watch will not give me more time with you, then I need to find another way."

Makenna stepped closer. "What other way?"

"I'm greedy, and I love you. You are sunshine to my darkness. I want all the time forevermore. Marry me?" He hadn't planned on saying those words today. They weren't in his schedule for the week or the next, although looking for a ring had made his private list of to-dos. Would she want something new, an antique, or a mix? That had been something he'd meant to ask.

Time stopped while he waited for an answer. Her gaze met his then moved to their clasped hands and back up.

*Please see this is real.*

"Yes." Tears leaked out of the corners of her eyes, her smile wide. She set the box on the counter and wrapped her arms around his neck. "I want to share all my time with you."

Her lips met his. Quin didn't need the watch to get time to stand still.

# EPILOGUE

The second Hawthorne First Night celebration was nearly over. Quin, Brant, and the board scaled it back, having only one firework show at 7:30 p.m. and closing the festivities at 10:00. By all appearances, attendance was up, and eliminating the second set of fireworks cut the overall budget by over twenty percent even after hiring an event coordinator. Quin checked with Makenna before going home. He would not miss getting his New Year's kiss from his wife this year.

A warm light from the parlor window reflected off the snow that refused to melt in their minuscule front yard.

"Sunny, I'm home." She'd become his sunshine in so many ways over the past year, and now that she slept normally most nights, everyone else could see her vibrant light within too.

Makenna sat on the couch facing the fireplace. Tonight, she wore a dress right out of one of those old black-and-white 1950s shows where women vacuumed in dresses. "Right on time. I'll get your hot cider while you change, and we can watch the ball drop."

Quin took a warm shower so his wife wouldn't complain

about chilly hands when they snuggled. The old pipes screeched, protesting their late-night use. They got moved up on his list of things to fix someday in the house. They'd made progress over the summer, and now all the rooms had working outlets. He bumped the silver-handled brush. The tradition had become one of his favorite parts of the day.

Makenna met him at the bottom of the stairs with a cup of steaming cider. "Complain all you want, but those pipes saved you from getting cold cider."

"I figured I'd get a better kiss if my nose wasn't frozen."

Makenna wrinkled her nose and kissed him on the cheek. "Probably."

She returned to the couch in front of the fire, curling her legs under her, and handed him an old box. "I found something for you."

"Christmas was last week." A Kewpie doll with a green sash lay between folds of tissue paper. "Oh, my own Baby New Year."

"Pick that up and read the sash again, California Boy."

"Baby this Year?" His chest swelled. An image of a baby wrapped in a blue and pink trimmed hospital blanket filled his mind. His heart swelled the same way it had on their wedding day when she walked down the aisle toward him. "Are you serious, or is this some kind of object magic?"

Although his wife couldn't control anything that happened between an article and its owner, she'd gotten much more adept at matching an antique with the person who needed it. Between her flipped furniture and increased sales, the store was doing better than ever.

Makenna reached for the doll. "Did you see something?"

"Me holding a baby in a generic hospital blanket." Quin was less surprised at seeing something than that he was seeing a baby. That wasn't any past memory he could place. It hadn't happened with a niece or nephew.

"Oh, broomsticks. I was hoping you could see the gender. I don't want to wait for the ultrasound." Makenna's lower lip pouted out.

"Really, I'm going to be a dad? I mean, you're a mom? We're having a baby!"

Makenna nodded and wrapped her arms around his neck. "Happy New Year."

During the middle of their endless kiss, Quin heard the bells of the church tower ring twelve times mingled with the chimes of the grandfather clock. For a moment, he wished he still had the pocket watch as he wanted to relish every minute of the new year.

He ended the kiss and looked into Makenna's eyes. He didn't need the watch. He could cherish every moment without magic.

# Acknowledgments

*I* love New England. Of all the places I've lived, I'd move back to the Commonwealth in a heart beat. When Maria told me her idea for a new series I practically begged her to let me write part of it. Working with her on Spellbound in Hawthorne has been amazing. I hope you love her imaginary town too. Thanks Maria for including me.

As always, thanks to Tammy, Nanette and Cami who are so willing to help make all my projects better and to read for all my mistakes. I would never make it through a day without Sally and Cindy whose advice keeps me going. Thank you wonderful ladies.

Thank you to my excellent co-writer for sharing her editing ability. And to my excellent proofreaders are not to be blamed for any remaining errors. Thank you ladies and gents!

My family, for sharing their home with the fictional characters who often get fed better than they did. And my husband who encourages me every crazy step of the way and puts up with all my messy spreadsheets.

And to my Father in Heaven for putting these wonderful people, and any I may have forgotten to mention, in my life. I am grateful for every experience and blessing I have been granted.

# ABOUT THE AUTHORS

*L*orin Grace was born in Colorado and has been moving around the country ever since, living in eight states and several imaginary worlds. She holds a degree in graphic design which comes in handy with creating book covers. Currently, she lives with her husband, four children, and a dog who is insanely jealous of her laptop. When not writing, Lorin enjoys creating graphics, visiting historical sites, museums, painting furniture, and reading. Three of her books, her debut novel, *Waking Lucy* (2017), *Mending Fences* (2018), and *Not the Bodyguard's Baby* (2020) have won Recommend Read awards in the League of Utah Writers Published book contest.

*W*hen Maria Hoagland is not working at her computer, she can be found combing used furniture stores and remodeling houses with her husband. She loves crunching leaves in the fall, stealing cookie dough from the mixing bowl, and listening to musicals on her phone. Maria has several published works in the sweet romance and women's fiction genres. Two of her books, *Still Time* and *The ReModel Marriage* have been Whitney Award finalists.